FOREVER IN MAGIC

IN MAGIC
BOOK SEVEN

KJ WARAWA

MYSTIC
CITY
PRESS

Edited by Jennia D'Lima

Proofread by Taylor Gonzales

Cover Designed by Sunset Rose Books

DEDICATION

For DBW

For believing in me.
One series down, many more to go...

AUTHOR'S NOTE:

Dear reader,

Forever In Magic is the final book and the exciting wrap-up to the *In Magic* series, and because it's bringing everything all together, the timeframes of the last three books in the series overlap. *Forged In Magic* (Kate and Isaac) started during the end of *Love In Magic* (Reece and Isabella) and finishes at almost the same time as *Forever In Magic (Sam and Mirek)*. But if you haven't read the other books, I suggest you do that first as this book wasn't meant to be a standalone. And if it's been a while since you read the other books and don't remember precise details, no problem—this book will bring you along for the ride—I promise!

When I began writing the *In Magic* series, I knew it had to start with Jack and Meredith, but before I'd even finished that first book, Ben Davis was telling me I had to write his story. Stella Finnegan, Ben's love interest, just came to me—as most characters do—but it was little Julia that threw me for a loop. She appeared so strong and intelligent, even at three years old, that I knew not only was I going to write her story, but that she would play a pivotal role in the series.

Julia—who you met again in *Found in Magic* and learned now goes by Sam—is going to wrap up the entire series, bringing it full circle. It's no secret that Sam is in love with Mirek, and although this is their book, it's more than that. You'll see how they fell in love, but you'll also see how the events over twenty years ago shaped their lives and continues to shape the lives of the other couples and what they're going to do about it.

That may deem this book to be more of a paranormal or urban fantasy than a paranormal romance, but there's still lots of love between all the couples, and I hope you love it all the same. *Forever in Magic* is about making mistakes, reflecting on them, and finding your forever love.

If you haven't read Ben & Stella's story with Julia, you can download it for free at the end of this book.

And if you're wondering about Rocky, Nate, and some of the FBI characters you met throughout the series… they'll get their own books… But first a family of brothers has a curse to deal with. I've included the description of *Cursed to Love* for you.

Happy reading,
KJ

PROLOGUE

Twenty-Two Years Ago

The tutor walked up the stairs to freedom, something Mirek Williams hadn't had in over a month. When the lock on the door at the top of the stairs clicked and no one came to take her place, he let out a breath of relief.

Listening for the lock clicking open and footsteps on the stairs had come to define his days, and those of his younger brother and two cousins. At the same times each day it clicked when the tutor arrived and left, and when meals were delivered. It was the unexpected times he heard the sound that he'd come to fear.

"I don't wanna do homework," Taren whined as he flopped onto one of the two couches in the room that had become their prison.

"We need to learn," Mirek said as he eased down onto a lounge chair, sucking in a slow breath to minimize his pain. In the shower that morning, he'd examined the bruising that covered his thigh, hip, and shoulder. Zeus had thrown him against the wall in anger the night before and then stomped away. Mirek had played off the pain, even after Zeus left, not wanting to worry the others. "It's September now, so that means we should be in school," he told his brother.

Molly dropped onto the cushions beside Taren. "It's not the same, and I miss my friends from school. And my mom and dad. And my sister." Her lip quivered, but she didn't make a sound as she picked up one of the couch pillows and held it against her face.

"Come here," he said, holding out his arm to Molly. She tossed the pillow to the side and climbed into his lap. At ten, Mirek was the oldest, though only two months older than his cousin Dylan. Molly was seven and Taren six, making Mirek the adult of the group. He missed his family as much as Molly did, but he promised himself that he would protect his brother and cousins at all costs.

Molly leaned her head against his shoulder, and he ran his hand along her hair, like he'd seen his mom do to his sister. "I know, Molly. I miss everyone too."

Molly reared back. "No! Don't call me that." She looked toward the stairs, her eyes wide as she put her finger on his lips. "You need to remember our new names," she whispered. "I'm Morgana now. If you call me Molly, they'll hurt you again."

He settled Molly back against him. "I'll try to remember."

"It's stupid," Dylan said. "I don't want to be called David. It's not my name. And I don't want to call Taren Tim. You—"

Taren pushed his too-long curls off his face. "I don't wanna be Tim," he said quietly.

Mirek glared at Dylan before turning to his little brother. "I know, Taren, but if you don't use the new name, they'll punish you."

"Then why won't you go by your new name?"

Mirek heard the challenge in his brother's voice. "I don't

want us to forget where we came from and I don't care if they beat me up because of it. You don't have to worry about using your new names because I'll remember our old names for all of us." His reasoning didn't sound as good out loud as it had in his head, but he would stick to it because he feared it might be the only reminder they had of where they came from.

"Okay," Taren and Molly both whispered, accepting that he would take care of them. Dylan didn't say anything but met Mirek's gaze and gave him a single nod.

Zeus, Maverick, and Snake had already taken so much away from them that Mirek refused to allow them to take this last small thing.

Even with their dumb nicknames, Mirek knew who the men really were. He'd seen them with his dad and uncles. They were council members who were supposed to protect all magic people.

Their parents and other siblings were dead. That's what Zeus said. He'd told them that every person in their families had died in a fire and only the four of them were left. Zeus said he and the others were protecting them.

Mirek might've been a kid, but he wasn't stupid. Forcing them to change their names and keeping them in a basement didn't make sense—Zeus didn't even say what he was protecting them from. Probably nothing. He didn't know why they'd been taken, but he would have bet his new Xbox that it wasn't to keep them safe.

As for everyone else being dead... he didn't know whether that was true. The last thing he remembered was a fire erupting in the cabin and his dad reaching for Taren and calling Mirek's name. Then he'd woken up in the basement with his brother and cousins. He shook off the thoughts because they wouldn't help their situation, and they had things to do.

He lifted Molly off his lap and set her on her feet. "Come on, let's get our homework done before dinner. Then we'll watch a movie."

"*The Land Before Time.*"

"*The Little Mermaid.*"

"*Rocky.*"

The TV wasn't connected to cable, but at least they had a DVD player and dozens of movies. He could already recite lines from their favorites.

"Sure." Mirek chuckled at Dylan's answer as everyone shuffled over to the dining room table. "I should just start calling you Rocky since you've watched that movie so many times."

Dylan shrugged. "Fine with me."

Homework didn't take long to get out of the way with Mirek and Dylan helping before tackling their own while Taren and Morgana read a book. They had settled into a routine even without parents.

After eating dinner, they sprawled out in the sitting area to watch a movie. Molly won rock paper scissors, so they were watching *The Little Mermaid*. The next time, they'd watch *Rocky*, and then the dinosaur movie.

As the crab started singing about kissing the girl, it made Mirek think about his dad, like it always did. His sister, Rowena, had picked the movie once during family movie night, and his dad had pulled his mom into his arms and danced her around the room while he sang along with the movie.

They'd all laughed because his dad was a lousy singer, but he'd loved them and their mom so much. He'd taught Mirek all about magics and told him crazy stories about his brothers conjuring things and driving their parents nuts. Mirek had been convinced he and Taren and his cousins

Dylan and Reece would do that to their parents when they were older. But now they were all gone.

He wished he and Dylan had their full magic because then they could have flashed out of the basement. And even knowing they wouldn't get more magic until puberty—however far away that was—they'd tried to flash anyway, until they were both too tired to move. His dad had told him all about magic and how he'd have to practice to master it and that some magics even got magic specialties. All the adults in their family had one, so his dad said that Mirek would likely get one too.

Mirek didn't know when he'd come into his full magic, but he was already pretty sure what his specialty was going to be—healing.

Two weeks ago, Taren had woken up screaming from a nightmare. Mirek had tried to console him but not fast enough to stop Snake from storming into the basement and grabbing Taren by the arm. He'd held Taren's small arm in his huge hands and squeezed until a loud crack sounded in the room.

Mirek would never forget the sound of his brother's deafening howl that followed. Snake flung Taren on the bed and sneered down at him. "Now you've got something to scream about." As he turned to leave, his gaze locked on Mirek's. "Keep them quiet."

As soon as Mirek heard the click at the top of the stairs, he kneeled beside Taren's bed, his brother's whimpers muffled by the blanket. Mirek had carefully lifted the blanket off Taren's arm, then swallowed the bile that sprang up his throat. A raised bump had formed, distorting its normal shape. The area around the bump was already turning purple.

He'd once again failed to keep his brother safe. Pushing

the thought aside for the moment, he focused on Taren and what he could do to help him.

As gently as he could, Mirek put his hands on the bump and closed his eyes. Taren didn't jerk away, but Mirek could hear his soft crying and blocked it out to concentrate. Using his magic, he looked into Taren's arm.

Mirek had never seen inside a body before, but once, when he'd had to wait at the doctor's office for a long time, he'd studied the skeleton standing in the corner. Just like the skeleton, two long bones ran from Taren's wrist and connected to the long bone in his upper arm, forming his elbow. One of his forearm bones, the one on the same side as his thumb, had a crack right through it.

Mirek's magic told him that the bone was called the radius, and the other one was the ulna. He only hoped his magic also told him how to heal it.

Calling up his magic, Mirek pushed it into his brother. When Taren moaned softly, he slowed his magic to a steady trickle.

"Remember last year when I fell and hurt my leg?" Molly asked, standing on the opposite side of the bed, stroking Taren's hair.

Mirek let his magic seep into his brother for a bit longer before he stopped to rest for a few minutes. He worried about draining all his magic at once.

When he went back to healing and watched as the two pieces of the bone came together, Molly talked to Taren. "Your dad fixed it," Molly said, awe in her voice. "He said healing hurts, but it doesn't last for long. And it didn't. Mirek will fix it."

After ten minutes, Mirek was beginning to think that Molly was wrong. His dad had never taken this long to heal someone. The bones were together, but he could still see the break.

"Can you fix it?" Dylan asked from beside him.

"I don't think I have enough magic to fix it completely."

"Remember when our dads told us about all three of them trying to do a McTwist at the skateboard park?"

Gently pulling his hands away from Taren, Mirek dropped his butt to his heels, suddenly feeling exhausted. He looked up at his cousin standing behind him, welcoming the break.

"Yeah. They said they each broke an ankle. My dad healed them so Grandma didn't find out they'd left the house when they were grounded." Mirek wished his dad was there to help him. But that was stupid. If his dad was there, they wouldn't be locked in a basement and Taren wouldn't be hurt. Mirek blinked against the burning behind his eyes. "They were teenagers though. They had their full magic."

Dylan rolled his eyes. "I know. But my dad said his break was really bad and Uncle Evan couldn't heal him all the way because he'd used up his magic healing himself and Uncle Thomas."

"Uncle Thomas helped him!" Mirek whispered when he remembered the story's details.

"Right." Dylan moved behind Mirek and laid his hands on his shoulders. "Put your hands back on Taren and tell me when."

Taren's face was pale as he lay still on the bed. "You okay if I try again?" Mirek asked him.

At Taren's nod, Mirek sat on his knees, laid his hands on his brother's arm, and closed his eyes. "Okay, Dylan, now." A weird sensation rushed into him, and he felt the power of Dylan's magic mix with his own.

Within a couple of minutes, Mirek's magic told him Taren was healed. He'd been both elated and drained.

Mirek wished everything could be that easy. He pulled

himself back to the present just as the prince and princess sailed away and the credits started to roll.

"Glad that's over," Dylan said as he powered off the TV and DVD player. Turning to Molly, he asked, "If we have to watch a princess movie again, can you pick a different one next time?"

"Maybe." Molly laughed as she walked toward the bathroom to get ready for bed.

A little while later, Molly and Taren were both in bed and Dylan was taking his turn in the bathroom when Mirek heard the lock click.

He rushed to the beds to stand in front of his brother and cousin, then watched the stairs. The footsteps descending it were heavy.

Snake appeared with a long white bag over his shoulder. He looked toward the beds, and his stare landed on Mirek. "Deal with this," he said as he dumped the bag on the couch. The only sound in the room was the click of the lock as he left.

Mirek moved to the couch, hearing the others behind him, and looked down at the bag. It was plastic, with a long zipper running down its length. He'd seen one in a movie before—but that one had been black, not white—a body bag. And judging by the lumps, it wasn't empty.

"Holy cow! Is that a body?" Dylan asked.

Mirek couldn't tear his eyes away from the bag. "I think so." An image of a comic, *Tales from the Crypt*, that his friend had brought to school the year before came to his mind.

"Aren't you going to open it?" Dylan asked, but he didn't sound any steadier than Mirek felt.

Terrified by what they'd find, he reached for the zipper, then pulled his hand back as he pictured a zombie jumping out at him.

"Open it," Taren whispered.

Taking a deep breath, Mirek grasped the zipper and slowly dragged it down. His plan was to zip it back up super-fast if something dangerous tried to escape.

Mirek continued to lower the zipper, but the top third of the bag was empty.

Then he saw hair and his hand faltered. He took another deep breath and dragged the zipper down a few more inches to reveal a little girl.

"What's that smell?" Taren asked before making a gagging noise.

"Burnt hair," Mirek answered without looking up from the girl. Her blond hair was singed on the right side of her head; little curled wisps with blackened ends stuck out.

Her face and the skin down to her neck and chest didn't look right. Red and black patches covered the area, and the skin had peeled away in places.

"Let me see," Molly said. Mirek moved back a step as Molly pushed in beside him. "That's Julia!"

Twenty-Two Years Ago—Two Weeks Later

JULIA FELT a hand on her face and opened her eyes to see a boy. "I've seen you before," she told him.

He pulled his hand back. "I'm Mirek."

"Molly's cousin?"

The boy nodded.

"I went to your funeral. My mommy didn't want me to go, but I thought it was important. You, Dylan, Molly, and Taren were buried with your dads."

He closed his eyes and dropped his chin to his chest.

Maybe she shouldn't have said that.

Julia didn't understand and wasn't sure if she should ask why he wasn't dead. Her mommy and daddy wouldn't have lied to her. Maybe if she waited, he would tell her.

She looked around and noticed she was on a bed, with Mirek sitting beside her. She counted six beds in the room, but it was too dark to see everything else. It must be nighttime.

A light came from a room on the side, like when her mommy and daddy left the light on in her bathroom. The dark wasn't anything to be afraid of, but her mommy said that it didn't matter—she could have the light on anyway.

She sat up and looked at the other beds. Three of them had blanket-covered lumps in them. She pointed to the beds and whispered, "Since you're not dead, does that mean that Dylan, Molly, and Taren aren't dead too? Is that them?"

Mirek lifted his chin and looked at her. "Yes."

He looked sad. Maybe because she kept saying the word *dead* and said she went to his funeral. She didn't like him being sad and wanted to cheer him up. "Mommy and Daddy said your funeral was really nice. I've never been to a funeral before so I couldn't make a comparison. I'd need more samples to know what a nice one looks like. Would you like me to describe it for you?"

"No, it's okay."

Julia wanted to turn more lights on so she could see the rest of the room. She needed to know more—she needed data. Without data, she couldn't figure out where they were or how to get home. Molly was her friend so she could ask her for answers.

Then she remembered when Mommy had told her she shouldn't wake someone up in the middle of the night to ask questions if it wasn't an emergency. Sometimes data gathering could wait.

She turned to Mirek since he was awake. "Why did you guys have a funeral if you're not dead?" she asked quietly.

"Because people think we're dead. I remember a fire, and then we all woke up in this basement. We've been here for almost two months."

"Don't you want to go home?"

"Yes, but we can't."

Julia tried to put all the pieces of information together. "Stranger danger," she whispered as she remembered something she'd been taught. "Did strangers take you?"

The corner of Mirek's lips lifted in a small smile, like she'd said something funny.

"Kind of. I know who the men are, so they're not really strangers, but they are dangerous. I wasn't sure if our dads were dead, but they must be if you went to their funerals."

"But I went to your funeral and you're not dead."

Mirek smiled bigger this time; she liked it because he looked happier. Then he frowned and the sadness came back again. "Yes, I'm sure they're dead. Are our moms and the other kids okay?"

"Your moms were at the funeral, but they were crying, so I don't know if they're okay. I saw Meredith, Rowena, Reece, and Jo. They were all crying too, except for Jo."

Julia wanted to ask Mirek a whole bunch of questions, but her mommy said that sometimes when people were sad, you had to wait to talk. Putting her hands in her lap she envisioned thermal physics equations in her mind to keep herself busy. She just hoped Mirek would talk soon.

"Do you remember what happened to you?" Mirek asked when Julia was working through her twelfth equation.

"I was at a big house with my friend Sarah." She looked at the beds and then remembered she'd only seen three being slept in. "She's not here, is she?"

When Mirek shook his head, his blond hair fell into his

eyes. "You need a haircut," she said, then jerked her hands up and covered her lips. She wasn't supposed to blurt things out like that.

Mirek laughed quietly. "Yes, I do. We all do."

She dropped her hands and smiled.

"What else do you remember?" Mirek asked.

Julia closed her eyes and pictured that day at the house. "Sarah and I were playing with Barbies. Connor conjured them. He's my cousin. He was talking to his friend, Drew. Then Drew got mad and threw a ball of magic. The couch was on fire, and I helped Connor conjure some baking soda to put it out. Connor didn't know he should do that. Baking soda is effective because it releases carbon dioxide when heated, which can smother the fire. You can also use—"

Julia stopped talking when Mirek put his hand on her knee. He didn't look mad, but maybe he didn't like science.

"You can explain that to me later, okay? What else happened?"

She was excited that she'd get to talk to Mirek about science later but focused on his question. "Drew was trying to stop Connor from getting help, and he made the fire worse. Then the curtains caught fire and my clothes..." She looked down, but she was wearing different clothes now.

Then she remembered the pain. She lifted her right hand to touch her cheek, but Mirek grabbed her hand and held it in both of his.

"You were burned," he said quietly. "When you came here, there were burns on your face, neck, and chest. They were really bad. I tried to heal you, but even with Dylan giving me some of his power, my magic wasn't strong enough."

He looked sad again, and she wanted to say something so he wouldn't feel bad. "I was told you're ten and my mommy and daddy said we don't get our full magic until we go

through puberty. That's when our bodies start to change..."
She trailed off because biology was science too.

"I know, but I wanted to heal you. I healed a lot of it, but you'll always have scars." Mirek let go of her hand and brought his hand to her cheek.

His fingers covering her ear felt warm, but she couldn't feel everywhere his palm touched her cheek—only in some places. Julia knew what that meant. Her daddy had a set of encyclopedias, and she could look through them anytime she wanted. There was a volume about the human body, and she'd read about burns. Since she couldn't feel Mirek's hand, she probably had a fourth- or fifth-degree burn.

He dropped his hand back into his lap. "That's what I was doing when you woke up. Every night I try to heal you a little bit more, but I don't think it's going to get any better now. The last three nights, it's stayed the same."

She wanted to look in a mirror and examine the burns to see if she could tell which level of degree she had—but it might be too late to tell now—and there was other data she needed more. "How many nights have I been here?"

"Fourteen."

Julia didn't need a bigger sample to extrapolate the possibilities of what her parents must think based on what had happened to Mirek and the others. "My mommy and daddy had a funeral for me too, didn't they?"

"I don't know, but I think so."

"What will the bad men do now?"

Mirek put his hand back on her cheek, but she didn't tell him she couldn't feel it. "I won't let them hurt you, Samantha."

She giggled. "My name is Julia."

"Not anymore. But I will always keep you safe, Sam."

CHAPTER ONE

Present Day — November 1

As Sam Davis packed up her textbooks, a patient walked by. She wondered if the drugs he'd become addicted to had been made by her. The same thought passed through her mind every time she came across a person addicted to drugs, which happened frequently since she spent most afternoons tutoring at an addiction rehabilitation center.

She bundled up, waved goodbye to the night staff, and braced herself as she walked outside into the cold, dark evening. Taking a deep breath of the crisp night air—a new ritual to acclimatize herself to Blue Mountain, Colorado—she let the temperature sink in.

Living in Mexico had never been her choice. Nor had being kidnapped and held captive for twenty-two years. When she'd been rescued a month and a half ago, she made several promises to herself, one of which was to do everything in her power to adjust to this second chance she'd been given.

Making the most of this new life was another promise she'd made to herself. The third one was to do everything in her power to find a way to pull the evil magic from Maverick and close it back into the box. Maybe then she'd be worthy of everyone's love… especially Mirek's, and they could plan a future together.

After a couple of minutes, she walked down the building's steps and turned onto the sidewalk that would take her to a safe place to flash home from.

When she was first rescued and reunited with her parents, life had been exciting. Her days had been filled with getting to know her brothers, spending time with her parents, and getting reacquainted with her other family members and friends. Her mom had been pregnant with her brother Nate when she had been taken, and Travis had been born two years later, and she had so much to catch up on.

Her family had accepted her with open arms and allowed her to adjust at her own pace. Because she hadn't revealed the horrors she'd had a hand in, that had been the easy part. Wondering where Mirek was, how he was doing, and if he was still being tortured was the difficult part.

But that wasn't anything new. Not a day, or even an hour, went by that she didn't think about Mirek. For twenty-two years, he'd been her reason for living. Even when she'd been forced to do unspeakable things, she kept going because of Mirek—he was her best friend and her lover, and he believed in her.

Turning into an alley, she headed to the spot where it connected with a path behind the buildings. The small space was secluded enough to flash to and from without worrying about being seen by non-magics. Sam pushed some magic to her eyes to enhance her vision, making the shadowed darkness a bit easier to traverse.

Her dad always offered to come pick her up and she

always declined, waving him off with a smile and saying she'd be fine. She loved that he offered, and he made it difficult to refuse, but she did. As much as she wanted to spend a few more minutes a day with him, to have his love and attention, she didn't deserve it. Rationally, she knew that denying her dad's attention could hurt him as much as it punished her, but feelings weren't always rational. Mirek had taught her that.

She sensed another presence in the alley, followed by the sound of footsteps behind her.

"What the hell, Sam?"

She turned to see her brother Nate stalking toward her and pulled her hair forward, around the right side of her face.

"Didn't you hear me calling you?"

"I was lost in my thoughts," she told him. When he stood only a couple of feet away, but he didn't reach for her, nor her him. She'd learned on the day she'd met her brother that he didn't touch anyone or let them touch him.

Nate's breathing was heavy as he stared down at her. "You're in an alley by yourself and not even paying attention. Don't you even give a shit?"

Sam didn't answer his question as she figured it was rhetorical. And she wasn't even sure if she did give a shit anymore.

Turning back around, she walked the remaining few feet to where she could flash. Nate followed her.

"I know what you're doing," he said quietly.

She doubted that. The only person who understood her was Mirek, and he wasn't around because of what she'd done.

"What am I doing?" she asked as one hand went to her owl necklace. Holding the familiar shape and everything it represented helped ground her and kept her tone neutral.

Even though Nate didn't fully know her, he was her brother and he cared. He didn't deserve her scorn.

"You're being reckless and putting yourself in harm's way because you think you deserve to be punished."

She'd give him that; he had her pegged. At only twenty-two, Nate was smart and observant, but him knowing wouldn't change the truth.

Sam was just about to flash when Nate held up his hand to halt her, still careful to keep his distance.

"I had a great childhood," he said quietly. "I'm guessing yours was pretty shitty, but I'm not telling you about mine to be a dick. It's just that a lot of kids in my position—the child born after the child genius was thought to have died—may have had a tough time living in their shadow. But Mom and Dad never made me feel that way. I knew they loved you, but they loved me and Travis just the same. It didn't matter whether we aced a test or did something dumb." He chuckled to himself. "Sure, Travis and I did a lot of stupid shit when we were teenagers and got in trouble, but it didn't change how much Mom and Dad loved us. And whatever stupid shit you did, whether it was to just survive or not, it won't change how much Mom and Dad love you."

Even though Nate and her parents truly believed that, it didn't make it so. If they knew the number of lives she'd destroyed, they would look at her differently. But that was the thing about beliefs—no matter how solid they seemed to be—a person didn't truly know how solid they were until they were tested.

"Thanks," she said quietly. "I'm going to flash to Uncle Joel's cabin. You want to come with me or go home?"

"I'll go with you for a while."

"Sounds good." Sam would cherish his love for however long it lasted. She scanned the area just to make sure they were alone and flashed.

Present Day — November 13

MIREK SUCKED in gulps of air even though his brain knew his body didn't need it. Lack of oxygen hadn't been the problem, just the illusion of it. But after another round of Eddie's torture, Mirek didn't have the strength to argue with what his lungs were trying to tell him.

If his body thought it needed air, it could take in as much as it wanted. Maybe he'd hyperventilate and pass out. That would be a welcome reprieve since his head felt like it had a bunch of jackhammers in it, all of them trying to escape at once.

"Okay?" Rocky asked.

"Just swell." Mirek turned his head to look at his cousin as he didn't have the energy to move anything else. They laid sprawled on the subfloor since the hardwood planks had been ripped from their moorings, thanks to Rocky.

Rocky let out a laugh that ended in a cough. "Fuck," he said when he finally caught his breath. "I've had enough of Eddie's torture. That guy's got to go."

Mirek had lost track of how many times Eddie had inflicted the silent death on him lately. That was the name Maverick had given it when he'd learned the nifty little trick after he'd consumed the ancient evil from the magic box a couple of months ago. As Maverick's protégé, Eddie had been given lots of new abilities, but the silent death seemed to be his new favorite.

It froze a person instantly, causing them to lose all control of their body. Mirek knew from firsthand experience that it felt like his brain was about to explode, then he'd drop to the floor and flail about. Silent screams would be forced out of him as his body flopped about helplessly. Eddie claimed that eventually the person's brain would implode. Yes, Eddie needed to go.

"Take my hand."

He looked up at Rocky standing above him with his arm outstretched. Mirek pushed a bit of his remaining power into his limb, giving him enough strength to reach up and grasp Rocky's hand. His cousin hauled him up and slung Mirek's arm over his shoulder, helping him maneuver around the hardwood planks strewn over the floor.

When they'd made it to the hallway, Mirek pulled away, determined to walk on his own. He turned into the next room, and Rocky followed behind, probably worried Mirek would do a face plant.

Twin beds sat against each of the side walls in the narrow, windowless room. The dresser positioned between the beds held nothing but a lamp. Lack of anything personal made the room seem like a transient space, instead of the place Rocky and Mirek spent a considerable amount of time in. Just like in the compound, they'd learned early on that anything kept in the open was fair game to the assholes who controlled them. An item could be taken because it was coveted by someone else or used against them.

They conjured what they needed and disappeared it afterward. And if Mirek didn't have the strength to conjure it, Rocky would do it.

Using what felt like the last of his energy, Mirek stumbled to his bed. Even with the familiar feeling of exhaustion pulling at him, he refused to give in and lie down. Needing to have some control over his own body for a change, he propped himself against the headboard. Over the years he'd come to yearn for the control—a sense that he wasn't completely helpless—after his power had been siphoned or he'd been abused, like when Eddie used his new, nasty trick.

"He won't be gone long. A couple of hours, maybe," Rocky said quietly from the other bed where he'd adopted a similar position.

Mirek didn't need to ask who he meant. Eddie lorded his power over them, and he couldn't seem to stay away.

"You did the right thing, Dylan," Mirek said softly. He rarely used his cousin's real name anymore, but at times like this, he wanted Dylan to remember he wasn't the person Eddie and the others had tried to mold him into.

"You mean the floor?"

"Yeah. When I realized what you were doing by lifting the floorboards and blocking Eddie and his zombies..." He shook his head in awe as he remembered. "It was brilliant."

Rocky met his gaze, his usual self-depreciation and sadness present in the lines around his eyes and mouth. "I could have gotten you killed. For a moment there, I thought Eddie was going to go too far with the silent death."

Mirek shrugged. "I doubt it. You gave Reece and Isabella the chance to escape, and that's what mattered."

Rocky conjured two bottles of water. He removed the cap on one bottle and passed it to Mirek.

"Thanks," he mumbled, grateful Rocky knew he didn't have enough energy to even unscrew a lid. He took the bottle and drank half of it in one go before taking a breath. When he finished off the bottle, Rocky handed him another before conjuring sandwiches.

Minutes went by as they ate in silence. By the time Mirek finished eating, some of his energy had returned. Not much, but enough for now. Rocky conjured another sandwich, and Mirek shook his head when his cousin held it up as if asking if he wanted another.

"Rocky. Next time you get a chance to escape, take it," he said in a serious tone, hoping Rocky would heed his advice for once.

"Don't start that shit again." Rocky glared at him. "Besides, you heard Eddie say he would use one of Maverick's spells on the building. There'd be no way I could get out."

"Not now, but maybe later. You still have your magic, so you'd have a chance. Even after Eddie figured out you betrayed him to help your sister, no one took your magic away. They'd never expect you to leave since they know you've stayed for me."

"And they're right; I wouldn't leave you."

They'd had this conversation a million times in the last decade. Mirek always gave up eventually and didn't push the issue, but not this time because all of Rocky's excuses had been obliterated and he knew it.

"Besides protecting me, you've always claimed that you couldn't go back to our families because they'd never accept you. Now you know that's not true. As soon as Reece saw you today, his love and acceptance was written all over his face."

When Rocky didn't respond, Mirek knew his cousin was hoping he'd fall back into old habits and drop the topic. "Dylan, when you get a chance to escape, take it!"

Rocky's eyes widened as he looked over at him. "You ordering me?"

"Yes."

"Funny," Rocky said without humor.

Mirek felt a bone-deep fatigue, but not only in his body. For years, he'd been looking out for others and fighting to survive. He wanted his cousins and Sam to be safe. It was his biggest wish because he'd given up on wishing for his own freedom a long time ago. Even if he got it, he wasn't sure how he'd feel—after years of abuse, he was a shell of his former self; he wouldn't be good to anyone. And he didn't deserve his freedom before Sam got hers. As far as he knew, she was still at the compound in Mexico.

"I kept you safe for years when we were kids, and now you've kept me safe. We're even. You need to get on with your life."

"Yeah?" Rocky swung his legs over the side of the bed and rested his huge arms on his thighs.

"And what about you?" Rocky's eyes narrowed. "You just planning on lying down and giving up?"

"Don't be an idiot. I've made it this far, haven't I? I don't plan on ever giving up as long as Maverick still has Sam. I'll keep fighting to make sure she's safe. You know that as soon as I leave, he'll use her to get me back, and I'm not going to give him that opportunity."

"Well… Now it's your turn not to be an idiot. Maverick can hurt Sam regardless of where you are. And even though you told me to escape… as long as Maverick still has you, I'm not walking away."

"Touché," Mirek said quietly. He let the topic drop, but Mirek would never forget how he'd failed his little brother. One day, he'd find a way for both Sam and Rocky to be safe and free. Morgana had escaped, which meant it was possible for the rest of them.

The problem was—free or not—the years had scarred Mirek, and not just his face. He felt too broken to have a future with Sam, but he wouldn't fail her and Rocky again. Not like he'd done for so long, starting seventeen years ago.

CHAPTER TWO

Seventeen Years Ago

Sam finished making her bed and looked up as Morgana walked over.

"You ready to go?" Morgana asked.

"Yes." Sam took one look around to make sure nothing in the girls' bunk room looked out of place and flicked off the light as she followed Morgana. "Do you think we're going to get a teacher?" They'd only been in Mexico a week and Sam was already itching to get back to learning.

Morgana giggled and put her hand over her mouth. "You're probably the only ten-year-old who would study every day and never take a break," she whispered.

"I know," Sam whispered back. Mirek said it was okay that she liked to learn all the time and that the other kids didn't. He'd told her to embrace her differences and so she did. Mirek had always seen things she didn't, and at fifteen, he was wise in a way Sam didn't think she'd ever be. When she'd questioned him about it years ago, he'd said there were different types of intelligence.

It had taken her a while to find what she'd sought from their limited textbooks, but now she knew what he'd meant. She had an extremely high IQ, but her EQ wasn't as high as Mirek's. Since that discovery, she'd decided to see if she could improve it.

She started by observing everything and everyone around her. When she got stuck in a book, her observation skills of her physical environment were horrible—in the shitter, as Rocky would say. That always made her smile.

Even walking down the hall, she had to remember to observe. The compound they were in was huge, and the all-purpose room they were going to was on the far side from their bunk room. They walked by room after room, and like always, they passed men with guns.

The men looked like soldiers. But their clothing was mostly solid colors, not camouflage patterned, and they didn't have insignia like she'd seen in movies. Mirek had told them not to make eye contact with the men because it brought attention to themselves.

As two men came toward them, Sam turned her head and pretended to look at the room on her right. As the men passed, Morgana let out a large breath. But some equipment caught Sam's eye and she was already headed into the room.

"What are you doing?" Morgana hissed.

Sam shot a glance over her shoulder at Morgana. "There's science equipment in here." Turning back, she tiptoed into the room, and then giggled at herself. Even she wasn't smart sometimes—as if tiptoeing would prevent someone from seeing her.

She estimated the room was twenty feet wide and at least forty feet long. It was the biggest room she'd seen in the compound so far. Burners and beakers with hosing lined the counters and pallets of boxes wrapped in cellophane.

"What is all this?" Morgana asked quietly from beside her.

Sam could depend on Morgana to be her partner in crime—she was always up for an adventure, even if it got them in trouble.

"I think it's a drug lab. Those are..." Her words trailed off as she walked over to inspect the respirators on a work bench.

Someone pulled on Sam's arm, spinning her around, and she squealed. If she'd been a cartoon, her heart would have jumped out of her chest and run away.

Mirek towered over her, but he looked more worried than angry. "You two shouldn't be in here. Hurry, or we'll be late." He headed for the door and held his hand back for her to hold. Morgana didn't like holding his hand anymore, said it was childish, but Sam loved it.

"It's clear," Mirek said before pulling Sam along with him after checking the hallway, and she had to run to keep up with him. As they turned the corner into the all-purpose room she glanced at the large clock on the wall. They were four minutes late.

Sam scanned the room. Rocky, Taren, and a couple of other kids were sitting on couches while Zeus and Maverick stood by the windows. The sun was at their backs, and Sam had to squint to see them properly.

"You're late," Zeus said.

"I saw—" Sam stopped talking when Mirek squeezed her hand. It was one of many signals they'd come up with over the years. Sometimes when they were sitting down, he'd give her leg a small squeeze instead.

"Sorry, Zeus. We'll try not to let it happen again," Mirek said. Then he pulled on her arm to direct her to the couch. She sat on the one with Taren and Rocky. Morgana crowded in beside her.

"Not good enough," Maverick said, his tone stricter than

she'd ever heard it. Sam looked to Mirek for reassurance, hoping they wouldn't get in trouble.

His head jerked up as his feet left the ground. He was suspended a few inches above the ground. His eyes looked too wide, and his fingers clawed at his neck as if trying to pry someone's hands from his throat, but no one held him.

"Mirek!" She jumped to her feet and reached for Mirek, but someone held her back. She tried to wiggle out of the grip, needing to help Mirek.

"Stop!" Rocky said quietly in her ear. "We need to sit down and behave, or Maverick will do something even worse."

Sam let Rocky pull her back down onto the couch, but she didn't take her eyes off Mirek. Counting the seconds gave her something to do, but it was the longest sixty seconds of her life. Small rivulets of blood ran down Mirek's neck. Then his eyes closed and his hands dropped uselessly to his sides.

Mirek fell forward and he caught himself on his hands and knees. His breathing sounded worse than hers after she ran the length of the soccer field while playing with the other kids. She wanted to reach for him but was afraid of what would happen.

"That was a nice little trick. I'll have to remember that," Zeus said as he walked over and stood behind Mirek. But Zeus didn't look down at him. His gaze landed on Sam, then Morgana, before trailing over the others.

"Do you know what Maverick did?" Zeus asked them, looking happy, like he was about to eat a bowl of his favorite ice cream. "Maverick suspended him and cut off his air. Any longer, and Mirek would be dead."

Zeus grinned at his pronouncement. Sam didn't think she'd ever seen him smile like that before. A few seconds later, his usual frown appeared, and he peered down at

Mirek. Grabbing the back of his shirt, he hauled him up. "Sit down."

Rocky scooted over, and everyone else did the same to make room for Mirek. He flopped onto the couch beside Sam, and she squeezed his leg to let him know she was sorry.

Maverick cleared his throat. When Sam looked up at him, she followed his path as he walked the few steps over to them. "I hope you've all learned that lateness will not be tolerated." He paused and looked directly at Sam. She couldn't look away even though he was the most terrifying man she'd ever seen.

"You will all continue to have a tutor as you did before, but you will also have jobs. Each morning, you will report to Maria." He gestured toward a woman standing beside the doorway who Sam hadn't noticed. "She will make sure your studying is done and then give you assigned chores or jobs for the day."

Mirek shifted beside Sam. She feared for him because she knew he was about to ask a question and it could lead to further punishment.

"WHY ARE WE HERE?" Mirek asked, doing his best to keep any signs of challenge out of his voice. "You said the council leader is dead and that you've killed our families. So why can't we leave?"

Sam squeezed his thigh again. He put his hand on top of hers and gave her a little squeeze back. He needed to know what Maverick, Zeus, and Snake had in store for them and why they seemed to need them. Without that knowledge, he couldn't protect Sam and the others from what would be coming next.

"We don't need you," Zeus sneered. "But since the council leader is dead and we no longer need to follow his plan for you, we're going to use you. Free labor."

"Exactly." Maverick smiled, like he had a devious plan. "I set up a nice operation here years ago, but it could always use a few extra sets of hands."

"The lab," Sam whispered.

"Yes, Sam, good girl." Maverick smiled again, his praise a twisted compliment, as he flung his hand toward them.

Sam cried out as magic lifted her several feet into the air. Mirek shot to his feet and gripped Sam's small hips, but Maverick's hold stopped him from pulling her back down.

"Thought you might need a reminder why trying to leave won't be a good idea. I control you all. Soon, you'll be working in the lab. Years ago, a seer told us Sam would be worth the hassle of taking her, and I believe that little prophecy is about to come true."

Mirek heard Sam's gasp but didn't let go of her. It would be just like Maverick to let Sam drop to the ground without warning.

"Maria," Zeus said, waving the woman over. "If any of them get out of line, just let me know."

Maria nodded. When Zeus and Maverick left, Mirek took the full weight of Sam into his hands, as the spell on her released. After he lowered her to the ground, he pulled her back so they were once more sitting on the couch, and shifted sideways so he could look into her eyes.

"I'm sorry, Mirek," Sam said quietly.

"It's okay. We'll just have to make sure we're not late again, but someday we'll find a way to leave. We're also going to find some time to practice with whatever magic we have. If there's ever a way we can fight back, we need to be ready."

Sam nodded as her eyes filled with tears, but she blinked them away. In the five years they'd been together, he'd realized the tutors and the bosses only seemed to notice Sam's intelligence. Even when she'd come to them at five, there had been no mistaking her genius, but what most people didn't see was how beautiful and strong a person she was—both inside and out—regardless of her scars.

"You don't have to hide your tears with me, Sam. You're like Athena, and I bet she never hid her emotions."

"Athena? Like in *Percy Jackson and the Olympians?*" She gave him a small smile. "She was the goddess of wisdom and warfare—battle strategy..." Sam shook her head. "I'm not like her, and the tutors and bosses said tears don't help anything."

Sam was now the same age Mirek had been when they'd all been taken—ten—and had lived half her life with assholes telling her how to behave. He brushed her hair off her face where she always pulled it over to cover her right cheek.

"You are like her. You're beautiful, strong, and wise. Plus, feelings aren't rational, and it's okay to cry when you feel like it. Whether tears help or not doesn't matter. You just need to accept your feelings because they make you who you are."

"Do you accept yours?"

He couldn't help but smile. Being super intelligent and yet innocent at the same time, she probably didn't even realize she was throwing his words back at him. "I try. And when I don't, I'll have you to remind me, okay?"

"Okay. Oh... Athena was the patron saint of heroes, and that makes sense because you've always been my hero."

Mirek didn't consider himself a hero, especially today. But before he could say anything Maria called to them in lightly-accented English, and they all moved over to the tables. Since they'd been studying together for years, they quickly fell into their routine with the lesson plans that Maria had for each of them, while she worked with some other kids who needed more help.

They worked for a couple of hours before Maria left after

giving them some more reading to do. She told them she'd be back the next day.

"Sam, look!" Morgana said from across the room. All the kids walked over to Morgana, who stood next to a bookcase, a big grin on her face. She was practically vibrating as she pointed to the bottom shelves. "Encyclopedias!"

Sam laughed and dropped to her knees to pull one of the heavy books into her lap.

"Let me help," Taren said as he grabbed a book. Rocky and Morgana took a book as well, but the other kids they'd met that morning, who obviously didn't get the same excitement from encyclopedias, left.

There'd been a time when none of them would have been excited over the thick tomes either, but Sam had made learning fun for all of them. Studying different topics had become part of their family time.

"Where do you want to start?" Mirek asked once they were all back at the table with the books open.

"These books were printed a long time ago, so I'm not sure they'll have what we need," Sam said as she ran her hand over one book's hard cover.

He frowned. "What do you mean? Are these an older edition than you had in the last house?"

"No, they're the same. But since they were printed years ago, they won't have anything about making drugs."

"What?" Rocky sounded like he was going to choke.

"The lab we saw this morning… I think it's for making drugs. Maverick mentioned his *operation*," Sam said while making air quotes. "I think his operation is a drug lab and he's going to put us to work in it. We need a plan to make sure we can take care of ourselves so we're not exposed to anything too dangerous."

There was no way they could protect themselves against

all the possible dangers in the compound, even if there hadn't been a drug lab.

Present Day — November 17

MIREK TOOK another sip of his coffee and savored the rich earthy taste as he watched the sunrise in the distance. He'd been drawn to the balcony after brewing a pot and had stepped out into the chill wearing only a pair of sweatpants and a hoodie he'd been given the night before. Leaning against the wall, the cold of the concrete floor against his bare feet made him feel alive.

The whoosh of the patio door opening sounded before Rocky took a spot beside him.

"Did you get any sleep?" Rocky asked.

"Some. You?"

"Same."

They were both quiet for a while as they drank their coffee and watched the sun rise. As it had been for years, the silence between them was comfortable. Eventually, one of them would speak, but neither worried about filling the quiet with useless chatter.

"It's surreal, isn't it?" Rocky asked, finally breaking the silence after a while.

"Yes, but which part?" Mirek huffed out a laugh. "That Eddie is dead or that we're finally in our parents' building after more than two decades?"

"All of it. I'm glad that fucker Eddie is dead. I didn't know when it would happen, but I knew it would eventually. Too bad his own greed killed him because I would have liked to do the deed myself."

Mirek looked at his cousin. "I'm not. You don't need that weighing you down."

"Wouldn't matter; it would just be one more thing." Rocky shrugged. "Either way, I'm glad he's dead and you were able to heal Isabella."

"Yeah, me too. It was touch and go there for a bit."

"Really? You didn't show it."

"I didn't want to let Reece know." Mirek faced the skyline again, and they lapsed into silence once more.

Rocky was right; everything felt a bit surreal. The last time Mirek had been in the building, he had been ten years old. His father and uncles were showing the family all the plans they had for the three buildings they'd purchased years before. The Magic Plate had come first, and then his dad said their progress had stalled because they'd gotten busy with raising families, but they were ready to move onto the next stage of their plans.

From the little he'd heard the previous night, it sounded like his cousin Meredith had moved on those plans in the last few years. He looked forward to hearing the details eventually.

The night before, he, Rocky, Isabella, and Reece had retrieved the sword, giving Mirek the possibility of a future. One that for the first time in years, didn't look bleak. Isabella and Reece had explained that they'd located three mirrors, and when working together, they would reveal a sword. Created and hidden centuries ago, the sword was the key to forging a lock that would seal the evil magic away forever.

When they'd left Maverick's building, leaving Eddie's body behind, the only thing on their minds had been escaping before they were caught. All four of them—almost completely drained of their magic—had been solely focused on going home.

Home. He hadn't thought about it for a long time. It

wasn't until Rocky had driven the SUV they'd taken up to the curb alongside his family's buildings, that Mirek's new reality had started to sink in. Freedom had been a foreign concept for decades.

During the short drive, Reece had reached out to Jack telepathically and let him know what was going on. That's when they'd learned that Maverick had created a diversion, which was why Jack and his wife, Meredith, hadn't been able to come to their aid when Reece and Isabella had reached out for help.

Jack and Meredith had greeted them and ushered them into one of the buildings. Isabella and Reece excused themselves and headed to his apartment. When Meredith led Mirek and Rocky to an empty apartment on the seventh floor, all they'd wanted was food and sleep to recharge.

While they ate, Jack conjured some clothes for them and Meredith gave them the bare-bones information about the new council. She said that it was the reason she and Jack were able to help replenish Mirek and Rocky's magic.

Past midnight and extremely exhausted, even with a new influx of power, he'd asked that a reunion with family wait until the morning. He wouldn't sleep long—he never did anymore—but he needed at least a few hours. Becoming a light sleeper had been a side effect of taking on the responsibility of the adult in his new, small family at ten years of age, always worried about his brother and cousins.

"Want a refill?" Rocky asked, breaking into his thoughts.

"Sure."

Rocky went into the apartment and brought back the coffee pot, setting it on the concrete once he'd filled their mugs. They resumed leaning against the wall as the sun crested on the horizon.

"Better than conjuring," Rocky muttered.

"True." Mirek had never been opposed to conjuring

coffee, but he hadn't had to when he'd first started drinking it. Being ten years of age when he was kidnapped, coffee was something he considered only an adult drink. By the time he'd come into his full magic, he and the other kids had been transferred to Mexico and rich, organic coffee was everywhere. There had been no need to conjure it.

Then he'd been brought to Blue Mountain, Colorado. Shuttled between a couple of apartment buildings by his captors, he or Rocky had conjured most of what they needed.

They'd been so close to home and yet… He cut off the thoughts of the last two years and focused on the present.

Jack said to be at The Magic Plate at ten in the morning. He'd promised to make sure no one bothered Mirek or Rocky before that, giving them a bit of time to rest and prepare for the reunion.

It wouldn't be a huge reunion as his parents and his aunts and uncles were all dead. Only his sister and cousins were still alive in his family.

He'd read once that after a long time apart, a person became fixed in their mind at the last age they saw them at. Last night he realized how true that was. Meredith, being Morgana's twin, had been seven the last time he'd seen her, and Jack twelve. Even though Meredith looked a lot like Morgana, Morgana had been spellbound the last time he'd seen her and hadn't looked like herself. Seeing Meredith all grown up had been like meeting a stranger.

Life had gone on, of course, but it was still going to take some adjustment. Thinking of everything he missed made him think of Sam. Although almost everything made him think of her since she was never far from his thoughts.

The night before, when Isabella's life force was dying, and Reece begged Mirek to save her, he'd said that Sam had been rescued. It was one more thing that felt surreal.

Mirek hovered his hands over Isabella and then dropped them to his knees. He'd looked up at Reece, feeling beyond exhausted, both physically and mentally. "To non-magics, she would be dead, Reece."

"What do you mean to non-magics?"

"Her body is dead, but her magic hasn't left her yet. As long as she still has some magic remaining in her body, she's still technically alive."

"Please, Mirek. Sam said you're an extraordinary healer," Reece had pleaded, a glimmer of hope in his voice.

"Sam?" As if he'd had adrenaline shot right into his veins, he'd sat up straighter. "You've seen her?"

"Yes, she's back home."

Relief hit Mirek so strongly that he'd slumped forward and hung his head.

"She said she loves you. Do you love her too?"

"I do," Mirek whispered, lifting his head to meet his cousin's eyes.

"Then you'll understand what I'm feeling. I love Isabella, but it's more than that. I've never felt anything like this before. I need her. I'll give my life for hers. Please, you have to help her."

With power from Reece and Rocky, Mirek had been able to save her. Although the future was a mystery, at least for now, Reece wouldn't have to know what it felt like to live without the one person who completed him.

For seven years, that had been Mirek's fate—separated from Sam when she'd been twenty and he twenty-five. Only seeing each other once, a time Mirek wishes he could have taken back.

"Hey, you okay?" Rocky asked, pulling Mirek back to the present.

He looked at his cousin. "Yeah, just thinking about seeing family." Mirek didn't need to mention Sam; Rocky knew she was always present in his thoughts. "Are you ready?"

"Yeah. Although Reece and I haven't gotten to catch up, at least I don't have to worry about his reaction. As for Jo…"

"She's your sister. She'll love you no matter what, and I bet she's grateful. Not only that you're alive, but that you saved her life. She won't care that you didn't let her see you. If you had, Eddie would have known you were never on his side, and you don't know what he would have done to her."

Rocky gave a large harumph. "Like he didn't figure it out anyway."

Mirek put his hand on his cousin's shoulder and waited until Rocky looked him in the eyes. "You saved me. You saved Jo. And you made sure Lucas was able to get help. And Jo knows that too."

"Okay. Let's go get ready," Rocky said as he opened the patio door, but he didn't sound convinced.

He followed Rocky inside and didn't say anything. Mirek had watched Rocky beat himself up for years and knew that nothing he could say right now would change how he felt. Maybe being around family would finally allow him to heal, but he'd bet money that Rocky already had his exit strategy planned.

His cousin likely wouldn't stick around, just like Mirek wouldn't, but for different reasons. Which meant he would see Sam and then he would leave. He would do whatever was necessary to protect Sam, even staying away until he was the man she needed him to be.

CHAPTER THREE

Sam reared back as two hands planted on the table
in front of her.

"Finally," Nate hissed in a low voice. "The entire family
has been looking everywhere for you."

Sweeping her hair around her face, the only protection
she had against his fierce stare, she fumbled for something to
say. "I—" She only got one word out before Nate interrupted
her, a strange panic lighting his eyes.

"Why didn't you answer your phone?"

"I—" Once more, Nate wouldn't let her speak and as he
ranted on, she pulled her phone out of her bag. There were
five missed calls and six unread text messages. A horrible
feeling crawled up her spine. In her experience any news was
bad news.

"Mom and Dad were checking with everyone at the
Williams's buildings and Uncle Joel went to his cabin looking
for you. I even went to the rehab center twice and finally
someone there said you like to come to the library."

She stared up at her brother, still leaning on his
outstretched hands and towering over her. He was tall, like

their father, and in the couple of months she'd been home, she'd spent hours looking at baby pictures of him and Travis. But she hadn't embraced them the way everyone wanted her to. She couldn't. They would reject her if they discovered what she'd done because she wasn't worthy of being in their lives. And when that happened, it could finally break her.

Nate frowned at her. "Aren't you going to say anything?"

"You going to let me?"

He straightened up. "Sorry. We were just worried." He looked down at the books she had spread all over the table. "Are those encyclopedias?"

"Yes." Sam ran her hand over one of the books like it was a precious gift. It didn't matter that the set wasn't the same one she'd had growing up. It wasn't even the same edition, as a new one had come out in 2010, but some of the historic pictures were the same. They made her feel closer to Mirek because it reminded her of the two of them going through the old books together.

"There's a thing called the internet, you know. These are even online," he said, gesturing to the books.

Explaining what the old encyclopedias meant to her would mean revealing some of the things she'd gone through, and she wasn't ready for that. Instead, she tried to get him back on track. "Why were you in a rush to find me?"

"Oh right. Reece rescued Mirek and Dylan... or Rocky... whatever... and everyone is meeting at The Magic Plate at ten this morning."

Sam reached for her necklace, rubbing the familiar pendant in her hand. Meredith had told her four days ago that Mirek was alive, but Sam had been afraid to hope. She'd been heartbroken so many times that she'd learned to shove any type of hope down deep. Now she'd finally get to see him —but would he even want to see her? Did he still love her? It didn't matter; she needed to see him no matter what.

Giving her head an internal shake, she shoved her chair back and stood as she grabbed her phone to check the time. It was already twenty past ten. "Quick, help me put these away."

It seemed to take forever to shelve the books and get to a safe place to flash, although it only took a few minutes. Then, not knowing if The Magic Plate was open to the public or not, Sam and Nate flashed to the back of the restaurant. They went in the back door of the empty kitchen and then pushed through the swinging door, into the dining area.

Once through the door, she stopped, forcing herself to breathe as a tightness in her throat threatened to cut off her air supply.

Nate brushed her shoulder and had to sidestep to avoid slamming into her.

"You okay?" he asked.

She nodded, her throat too constricted to speak, but it must have been answer enough since Nate nodded and walked away.

The air she'd been forcing in and out of her lungs didn't feel sufficient. The constriction in her throat had slid to her chest and she felt like she'd never be able to get enough oxygen again. Her feet felt frozen to the floor.

She wanted to run forward but couldn't.

Mirek stood within a circle of people off to the side of the restaurant. He had an arm slung around Rowena's shoulders, holding his sister to his side.

Instead of moving forward, Sam took him in. Like memorizing the pages of the encyclopedias so long ago, she just wanted to observe every detail and change in him.

His hair was longer on top than it had been, but the sides were still short. Covered with a few days' worth of blond beard, his gaunt cheeks made the scar on the left side of his face stand out.

Like it had a mind of its own, her hand came up and rubbed her own cheek as memories flooded her all at once. She saw ten-year-old Mirek in the dim light from the bathroom as he looked heartbroken at not being able to heal her more. Then an image of him at sixteen when his own face had become scarred.

They both had so many more scars, most of which weren't even visible.

Sam continued to soak in Mirek's appearance. Even thinner than the last time she'd seen him, his skin pale. She still thought he was the most beautiful man in the world.

As she watched him laugh with his cousins, his sister looked in Sam's direction, as if sensing her presence. Rowena elbowed Mirek and lifted her chin in Sam's direction.

Mirek's gaze locked on hers.

For years Sam had been surviving day to day. Her life had been upended many times over and her heart shattered. She'd struggled to keep going and come to terms with everything she had been forced to do and fought to make up for all her wrongs.

Now, for the first time in years, her world righted itself. The wrongs hadn't been fixed, but as Mirek walked toward her, it felt like he was picking up the pieces of her heart along the way and putting them back together.

She'd imagined this moment a million times and had rehearsed everything she would say, but looking up into his face, she had no words. Instead, she took a step forward, and then another.

Mirek stopped and opened his arms, and she walked right into them.

There weren't any kisses.

No words were spoken.

But she would never forget the moment for as long as she lived.

She was finally where she belonged.

They stood in each other's arms and held on.

When Mirek finally pulled back, Sam looked up into his eyes and felt every emotion she'd been holding onto for three years let go.

Tears welled in her eyes, but she didn't bother to wipe them away because they were tears of joy.

Like they'd done so many times in the past, she lifted her hand and cupped the left side of his face as he mirrored her movement and cupped her face's right side. They'd once joked that between them, each with half a scarred face, they made the perfect whole.

"I've imagined this a million times," he whispered as if he'd read her thoughts.

Before she could respond, he took her hand, pulling her with him as he headed toward the back of the restaurant. She didn't ask where they were going because it didn't matter. She would follow Mirek anywhere.

SOME PART of Mirek knew he shouldn't be pulling Sam along like he was a caveman and she was his possession, but he couldn't help himself. He felt nothing like he'd imagined he would when he saw her again for the first time in years.

He'd envisioned holding her while they talked, kissed, and got to know each other after so many years apart. The sex between them had been exciting and fun, but not like the overpowering desire now consuming him. His need to be inside her was driving him like an addict who had gone days without a fix.

Mirek pushed through a door to a stairway off the side of the kitchen that led to a walkway connecting the buildings.

He and Rocky used to hide in it when the younger kids wanted to play hide and seek.

Hurrying up the stairs, he still held Sam's hand, her keeping pace with him. When he got to the second floor and found the alcove he remembered—just a small, partially hidden, empty sitting area—he pulled Sam into it with him.

Taking her in his arms, he spun them, putting her back against the wall, and lifted her. She wrapped her legs around him, like they'd done so many times in the past, melting away the time they'd been apart.

Without missing a beat, he leaned forward and their lips met; sparks flashed between them with the same intensity they always had. Sam parted her lips for him and when their tongues met, he felt like he was finally home.

Sam smelled like honeysuckle and orange, scents that always reminded him of her.

When they finally pulled apart, gasping for air, he worried that he'd moved too fast. Had he let his need for her override his love?

He rested his forehead against hers as their breathing slowed down. "I should have talked with you before dragging you here."

"No. What you did was perfect. Please don't stop. I need you, hero."

The old nickname made him smile, but before he could comment on it, a breeze rushed over his body. He looked down; they were both naked. He'd taught that trick to her years ago, and he would have laughed if his lust and love weren't driving him to make her his again. "Are you sure, Athena?"

"More than I've ever been. I haven't been with anyone but you, and I'm on birth control."

She looked down for a moment, a response honed in her from years of worrying about speaking up. Before he could say anything, she lifted her chin, and he saw his strong, independent Sam break through the conditioning. "I wanted to be prepared. I knew you would come back to me."

Mirek felt a small ache in his heart, and he knew it was only a precursor for the pain to come when he had to leave her. "Sam, I…" He paused, unsure how to tell her what he needed to.

She placed a finger on his lips. "We can talk later. Please, Mirek."

He kissed the tip of her finger, then leaned his head forward again and captured her mouth with his. There was nothing tentative about their kiss as they came together like lovers long familiar with each other.

Sam reached her hand down between them, and Mirek pulled back just enough to give her room. He let out a groan when she gripped him and felt his breath catch as she positioned him against her wet heat. At the same time, he pushed some magic into his arms to give himself more strength to support her as she lowered onto his length. She used his shoulders for leverage to lift and lower herself as he rocked up into her. They didn't take long to establish a fast rhythm.

"I'm not going to last," he gasped, dropping his forehead to hers as he continued to thrust up into her. "Rub yourself," he said.

Sam put her hand between them, and her body tightened around him. Tilting his hips at an angle he knew she loved, she detonated and took him with her. An intensity of pleasure he hadn't felt since he was last with her exploded inside him.

"That's not how I imagined our reunion," he whispered, kissing her forehead. "I wanted to take it slow and worship you."

Sam huffed out a laugh. "Later. Besides, I'm heavy." She

took her hand off his shoulder and flicked it behind them. "There."

With her legs still wrapped around him, he turned. A large armchair that hadn't been there before was snugged into the corner.

"You're not heavy, but you make my legs weak," he said with a smirk, and as he eased down into the chair, his cock slipped from her body. She giggled and wiggled back and forth in his lap, smearing their juices across them both.

He'd taken a risk, making love to her in a stairwell, and didn't want to imagine what would have happened if her parents had come looking for her. But he had no regrets.

Using his magic, he cleaned and dressed them without either of them standing up. He wanted her again, but he felt drained, even though Jack had done so much to heal him the night before.

Sam snuggled into his chest, and he tightened his arms around her, wanting to hold on and never let go. If only he could, but Mirek knew better. This couldn't last. He wasn't the man she needed right now.

Her fingers stole between the opening of his Henley, and she rubbed small circles on his skin. "I love you, Mirek," she whispered.

"I love you too, Sam. I always have and I always will."

She looked up at him. "You're going to leave, aren't you?" she whispered.

He kissed her forehead and pulled her back against his chest. The look of sorrow in her eyes was too much to take, and he needed to hold her for just a little while longer. "I have to." She didn't push away, only continued to caress his skin with her soft fingers. That was his Sam. She'd wait and listen until he was finished and then carefully weigh his words before speaking.

He took a big breath, knowing no matter the pain it

would cause them both, he had to leave. "Eddie is dead, but Maverick is still out there. You know what he can do. I thought I would need to leave you because as long as we're together, he'll hurt you to get to me. I—"

Sam cut him off. "If Maverick wants us, it won't matter where we are."

"When I told Rocky I would leave to keep you safe, he called me an idiot. You're both right."

He'd had a lot of time to think in the past four days and realized he'd been using keeping Sam safe as an excuse. Although he always wanted her to be safe—and that hadn't changed—he had finally admitted to himself that he wasn't in the right frame of mind to make sure that happened. Chances were he'd always feel like he'd failed in the past, but if he didn't find a way to heal himself, he would fail again.

Just seeing Sam in person again had his emotions raging out of control. Being passionate with the woman he loved was one thing, but what would happen if it was his anger or hatred he couldn't get a grip on? His losing control had led to Taren's death and Sam and his cousins being tortured countless times because of him. He refused to allow another of his mistakes to lead to anyone else being hurt, even if that meant staying away from Sam.

It would be the hardest thing he'd ever done. Not even being tortured, siphoned of magic, or forced to heal until his life force was almost drained, could compare to making himself stay away from Sam. To not see her smile, hear her laugh, or listen to her go on about things that fascinated her, when he was so close, might just kill him. But it was better than losing control and hurting her.

"It's going to sound selfish... but I need some time by myself. I... what..." His throat burned at the thought that Sam might think he was pushing her away, and he fought against a lump to swallow. "I need to process everything I've been through... I feel like I wouldn't be able to be there for you the way I should… until I can heal myself."

"I want to be there for you too," she whispered against him, making him feel like he'd failed her again.

Holding her shoulders, he pushed her away from him a few inches so he could look into her eyes. "I love you so much, Sam. My Athena. I'd do anything for you. I just need to get myself together first."

"I've waited years for us to be together," she said quietly. Her tone reeked of sadness, and the ache in his chest turned to pain.

"I've waited years too, and one day we will be together," he said softly when she laid back on his chest. "Because you're my patron saint and I'm your hero."

She shook in his arms, her sobs silent after years of being punished for making a noise. All he could do was hold her and hope that his words wouldn't prove him to be a liar.

CHAPTER FOUR

Present Day — November 23

irek picked up the water bottle he'd refilled and chugged the ice-cold liquid. When he'd drained the bottle dry, he tossed it onto the small pile with others to refill later and lifted the hem of his shirt to mop the sweat from his face.

Six days ago when he arrived, he'd been so sure that he would find the answers he needed. Even though it was the site of huge tragedy, before that, it had been a place of happiness. His parents and aunts and uncles had loved coming out here. They'd said it was a place that allowed them to let the rest of the world fall away.

Placing his hands on his lower back, he arched into a stretch. His gaze wandered over the meadow where his family's cabin used to be and then across the lake. The blue water stretched for what felt like forever, and for brief moments, it gave Mirek a sense of calm. Then his emotional exhaustion returned.

Each day Mirek pushed his body and felt physically stronger. If only that were enough.

"What's the rush?" Rocky asked.

Mirek turned to see Rocky walking toward him from where he must have landed about twenty yards away.

Rocky had visited a couple of times, but he never stayed for more than a few hours. There was a restlessness about his cousin that had gotten worse in the last year.

"Rush?"

"Yeah. You seem like a man hellbent on a mission. I was just here two days ago and it looks like you've done a week's worth of work."

Mirek had cleared and prepped the area, both by hand and with magic, and used his magic for the excavation. "You want to help me with the footings?"

"Sure."

They worked together for several hours, only talking when required, until Rocky stopped and bumped his shoulder.

"When did you conjure that?" Rocky smirked, tilting his head toward the tent off to the side of the cabin. "Got cold?"

"Fuck off," Mirek said, but there wasn't any heat in his words.

Rocky had told him on his first visit that it was too cold to be roughing it out under the stars. Mirek had ignored him, needing to be here.

A warm front had settled into the area, and for the first few days, a winterized sleeping bag and his campfire had been enough. Then regular November temperatures had settled in, bringing snow. Walking through the cold slush had made him question his own sanity, and that's why he'd come to the remote location to begin with. He needed to be with his own thoughts and away from people, even Sam, although she was always on his mind.

"Do you feel closer to them by being here?" Rocky asked out of the blue.

Putting down the shovel, Mirek looked out over the field and contemplated how to answer the question. He didn't remember much about the fire, just the odd flashes of his father and brother. Over the years Zeus would bring it up every now and then. The older man would taunt Mirek and the others, saying that their fathers had died helpless and screaming. That their mothers and the rest of the children died trying to save them.

Zeus had been a sick bastard and reveled in providing details about the burned-out shell and ashes—all that was left of the cabin Mirek's dad and uncles had built. From what Mirek could tell, Zeus's rants never had a purpose beyond wanting them to wallow in their sorrow, but perhaps that alone gave Zeus a sense of power. Although why he needed it over a bunch of kids, Mirek never knew.

When he'd arrived, he hadn't known what to expect—maybe the destroyed remnants of the cabin. "I thought I'd feel closer to them here," he said as he surveyed the area. "I remember our parents saying that when they came up here, all their troubles fell away. I can imagine how they felt… the area is familiar—even with the cabin gone—and the solitude is a refreshing change…" Mirek let his voice trail off, not knowing what else to say since he still felt such turmoil inside.

"I get it. I thought coming here would make me feel closer to my dad, but with the cabin gone…"

"It's like one more reminder of what we missed, isn't it?"

Rocky nodded before pointing to the log they'd just prepped. "Let's get this into place."

They fell silent again, only talking as needed to work, but even that wasn't much. He and Rocky had spent years together, and in situations most people would never be able to comprehend. Even when it looked like Rocky was working for the wrong side, they'd trusted and relied on each other. They'd come to know what the other was thinking.

When they had the footings laid with help from their magic, they took a break. Mirek started a fire in the pit he'd built, and Rocky conjured some sandwiches and a couple of beers.

"Cheers," he said, lifting his beer to Rocky and taking a long swallow. Beer had been foreign to them until a couple of years ago when Mirek had been taken back to Blue Mountain and Rocky made sure he got invited along. Before then, they'd been treated like children. Although Mirek was still held by a very short leash and drained of his magic, drinking it now reminded him of those days.

"Remember the first time you got us beer?"

Rocky chuckled. "I was so nervous. Hell, almost thirty years old and buying beer for the first time. I had no idea what to get."

"Fuck." Mirek almost choked on his beer and wiped his mouth with his sleeve. "The first brand wasn't too bad. It was that shit bought next that tasted like… well… shit." He laughed at the memory. "Drunk for the first time at thirty—we were pathetic."

"Yup, but not the last time being drunk… or pathetic." Rocky's lips twitched in a semi-smile.

"That's for sure. You were crazy, bringing home a different type of alcohol to try every couple of days."

"Yup, and you were crazy right along with me, trying each one."

"Well, a good friend wouldn't let you try all those by yourself," Mirek teased, wanting to keep the mood light, but when he met Rocky's gaze, their expressions sobered.

Always close as cousins, they'd become more than that over the years. They were each other's confidants, the ones they confessed their sins and deepest fears to. Each of them had seen and done things neither of them could have ever imagined. Rocky knew him better than anyone, even Sam. It was a big reason for him needing to get his head on straight before he could return to normal society. How could he explain to her that he was too broken to be of any use?

Mirek disappeared the remnants of his lunch and stood, ready to get back to work. The physical outlet let him exhaust himself until he was too tired to think of Sam. Well... not think about her as much.

"Is it working?" Rocky asked, as if reading his mind.

"No," he muttered and picked up the ax. He still didn't feel whole, and after almost a week without people, except Rocky, he felt like he hadn't made any progress.

Rocky flashed in front of Mirek, making him jerk to a stop. "Drop it," Mirek said, barely holding in his temper.

He tried to push past his cousin, but Rocky put his hand on Mirek's chest. "No. I get that you feel like shit inside. I'm right there with you, but you're missing the big picture."

Mirek raised his brows, hoping Rocky would get on with it. "Spit it the fuck out, Rock."

"Sam. She's the big picture."

"I know! That's why I'm staying away!" He knocked Rocky's hand off his chest, but that wasn't enough; he wanted to hit something. Anger at himself for his own lack of control and how it was hurting not just him but Sam, burst free.

One second Rocky was standing in front of him and the next he was on the ground. As if Mirek's hands had a mind of their own, he had thrown the ax to the ground, then struck his cousin's chest with so much force, he'd knocked him to his ass. Mirek stood speechless, his breaths sounding like he'd just run the one-hundred-yard dash as they sawed in and out of his lungs.

What the hell was wrong with him? Mirek sank to his knees in the cold grass. He scrubbed his face with his hands and felt so many of the feelings of failure he'd been holding in for so long, now bubbled to a boil inside him. The rage that he'd been holding in for so long had craved an outlet and he had been weak enough to give it one.

A familiar tightness squeezed his throat, but he didn't cry. After spending years hiding his feelings, he felt too numb to cleanse himself with tears—another part of himself that was broken.

"Mirek?" He felt Rocky kneel in front of him, and he dropped his hands.

"This isn't about you staying away because of Maverick, is it?"

He met his cousin's gaze and saw a tenderness he hid from most people. "No. You told me I was an idiot for having that plan anyway."

Rocky smirked. "You were, but I didn't think you'd listened."

He made a small huff. "I did. I... I realized I'd been using Sam's safety as an excuse to avoid the real issue."

"What's that?"

"I'm broken, Rocky."

"Ah, fuck." Rocky placed his hand on Mirek's shoulder. "Anyone who went through what we did would be broken."

"Exactly. And I don't see you getting all lovey-dovey with our family either."

Rocky dropped his hand. "This isn't about me... I don't have a Sam."

Mirek felt like an even bigger idiot. "Hey, man. I'm sorry. I didn't—"

"Don't pity me," Rocky snapped. "That's not what I meant... You're not getting it. Sam's the big picture, but not because of you. Because of what she'll do."

"What d'you mean?"

Rocky let out a large sigh. "Nothing specific, just a feeling. Even though it's been a while since I've seen Sam, I know that her guilt is as massive as ours. The difference is, I think that big brain of hers has always been calculating a way to make up for everything she's done. Even when she was little, she was always looking into the future to try to find a way to make things better... I remember..."

Rocky paused and shook his head.

"Tell me, Rock."

"I said I wouldn't bring it up again, but... remember what you told me one of those times we were drunk and you were missing her? You weren't drunk enough to give me specifics, but you said there was a reason why Sam came to us in a body bag and that she has a secret. I don't know for sure, but I can guess because I've seen things."

"I shouldn't have said anything. I can't break my promise to Sam."

"I'm not asking you to. But whether you're staying away because you think she'll be safe or because of your guilt for all the shit you've gone through, it doesn't matter. I wonder if she'll do something to appease her guilt *and* yours—like take out Maverick?"

"I don't know." It was possible, and one more way in which he'd failed her. He looked up. "Are you going to stick around?"

"Jack gave me a key to an apartment downtown. I'll stay there until I figure things out. Staying with the family is too hard."

Mirek stood and slapped his cousin on the back. "I get it. Help me finish this part of the foundation before you take off?"

"Sure."

He and Rocky worked together, but even with the

physical labor, thoughts of Sam always intruded and made him worry about her. He stayed away to protect her from himself—at least until he felt like he could be amongst people —but maybe Rocky was right... Mirek might need to protect Sam from herself too.

Over the last two decades he failed to protect her more times than he could count. This time, Mirek just had to trust that he was making the right decision by getting his own shit together first.

CHAPTER FIVE

Present Day — November 25

Sam whisked the eggs and then turned to her dad as he measured out dry ingredients in another bowl. "What made you suggest baking?" She laughed before he could respond. "That didn't come out right. I'm not complaining. Just curious."

"It's something we used to do together when you were little." He leaned his hip on the counter as he faced her. "You were baking a cake when we met, and you asked me to join you. When you and your mom moved in with me, you would bake with your mom and then it just became something you and I did together on Saturday mornings to give your mom a break."

"I don't remember," she whispered. A feeling of guilt at forgetting piled on top of the massive mound of guilt that already threatened to crush her every day.

"Aw, sweetheart, I wouldn't expect you to remember. You were only three when we met and five when you were taken." He cupped her scarred cheek, just like Mirek did, and looked at her with so much love. She pulled away gently and picked up her bowl. If he knew what she'd done, he'd probably never look at her like that again.

Since being home, she'd learned that her dad was intuitive and more observant than she would like, but he had a sense of when not to push. At least with her. She'd told her parents bits and pieces, and as always, they let her divulge information at her own pace, but she guessed they had figured out more than she'd said.

Now, as she and her dad worked together, he asked about dishes she liked to bake and cook and who had taught her. She knew it was her dad's way of learning about what she went through in captivity without asking questions she might not want to answer, and she loved him even more for it.

"How many minutes does it—" He stopped talking and held up his hand for her to stop. She didn't mind, figuring he was talking telepathically to someone. Since her mom was reading and her brothers were out doing their own things, she guessed it was most likely Jack or Meredith. They were the only ones who could communicate over distances longer than the length of a room or two.

After less than a minute, her dad turned to her, and she knew by the look on his face something terrible had happened. "Is it Mirek?" Even with so many people at risk, Mirek was always her first thought.

"No. It's the Williams's buildings. They've been attacked. Jack's sending people out to different locations to help; I've got to go."

She reached over and turned off the oven. "I'm going with you."

He hesitated for just a moment. "Okay. Jack said only minor injuries have been reported," he said, as if calculating the risk to her. She couldn't tell him that any situation would likely be safer for her than him.

"Flash to Isaac's tattoo shop. You know where it is?"

She nodded and then put her hand on his arm before he flashed away. "Since there aren't any serious injuries, I think the blasts are a distraction. Maverick is up to something. Except for that narcissistic message he blasted into our heads, I don't know how the magic from the box has changed him, but he always had a game plan. You can't underestimate him."

"We won't."

She flashed to the front of the shop, and her dad landed beside her.

"You both okay?" her dad asked Kate and Isaac as they all walked toward each other.

"We're good. It's just me and Kate here. Can we help somewhere?" Isaac asked.

"Jack has the rest of the buildings covered. No one was seriously hurt, just minor injuries from falling debris," her dad told them.

"My shop and the bakery are the only businesses in the buildings open right now, so there can't be many people around."

"Then we got lucky, but Maverick is up to something and likely wanted to make a distraction, or he would have done more damage," Sam said.

"You're thinking it has something to do with Kate?" Isaac asked.

Kate jerked her gaze to Isaac. "But I don't have the sword. Jack does."

"Not right now, you don't. But it doesn't mean you won't soon. Plus, Maverick might not know that," her dad said. "Unfortunately, Sam had a lot of opportunity to study

Maverick..." Her dad's voice cracked, and she saw him swallow.

She leaned into him, wrapping an arm around his waist, giving him a quick hug. "It's okay, Dad," Sam whispered.

Dropping her arm, she turned to face Isaac and Kate. "We can't underestimate Maverick. I don't believe he had a conscious, even before he consumed what was in the box. He's an extreme narcissist, believing he should have whatever he wants, and he refuses to let anything stand in his way. So, my guess is, whether or not he thinks you have the sword, he knows you have the ability to forge it into something else, so he'll come for you."

"I believe Sam is right," her dad said, his eyes clear and focused when she looked at him. "Once the council members and those working with us have secured the other buildings, we'll come up with a plan."

"That won't be necessary, Ben," someone said from behind them, and the familiar voice made Sam shiver.

All four of them spun to see Maverick's feet touch down on the floor.

The last time Sam had seen Maverick he'd drained her magic, broken her leg, gagged her, tied her to a chair, and held a gun to her head. If all that wasn't enough, the building had been collapsing around them because he'd set timed bombs.

Looking at the man brought back so many memories—none of them good—but she shoved them down. She was no longer the same person he had tortured and manipulated over and over again for his own personal, twisted gains.

"Your protection spells are amusing but not even worth the magic it took to cast them," Maverick said, smiling like he came for a friendly visit. "How are you feeling, Ben? Recovered from your little incident in Mexico? I see you've gotten acquainted with your daughter again after you abandoned her for more than twenty years."

Out of the corner of her eye she saw her dad take a step forward but kept Maverick in her sight. The man always claimed to be patient, but a challenge to his perceived superiority would light his fuse in a heartbeat.

Maverick lifted his chain, his gaze looking past Sam. "Oh, Kate. You're so cute, thinking that charging your measly magic will help you. If I want something, I'll take it. Right, Ben?" he jeered.

Sam kept her gaze locked on Maverick. His cheek pushed out on one side as if someone had pinched the skin and pulled. Just as quickly, the bulge disappeared, and one appeared in his neck before it too vanished.

"What do you want, Maverick?" her dad asked. "Or maybe you're here to brag. You always were an arrogant asshole. I see nothing has changed."

"And you always were a self-righteous bastard, Ben." Maverick smiled, his teeth looking Hollywood-white. "And as for what I want?" He grinned wider.

When Maverick raised his arm above his head, her dad slammed into her, taking them both to the ground. The snap of Maverick's fingers reverberated through the shop with the sound of a million fingers snapping at once. The building shook and the floor moved beneath her, but all she felt was her dad's warmth as his arms came around her head.

"How's that for fun, Ben?" Maverick asked, his voice carrying over the sounds of shouts and banging coming from the other buildings.

"Are you hurt?" her dad asked softly as he rolled off her, then reached a hand down to help her up.

"I'm fine." Sam gave her dad a small smile and raised her brow in question.

He nodded he was okay before turning to Maverick. "Not

my kind of fun. Just tell us what the fuck you want, Maverick, and then you can go on your merry way."

Maverick's face contorted again; a portion of his cheek bulged out, and then another. "Stop!" he shouted, frantically looking around the room. "Shut the fuck up!"

Sam watched Maverick's face with fascination. The man had a short fuse, but she'd never seen his face distort as a result of his anger. She suspected the magic he had consumed from the magic box had something to do with it.

While Maverick and her dad passed taunts between them, she listened with half an ear as she wondered about the properties of the magic inside him. If she could calculate the volume and how it interacted with his own innate magic, she might be able to hypothesize its outcomes. That would assist her with ensuring her plan to trap the magic would be successful.

Running calculations through her mind, she hadn't noticed her dad had moved until he was almost in front of her, blocking her direct line of sight to Maverick. It was then she fully tuned into his words.

"Nice chat, Ben," Maverick said with fake kindness, a voice she knew all too well. "Now, I really must get on with what I came to do. But I think I'll alter my plans slightly. At first, I thought I'd just kill Curtis's daughter, but now I think I'll add a twist to it."

As Maverick finished his sentence, Sam copied a move out of her dad's playbook and slammed into him, pushing him to the side. As she fell on top of her dad, she turned her head in time to see a colorful blast of magic headed toward Kate.

Isaac reached for Kate as the magic hit her from the side, sending her flying backward. Isaac lunged forward, and the wall absorbed them both.

Sam shot to her feet and flashed to the wall. As she ran

her hand along the drywall feeling for cracks, she looked for a seam. Anything to indicate how Kate and Isaac had disappeared. Could they have flashed?

She pivoted looking for other clues as to where they could have gone. Her dad was beside her now but kept his eyes on Maverick, who still stood at the front of the room.

"Look down, Sam. Do you like my little twist?" Maverick asked, amusement clear in his voice.

Sam braced herself before doing as he asked.

Her heart felt like it skipped a beat and then she dropped to her knees. A large pile of ashes stood in a mound at the base of the wall.

"You incinerated them!" her dad barked, angrier than she'd ever heard him. His hands balled into fists, but he didn't move forward. Maverick had almost killed her dad the day she'd been rescued, and he hadn't been anywhere near as powerful as he was now.

"It needed to be done." Maverick shrugged with a casual attitude as if he hadn't just killed two people. Then, as if he'd flipped a switch, his countenance changed. She'd always feared his brutality, but his lack of control made him even more dangerous.

He locked eyes with her and held out his hand. "Come, Sam. I need you."

Her feet lifted off the floor as an invisible tether pulled her toward him. She pushed down her panic, knowing Maverick thrived off other's fears, and pulled on her magic. Nothing happened. She had no control over her own body, and she felt like she was ten years old all over again.

"No!" she heard her dad shout as he flashed in front of her and shot his arms forward.

Maverick stumbled backward, and the tether holding Sam snapped like a dried-out elastic band pulled too tight.

Her knees hit the floor, and she sucked in a breath as a sharp pain zinged up her thighs.

"Out of my way, Ben. I want Sam and you can't stop me from taking her!"

Sam felt the shift in the air as her dad absorbed the energy around them.

Her gaze flicked back and forth between her dad and Maverick, trying to calculate who would strike first. She knew without a shadow of a doubt that her dad would sacrifice himself to save her.

What he didn't know was that she could save herself, because even when he wasn't with her, Mirek had taught her how to protect herself. And if that wasn't enough, her magic gift would be.

Thrusting her magic into her feet with enough force to lift her, Sam flung her body up and to the side. As she went airborne, she wrapped one arm around her dad and shot her other hand toward Maverick, shooting a blast of magic in his direction.

The pain in her side registered first.

Maverick's scream penetrated next.

Then her lungs ceased as she came to a jarring halt on top of her dad, knocking the wind out of her.

Her dad yelled, but his voice sounded far away.

An image of Mirek sixteen years ago, and his newly scarred cheek, popped into her mind. She had to hold on because she couldn't have him blame himself for not anticipating this too.

But the world around her faded away.

CHAPTER SIX

Sixteen Years Ago

Mirek reached across the table for a puzzle piece when something across the room caught his eye. He shoved against the table and stood, the momentum knocking his chair backward. It hit the ground as he strode across the room.

Drew stood in the doorway, his hand tightly gripping Taren's upper arm.

"What the fuck are you doing?" Mirek barked at Drew.

"The little shit was listening in on a private conversation."

Drew shoved Taren into the room, sending him flying forward. His head hit a table before he landed in a heap on the floor.

"Leave him the fuck alone," Mirek hissed as he gripped Drew's shirt in his fists and pushed the asshole up against the wall. At sixteen, Mirek was a year or two younger than Drew, but Mirek had a few inches of height on him. Using it to his advantage, he stared down into his eyes, wanting Drew to see he'd had enough of his bullshit. "Don't touch him."

Drew threw up his arms between Mirek's and knocked his hands away. "Fucking make me." He lifted his chin to where Taren lay on the floor, "The stupid ass was eavesdropping."

Mirek didn't turn around, knowing better than to ever turn his back on Drew. In the year Drew had been coming around, he'd made their lives even worse than they'd been before, which was a feat. The guy seemed even more volatile than his dad and they'd discovered the hard way that he had the magic ability to alter memories as they occurred, to distort events.

"I don't give a shit what he listens to; don't fucking touch him." Another thing Mirek had learned over the last year was how to curse and sound tough. Drew was never going to respect him, but the swearing at least elevated him above pathetic status in Drew's eyes.

Sam and Morgana gasped behind him, but they wouldn't interfere because they knew it could make things worse. Even if instinct told them to go to Taren to make sure he was okay, everything Mirek had taught them and all their lessons from living with monsters for six years would keep their feet rooted to the floor.

Out of the corner of his eye, Mirek saw Rocky stand beside him.

"Yeah, he's a whiny little shit," Eddie said as he came around from behind Drew.

Like with Drew, Mirek knew better than to underestimate Eddie, but he didn't give the kid the satisfaction of a response. Eddie had shown up at the compound a few months ago and had been a pain in the ass from the start. He couldn't have been more than thirteen years old, but already he was a punk and a shit-disturber.

Drew took a step toward Mirek. "You think you're so tough?" Drew asked as he gestured with his arm. "Take a look around you. You're in a classroom with a bunch of kids and your parents are gone. You're pathetic."

Everything he'd endured for the past six years—all the torture and bullshit—came barreling up inside Mirek, giving him blinders. Pushing some power into his arms, he lunged forward, and shoved Drew against the wall.

"Fuck!" Drew yelled as the force of Mirek's hit propelled him into the drywall, dust and plaster falling around him.

Mirek stood with his fists clenched waiting for Drew to come at him.

Drew thrust off the wall, a killer look in his eyes. "You'll pay for that, asshole."

"No, I won't. I've had enough of your shit. No more hiding behind your daddy," Mirek said, his tone a low hiss. He'd had enough of young punks.

"Ya think?" Drew asked. He shifted, as if to take a step forward, when Eddie stepped in front of him brandishing a blade.

"See this?" Eddie asked, holding up his knife. "It's special. I got it from an old magic. He didn't want to give it to me, but I convinced him. The hard way."

Mirek looked at Eddie, a gleam of pure, twisted joy shining in his eyes.

"Eddie. Come on, man. Put the blade down," Rocky said as he took a step forward.

"Back the fuck off, Rocky, or you'll regret it," Eddie said, waving the knife in Taren's direction.

Keeping his gaze on Drew and Eddie, Mirek didn't know what to do next. He'd never been in a standoff before. He was trying to figure out what to say to de-escalate the tension when Taren whimpered.

Mirek turned toward his brother as Drew yelled, "Shut the little shit up!"

Eddie lunged at Taren.

Mirek flashed in front of his brother just as Eddie's knife came down in an arc.

The blade tore through Mirek's flesh starting right above his left eyebrow, catching the outer edge of his eye, and all the way down his cheek.

He threw his hands over his face, but blood poured through his fingers. Dropping to his knees, he sucked in air, trying to breathe through the fire-like pain consuming his face.

"Get the fuck up!" Drew yelled.

Caught up in his own agony, Mirek didn't know who Drew was yelling at until a kick landed on his hip, knocking him over.

Mirek pushed up onto his hands and knees, transfixed by the blood dripping down and covering his fingers in a macabre scene.

"Look out!" Sam yelled as Morgana screamed.

Hearing their panic pulled Mirek out of his trance.

He struggled to his feet and turned but couldn't focus through his blurred vision. Then he watched through a haze as everything seemed to slow down.

Eddie shoved Rocky in the chest, and he stuttered on his feet before hitting a desk and crashing to the floor.

Drew yelled at Eddie, his words unintelligible.

The girls shouted in terror.

Taren scooted backward until his back hit a table leg.

Eddie raised his arm again and thrust the blade into Taren's chest. Then Eddie pulled it out, blood dripping from the blade.

Rocky reacted first, his fist hitting Eddie in the jaw, sending him flying backward.

Mirek dragged his arm across his face to try to clear his vision as he dropped down in front of his brother. "Taren, hold on! Taren? Can you hear me?"

Mirek shouted at his brother as he flattened his hands on Taren's chest. Closing his eyes, Mirek pulled on his magic and looked into Taren's body.

"Taren," he whispered as he saw the blade's destruction. His heart was torn almost in two.

Mirek pulled in more energy from around him, using everything he could, and amplified his magic. As he pushed it into his brother, trying to repair his heart and wishing for a miracle, he opened his eyes.

Taren's eyes were closed, but his lashes were still wet from his tears. His usual flushed cheeks were slack and becoming more ashen by the second.

Even knowing Taren was already dead, Mirek refused to give up. Closing his eyes again, he focused on Taren's heart and forced more magic into him.

Locked in a fog of desperation, he didn't hear anything until his magic spoke to him—*Stop.*

He ignored the voice, but a few seconds later, it spoke again. *Stop.*

Once more he ignored it, fixated on Taren's heart, until his flow of power stopped. His magic had cut itself off.

Mirek opened his eyes and looked down at his brother. He brushed the curls off Taren's forehead and realized he hadn't given him a haircut. He'd been meaning to do that.

A sob tore from deep within him, shaking him to his core. A drop of blood landed on Taren's cheek, the contrast vivid with his ashen skin. The shock of seeing the blood awakened something within Mirek—his facial nerves lit up like they were on fire—reminding him of the slash across his face.

"Mirek?" Sam whispered.

He turned his head, his hands still on Taren.

"Eddie said the knife was *special*"—Sam winced as she said the word—"because it was magically imbued with poison."

"The knife did enough damage without the poison," he

said, his voice sounding dead to his own ears. Maybe that's the way he would always feel now.

Hours later Mirek lay on his bed, the wound in his face pulsing like a heartbeat. He couldn't stop thinking about Taren and then what followed, playing like a loop in his mind.

A few minutes after Mirek's magic had cut off, Snake stormed into the room and ordered two of his goons to take Taren away. He instructed them to take his body back to Blue Mountain and bury it in his gravesite.

When the men lifted Taren, Snake kicked Mirek's leg. "I knew this day would come. Just didn't think it would take six years. Your brother's body will go back where it belongs. When Knight first took you kids and weighted the coffins, the plan all along was to return your bodies to your graves when you died. It's a pain in the ass, but it covers our tracks... Now, get the fuck up, or I'll be sending you there today too."

Rocky appeared at Mirek's side and pulled him up. Mirek swayed on his feet, grateful for his cousin's support.

"Go get cleaned up," Snake said.

As Mirek was walking through the door, Snake called out, stopping them.

"Your knife wound? Don't bother trying to heal it. The poison embedded in the blade prevents wounds created by it from being healed with magic."

Mirek didn't care about the scar—it would be a good reminder of how he'd failed his brother—and it was the least of what he deserved.

"Mirek?" Sam whispered as she sat on the bed beside him later that night.

"Sam, you shouldn't be here."

"I know, and I'll leave, but..."

He heard the pain in her voice and felt like an ass. She, Morgana, and Rocky were suffering just as much as he was.

They'd loved Taren too.

Mirek sat up. "Just for a minute," he said as he pulled her into his arms.

"It wasn't your fault," she whispered against him. "You're the one who taught me we can't control other people's actions."

Mirek still believed that, but Sam was wrong. Taren's death was Mirek's fault because he hadn't controlled his *own* actions. He'd provoked Drew.

He didn't say anything to Sam, only vowed to himself that he would protect her—do whatever he needed to do—and would never fail anyone he loved again.

CHAPTER SEVEN

Present Day — November 25

Sam came back to consciousness with a jolt, like all the caffeine from a hundred cups of coffee had suddenly taken effect. Her eyes popped open.

"Sweetheart, thank Christ," her dad muttered. His hand trembled as he ran it over her hair, as if reassuring himself she was alive. "I thought I'd lost you again. I—"

"I… I'm okay." She wasn't yet, not really, but she wouldn't tell her dad that and have him worrying more. Even with the jolt back to consciousness, she felt drained and exhausted.

"I messaged Jack. He should be here any minute to finish healing you. Healing isn't my strong suit. When you were hurt in the fire—"

Her dad choked on his words again and tears welled in his eyes. She only ever remembered him crying once before —the day she was rescued. She wondered how many times he and her mom had cried for her over the years. One more thing to add to her pile of guilt.

"Really, I'm okay," she lied, still too weak to sit up.

"Where's Maverick?" She could feel her internal wounds knitting back together. Even though it was part of her magic, she'd luckily only had to experience it a couple of times in her life.

"When I rolled you off me, he was already gone."

"Oh no!" Sam looked at the pile of ashes as the rest of her memories came flooding back. "Kate and Isaac! He killed them."

"Yes. We need to gather their ashes. I was just so worried about you. It felt like…"

He didn't need to say any more. Over the years, Sam and Mirek had spoken many times about what her parents and the Williams mothers must have gone through. She'd do anything to stop her dad from reliving that again.

"What happened?" Jack asked as his feet touched down right beside her and he crouched at her side.

Her dad sat back on his knees and took her hand in his. "Maverick hit Sam with a blast and her heart stopped."

"Sam, can I check you out?" Jack asked with his hand hovering above her.

She hesitated for a moment. For eleven years—since she and Mirek had learned about her secret—they had safeguarded it, not knowing what would happen if it became public knowledge.

Now, she had a choice to make. If she refused Jack's help and said she was fine, her dad would worry and wonder why she was making such a big deal about Jack healing her. But if she let Jack heal her, he would know she was different. Jack knowing about her wasn't her biggest concern. Jack telling her parents was. They would question why they didn't know and blame themselves for everything that had happened to her. The last thing she wanted was to pile more guilt on top of what they already carried.

Her dad rubbed her hand between both of his. "Sweetheart, Jack's a powerful healer, you'll be okay."

Since most magics, like her dad, had only basic healing abilities, she didn't have to worry about them tending to her injuries and sensing something was different about her. Not so with Jack. Her injuries healed quickly, but her dad didn't know that. As far as he knew, his daughter's heart had stopped, so she needed to reassure him.

Sam nodded at Jack and hoped he wouldn't tell her dad the truth about her.

Jack placed his hand on her stomach and closed his eyes. She felt his push of magic and held her breath. The moment she felt Jack's magic withdraw, she met his eyes.

He knew.

Maybe not the details, but he knew enough and would have sensed the last of her injuries repairing themselves.

"Are her injuries too much?" Her dad's grip on her hand tightened. "Call Mirek. I know you can reach him no matter where he is. He can heal her."

"No!" Sam shouted, then took a deep breath to make sure her next words came out in a normal tone. "Dad, I'm fine. Right, Jack?"

She hoped he saw the pleading in her eyes. Not only did she not need healing, Mirek couldn't see her like this—it would reinforce his belief that people got hurt because he had failed them. Then no matter how hard she worked to redeem herself and be worthy of him, it would never be enough.

"Yes. Sam is almost as good as new," Jack said looking at her dad. "I think what you did healed most of her injuries."

"Really? Jack, she was..." Her dad's words trailed off. He couldn't seem to say the word, but she had died.

She squeezed her dad's hand. "Maybe my heartbeat was just slow and you missed it. I'm fine."

"She is. I've never lied to you, Ben." Her dad must have seen some kind of reassurance in Jack's eyes because he gave him a small nod and placed his hand back on her stomach. She waited for his push of magic, but it didn't come. Jack was pretending for her dad's sake.

After another minute, Jack lifted his hand and helped her sit up. "You're going to be fine, Sam."

I won't say anything, Jack said into her mind.

"Thank you," she told him, knowing her dad would think she was thanking Jack for healing her.

Her parents had lost over twenty years with her and had to live with that every day. She couldn't imagine what it would do to them to know her secret, and think they could have prevented her from being taken all those years ago.

Sam pulled herself out of her thoughts, realizing Jack and her dad had moved over to crouch by Kate and Isaac's ashes. Sam only caught the tail end of their conversation. "… tell Fiona," Jack said.

"I'll go with you," her dad said as he and Jack stood. "This isn't about you being the leader of the council; this is family."

Jack nodded and turned to Sam. "You okay?"

His words were kind, but his stare was so intense, she pulled her hair forward, covering the right side of her face before she answered.

"I'm fine. Did you protect their ashes or are you taking them now?" Sam had seen a lot of death in her life, but it didn't make the loss of Kate and Isaac any easier. She swallowed against the burning in her throat.

"I've put a protection on them and don't want to touch them until I know what Fiona wants to do," Jack said, his tone deeper than she'd ever heard it.

"I'll wait here for… uh… I'll wait until you come back."

Her dad kneeled and pulled her into a hug. "You sure

you're okay?" he asked when he pulled back and met her gaze.

"I'm good."

"I texted Nate to come so you're not alone."

"I'm here," her brother said from the front of the shop as he walked through the debris to reach them.

Jack and her dad said their goodbyes and were gone a moment later.

Nate walked over to the back wall and stared down at the ashes. "Dad told me." He waved his hand in front of his eyes and turned to face Sam. "I can't believe it."

His magic dried his tears, but it didn't erase the sorrow etched into his young face. "I know," she whispered as her throat burned and she blinked back the tears.

"Hey, give me a hand," Sam said as she raised her hand to her brother.

Nate walked the few steps to her but shoved his hands in the front pockets of his jeans. "You can't get up?"

"Come on, it's just a hand. I'm not going to give you a full-on bear hug or anything."

Nate hesitated for several seconds before he pulled his hand from his pocket and gripped hers, hauling her to her feet. The movement was so fast, Sam stumbled a bit before throwing out an arm to catch herself on the wall.

"Hey, baby brother, not so much strength next time." She chuckled and turned toward him, expecting to see him grinning. Instead, he was pacing back and forth in a small patch of the floor that had escaped debris and running his hand through his hair. His movements were so similar to their father's, her breath hitched for a moment.

"Nate, what's wrong?"

He stopped pacing and whirled to face her. "I shouldn't have touched you, and now I can't take it back."

"Uh, okay, sorry. I won't ask next time."

"No. I... That's not what I meant..."

When his words trailed off, Sam reran his words in her mind. "You said you can't take it back... Mom and Dad told me you don't like being touched, but that's not it, is it?"

"No." Nate's gaze held more than sorrow now, he was clearly regretting touching her.

Growing up, she had never had access to ancient magic books to learn their history and specialties, but because she loved collecting data she had questioned every magic person she could. Specialties were as varied as the magic people who wielded them. "What is your specialty, Nate?"

"I... when... I touch people, I can see their future."

"And you saw mine?"

He hesitated for only a moment and ran his hands through his hair again. "Yes."

"Did you see my death?"

"Yes," he said, his voice quiet, but full of regret.

Sam walked over to the couch by the wall and used her magic to disappear the evidence of Maverick's destruction and sat down. She was healed, but still weak.

Nate cleaned off the other couch and slumped onto the cushions like the weight of the world rested on his shoulders.

"What you saw... I wasn't an old lady with grandchildren at my side, was I?"

"No."

"Not even middle-aged?" she teased.

"Sam, this isn't a joke!"

"Do you know a date?"

"It's not that specific, but I know it wasn't this time of year, there were Christmas decorations around."

Sam wasn't surprised by her impending death, only the timeframe. It was November twenty-fifth. She had one month until she died.

MORGANA LOOKED out the passenger window as the scenery flew by and wished that something looked familiar. In the two and a half months since her spell broke, a lot of her memories had returned, but not all. Some days, something would jog her memory, but those instances had become fewer and fewer in the last month. Perhaps age, and not just the spell, had locked away some of her memories forever.

"Angel? You okay?" Damon asked as he reached over and grasped her hand that was resting in her lap.

She rotated toward him. "I'm fine. I just keep waiting for something to look familiar."

His eyes met hers for a moment before he looked back at the road. "I wasn't spelled, and I don't have a ton of memories from when I was seven. I think that's normal."

"I know. I was just telling myself that. But..."

"We're going to the last place you saw your dad."

"I don't have a lot of memories of him left," she said more to herself than Damon. When she thought of her dad, she remembered him laughing, but not what he'd been laughing about. For years she'd tried to hold onto the memories, but the spellbinding had erased them all.

She swallowed against the sudden tightening in her throat. "It's also the last place I saw my mom... Kind of. I mean..." She saw her mom moments before her death but didn't even know who the woman was to her then, only that she was Meredith's mom.

"You don't have to explain, angel."

They lapsed into silence for several minutes, but silence was always comfortable with Damon.

She looked at him as he drove, and like she so often did, she wanted to pinch herself that he was hers. He was everything she'd ever dreamed about in a man, even his overly protective and persuasive side that drove her nuts now and then.

Most days, she didn't notice the scars on his right cheek, but they were facing her now. He got them because of her. Because she wouldn't listen and made him go into Maverick's compound without backup. In the days since, she'd run every possible scenario through her mind. If faced with the same choices, she couldn't say she'd do anything different because it led to them rescuing Sam. She didn't hate Damon's scars because they were ugly; they made him look rugged, and she liked to tease him that they made him a little less pretty.

He gave her hand a small squeeze and she looked down at their hands clasped in her lap. Morgana traced her fingers over the tattoo on his forearm. The serpent in the design was like the small one she had, but his covered most of his forearm. Her finger moved across the dark lines and shading, almost petting it because it looked so real. Then she traced the bigger versions of the sunflowers Isaac had originally tattooed on her. She'd loved how bright and pretty they'd been, but each one had disappeared when they transformed, just like she had.

Damon had mentioned that Isaac had finished his design the night before, just before Jack had called a meeting. When they'd gotten home after the meeting, and learned about the attack on Kate and Isabella, Damon had healed his skin because Isaac hadn't had time.

It didn't seem to matter that she'd been rescued and two of her captors were dead. There were reminders everywhere and Maverick was still a danger to all of them.

"Hey, angel. Don't you like the design?"

She looked up at him just as he turned back to the road. "What?"

"You're running your fingers over my tattoo and frowning."

"Oh." She bent over as she lifted his arm off her lap several inches and kissed the design. "I meant what I said last night when I told you I loved it, and I still do. Isaac is an amazing artist. I... I was just thinking about why I needed the tattoo... not just the spellbinding, but the kidnapping too. I missed out on so much."

"Aw... angel. If I could give you the time back with your family and prevent all the horrible things you had to go through, I would. But no one can escape their past. It shapes us, and I love the woman you are. But... are you talking about something more specific?"

"Yes and no." She looked out the passenger window again as she tried to formulate her thoughts. "I want to remember some things, like this drive to the cabin and the good times we had, but... I also want to forget other things. Like Maverick."

"I think everyone feels that way about some things. And who wouldn't want to forget Maverick, really?"

"I guess."

"Tell me again why we're going to see Mirek. Just to catch up? Don't get me wrong... I'm happy to drive you anywhere, even after you get your license, or maybe especially after that," he teased.

"Hey!" She playfully swatted his stomach. "I'm going to be a good driver. I just need a lot more practice."

"I know. You've always been determined. Now... I know you want to see Mirek, but it's more than just seeing him, isn't it?"

"Yes, I want to apologize."

"For?"

"For that time I cried wolf."

Damon brought her hand to his lips and kissed her, like

she'd done to him. "Angel, no one is going to judge you for what you did to survive."

"For the longest time I thought I'd killed him. It wasn't until Simon mentioned a healer that I knew he was alive."

Damon was quiet for a moment as he kissed her hand again before putting both their hands back in her lap. "I don't think you need to apologize to Mirek, but I understand why you want to. He'll forgive you."

She knew he'd forgive her, but she hadn't yet forgiven herself.

A few minutes later, Damon turned the SUV on a gravel road and parked on a dirt landing off to the side of the road. She couldn't see much through the trees, but Rowena had said Mirek was here. She'd wanted to come out and see him the week before, just after he was rescued, but he'd asked her for some more time alone.

Morgana undid her seatbelt and got onto her knees to lean over to Damon. Their kiss was heated, but not long. "You sure you don't want me to go with you?" he asked.

She dropped back into her own seat and reached for the door handle. "I'm sure. I need to do this on my own. Did you bring a book?"

"Yes." He grinned and held up his eReader. "I downloaded the new release from our favorite PNR author. It came out this morning."

She laughed, something she did a lot more of now thanks to Damon. "When we drive back, you can't tell me anything. I'll have to download it tonight."

"You have your phone on you?"

"Yes, and I'll call you if I need you." She smiled and shut the door. Only a couple of months ago, she had hated his protectiveness, but now she understood it was done out of love.

Morgana hadn't gone far on the well-worn path when the

trees opened up to reveal a meadow and she caught sight of her cousin.

Mirek looked so much different than he had when he'd healed her. Less than two weeks ago, she'd seen him from a distance after he'd been rescued. She hadn't been ready to talk to him with so many others around. He'd been even gaunter than she remembered. Now, he looked like the man he used to be, fit and strong, though a few years older.

He must have sensed her because as soon as she cleared the trees he opened his arms for her. She ran into them like she was still seven years old and he could make the entire strange world that they'd been dropped into safe. When tears welled in her eyes, she didn't bother to hide them.

CHAPTER EIGHT

$\mathcal{M}$irek didn't know how long he held onto Morgana, and he didn't care. There had been a time when he thought he'd never see her again. When he believed she was one more person he had failed.

When she finally pulled out of his arms, she waved her hand in front of her face and looked up at him with dry eyes. So many memories of her drying her eyes, or holding back tears trying to be tough, swam in his mind. He had hoped it was something she'd never feel the need to do again.

He conjured two cups of coffee and passed one to her, then motioned to the logs by the fire.

"Delicious." She laughed, and he saw the old Morgana in the glint in her eyes. "I remember the first time you conjured coffee. It was before we were allowed to drink it, and wow… it was disgusting."

His lips hitched up at the memory. "Yes, but you and Sam were determined to try it anyway." The memory was bittersweet as it brought back both the joy of the event and the pain of knowing he had missed out on so much with Sam. Until the last seven years, she was in all his memories.

Sam had been a part of him since he was ten years old, and he knew that even if he never saw her again, she always would be. Sam held half his heart.

"I thought I'd killed you. I'm so, so sorry," she whispered.

Morgana's comment pulled him from his thoughts. She'd always thrown out comments as her brain processed them. They would seem random thoughts to others, but he'd gotten used to how her brain worked, and he wouldn't have her any other way. She'd been a different person when she'd been spellbound—like it had taken her spirit away and made her feel lost. Left her floundering as she tried to find her true self.

Their time together before she was rescued had been so rare that there were only a few incidents she could be referring to. "When I healed you at the apartment?"

"Yes. I cried wolf because I was bored, and you gave me so much of your power that I thought I'd taken your very essence. They had to carry you away."

Mirek disappeared his coffee and held out his hand. "Come here." She put her coffee mug on the ground and sat beside him on the log. Wrapping his arm around her, he tugged her to his side. "You don't have anything to apologize for. I should be the one apologizing. I couldn't stop them from spellbinding you. I'm the one who let you down, Molly."

"I'm Morgana now. I don't know who Molly is anymore."

"Another way I failed you."

Standing, she faced him, her hands on her hips. She might think of herself as Morgana, but he could still see Molly—proud and stubborn, with pieces of insecurity.

"You never failed me, Mirek. I'm alive because of you, and so are Sam and Rocky."

She didn't mention Taren, but she didn't have to. He'd failed his brother like he'd failed the others.

Morgana turned away, but she sniffed before she turned back. "Show me around."

Chuckling as he stood, he waved his hand in an arc. "Well, there are trees, more trees, a lake, wildflowers, and more trees." Mirek didn't mind that Morgana had changed the topic; he didn't need to be reminded of his failures since he lived with them every day.

He walked Morgana around the cabin, showing her what he'd done so far.

"This is amazing." She turned to him. "What's next?"

"I've got some logs ready, but even lifting them with my magic, it's difficult to keep them steady, so I'm making a pulley system. I was just starting when you arrived."

"What has to go where?"

Mirek pointed to a couple of logs he had already prepared and notched. "See those? They need to go over there," he said indicating the frame he had started. "I can move the logs, but with their weight, my magic isn't controlled enough to position them well. Mostly, I just whip them around."

Morgana walked over to the first log and held out her hands, palms up. "Not like this?" she asked as she grinned, and the heavy log raised in the air, completely steady.

"Holy shit! When did you learn to do that?"

"After the spell broke. I still can't flash, but I can do other things." The log raised higher. "Up here?"

"Just a second." He flashed onto the subfloor. "Bring it closer." Morgana was able to maneuver the log in a way he couldn't, and in no time, they had another layer of the log shell in place.

They were taking a break when a telepathic message came in with an update from Jack.

Morgana sat on the log by the fire. "I hate waiting for Jack to come back with his full message. It's always bad news lately."

Mirek had heard the message from the night before but hadn't gone to the conference room. He wasn't ready to put himself in a position where others might need to rely on him.

The Williams's buildings have been attacked. The fight is over. Make your way home.

Morgana looked wide-eyed and lost, so reminiscent of times when she was little. "He didn't say if anyone was hurt."

"I've got to go," Damon said as soon as he flashed a few feet from where Morgana sat. She stood and walked right into his arms.

Mirek stood as well. "Did you get any details?"

"Not really. Just that I need to go home for my sister." Damon turned to Mirek. "I'm going to flash home; can you drive Morgana back? Ah… do you have a license?"

"I can drive." Mirek didn't explain why he'd had to learn to drive. Being able to drive supplies and the injured in case the driver was taken out when they were on a drug run wasn't something he wanted to explain to Damon. "I have a Colorado license."

"Thanks." Damon kissed Morgana and then he was gone.

Mirek hadn't expected to be heading back to Blue Mountain so soon, but it would give him a chance to see Sam. Since being with her again, their time apart was almost worse than it had been before. The years they'd been apart hadn't been easy, but they had become the norm. Now that he'd had a taste of Sam again, he wanted more. Even though he wasn't ready to be thrown into the thick of things, he didn't see he had much choice.

Morgana hadn't said anything since they'd started the drive, but she'd been texting non-stop.

"Any news?" he asked.

"Sam was injured, but she's fine," she said.

Mirek hated that Sam got hurt, whether she could heal herself or not. It was seeing her in pain, even temporarily, that killed him. "Glad she's okay. Anything else?"

"When I asked about Kate, Meredith only said to hurry home."

He and Morgana didn't speak for the rest of the trip, both lost in their own thoughts. A sinking feeling had settled into the pit of his stomach. Jack was a skilled healer, as evidenced by what he'd done for Mirek. But if Kate was injured severely enough for Damon to need to go home, why hadn't Jack reached out to Mirek? The only conclusion he could come to was that no amount of healing would be enough.

As the miles passed, his thoughts returned to Morgana's apology about calling wolf. Mirek didn't blame her. She'd been in an untenable position. They'd all been.

The thought stuck with Mirek as the SUV ate up the miles. Morgana had been in a no-win situation the same as he and Rocky. If he could forgive Morgana, why couldn't he forgive himself? Did he need to stay away to get himself under control, or did he just need to let himself feel?

Mirek ruminated all the way back and decided that maybe it was time to stop running.

CHAPTER NINE

Sam sat off to the side as everyone arrived at The Magic Plate. Each person approached Fiona, hugged her, and gave her their condolences. All the vibrancy Sam had come to associate with Fiona was gone. She looked numb as she went through the motions of talking to friends and family. Damon stood with his mom, protective and stoic.

The first time Sam met Damon, that she remembered, they were in the market in Mexico. She hadn't spoken to him then, only saw a massive-looking guy, all broody and protective of Morgana. He was still that guy, but now his eyes were red and puffy from crying. A bit of magic, such as a glamour, would have rid him of the evidence of his tears, but he didn't bother. Or perhaps he was so caught up in his grief that he just didn't care what he looked like. He must be comfortable enough not to hide his feelings because he was around family.

For years, Sam's family had only consisted of Mirek, Morgana, Rocky, and Taren. But one by one, they'd been taken from her until she'd been alone. She'd forgotten what it felt like to be around people who accepted you just the way you were.

She felt a hand on her shoulder and looked up to see her dad. He gave her a sad smile, and then her mom was hauling Sam up into her arms. "I'm so glad you're okay," she whispered in Sam's ear.

When her mom released her, her uncles gave her hugs, first Joel and then Frank. Travis, her younger brother, was next.

"Please take a seat," Jack called out.

Her family shoved a couple of tables together and pulled out chairs, her mom sitting on one side of her and Nate on the other. "We're heartbroken over Kate and Isaac," her mom said quietly, leaning into her, "but that doesn't mean we can't be thankful you're alright."

Sam gave her mom what she hoped was a small smile and looked over at Jack as her dad and Uncle Frank walked up beside him. They were a line of solidarity, standing beside Damon for support.

In a solemn tone, Jack briefly described the events that led to Kate and Isaac's deaths. Their ashes had been collected, but Fiona wasn't ready to talk about a funeral.

"If you haven't received the protection spell, please say it after me," Jack said. "Now that I think about it… It probably wouldn't hurt for everyone to say the spell, whether you've already done it or not." He proceeded to recite the spell one line at a time with everyone in the room repeating it after him.

Afterward, Jack, her dad, and Uncle Frank welcomed questions.

The reprieve gave Sam a chance to let her mind wander to something Fiona had mentioned earlier—that she didn't want to talk about funerals. That had struck Sam as strange. She'd seen a lot of death in her life, but she'd only been to two funerals—the one for the Williams family and the small ceremony some of the staff, her, Mirek, Rocky, and Morgana had for Taren in Mexico. Perhaps Fiona needed more time to come to terms with their deaths.

While only partially listening to the questions and answers being volleyed back and forth, she didn't miss the sudden silence in the room. Sam looked up and followed everyone's gazes to the front doors of the restaurant where Mirek and Morgana walked in.

Damon flashed over to them, but he was too far away for Sam to hear his words. Sam thought about using magic to amplify her hearing, but that may have been considered rude. She'd have to ask her mom about the etiquette of that later. When Morgana collapsed in Damon's arms, Mirek walked toward Sam, and low murmurs started up around the room.

Sam's mom hugged Mirek, then she and her uncle Joel took her brothers over to her dad. Without a word, Mirek took Sam's hand, and she followed like she had the week before and all the years before that.

"Flash to the seventh-floor apartment," Mirek said when they reached the back of the restaurant. Sam flashed without responding.

At the apartment, Mirek led her inside. An awkward silence descended upon them as they stood unmoving in the foyer. It didn't used to be this way between them, but time and separation could do that. Their sexy reunion last week had been in the moment. Now, things felt different. She looked up at him and felt so much love she thought she might burst. "Are you back for good?"

"Good question. Morgana came to see me, and then we got Jack's message and Damon flashed back. I drove Morgana home, and since I was here, I couldn't not come and see you."

Sam turned to the kitchen to get a glass of water, keeping

her back to Mirek. She'd never been good at hiding her emotions from him, and she didn't want him to see how hurt she was that he was only here because of Morgana.

"You weren't planning on coming home, then," she said without facing him, and took a few gulps of water.

"On the way back, Morgana got a text that said you were injured, I…" His words were so quiet, she finally turned to him, and he took a step toward her. "I was staying away to protect you. I needed a break—to slow down and self-assess —because I knew with my emotions a jumbled mess, I could do something to get you hurt."

He took her glass, placed it on the counter and he clasped both of her hands in his. "I worry that I might react without thinking or that my emotions will prevent me from making the best decision in the moment," he said, his tone filled with regret. "I… I don't know what I'd do if something happened to you."

Sam pulled her hands from his. "Your argument doesn't hold weight, Mirek." She'd always let him lead—be her hero. Maybe this time he needed a push. "It's not your job to protect me, at least not yours alone. This morning proved that."

"I know."

"You weren't at the compound when Maverick blew it up and you weren't in Isaac's shop this morning, but that didn't stop my life from being endangered both times. Things happen and all we can ask of ourselves is to react the best we can in the moment. Whether you've got your emotions in check or not doesn't matter."

"I know."

"You keep saying that. Does that mean you understand I had no choice but to protect my dad? I reacted in the moment because I couldn't let him die, and I knew I could handle Maverick's blast."

Mirek moved to the kitchen island and sat on a stool before conjuring a cup of coffee. She nodded when he raised his eyebrow in question.

She took the proffered cup, but instead of sitting down she leaned back against the counter and faced him.

After taking a sip of coffee, his eyes met hers. "I understand you wanted to protect your dad, but he's a grown man with lots of magic experience. You can't keep playing martyr or Russian roulette with your magic. The seer never said how long you have; what happens if the next time is the last?"

"Oh, that's rich coming from you, Mirek. Pot meet kettle. How many times are you going to drain your magic to save someone?" Sam lunged forward and slammed her mug on the kitchen island, only sparing the spilled coffee a quick glance before she glared at Mirek.

They'd had this conversation so many times before, and it was always the same—he worried about her as if she didn't do the same for him. She didn't yell, that wasn't her, but she could get angry and speak her mind.

"For years I watched you sacrifice yourself, and when we were separated Rocky would give me updates when he could. I know he didn't tell me everything, but it was enough to know you were playing with fire. Because you think it's up to you to save everyone, you made decisions that affect both of us, and you did it without asking me. If that's not being a martyr, I don't know what is. If you're not sacrificing our love, then you're sacrificing yourself physically by healing past your limit. So, don't you dare tell me—"

"You're right," Mirek said, interrupting her tirade.

His quiet words knocked the wind right out of her sails. "I'm right?"

He came over to her, gripped her upper arms, and looked down into her eyes. "Yes. I've been trying to keep everyone safe and have sacrificed myself for it, but it didn't matter. I still failed. There wasn't a way to win."

She could see the torment in his eyes before he bent his head and kissed her. It was different from the week before, less urgent. Their hands roamed like they were once more reacquainting themselves with each other.

After a few minutes, Mirek pulled back. "I'm sorry, Sam. You're my Athena, so I should know you can take care of yourself. I just want to make sure I have a grip on my emotions and don't do anything to endanger you. I just… Seeing you hurt tears me apart inside… and I don't ever want to be the reason for it… I've wanted to protect you since the day I met you, even when I couldn't."

As Mirek said the words, she knew what he said was true. It hadn't mattered what they'd done, the odds had always been stacked against them. First, they were kids in an untenable situation, and then they were adults trying to survive while being used against each other. But none of it changed the way they would both still fight for those they loved and that, because Maverick was still out there, their biggest battle had yet to come.

Leading them to the living room, Mirek turned Sam around. Her knees hit the back of the couch, and he eased her down. He knelt in front of her and cupped her cheeks. "Yes, I may have been a martyr, because I fear making an error that will lead to you being hurt or worse. And this isn't something I could live with… Don't you get that I've loved you since I was ten years old?"

Mirek's lips twitched. Even though their love was the caring kind to begin with, they'd played this game a thousand times and she knew he was waiting for what she would say next. She'd been throwing the argument back at him for years.

"I've loved you since I was five, so for far more of my life," she said with mock superiority, biting the inside of her cheek to stop the grin.

"Yeah, yeah, so you say." Mirek pushed her back onto the couch and crawled on, pulling her down to lie beside him. "You know, as we get older, there won't be as much of a difference in the percentages of time we've loved each other?"

She did the calculations in her head, advancing them five years at a time. "Well, actually—"

Mirek pressed his lips to hers, and all thoughts of percentages fled.

The urgency of the week before hit them. Their clothes were gone with a single wave of Mirek's magic, and then she felt his hands everywhere as his mouth continued to devour hers.

His fingers found the wetness between her legs, and she arched back, groaning as sensations barreled down on her faster than ever before. "Oh god. Oh... Yes! Oh..." Sam couldn't speak as her legs stiffened and her body erupted in the most delicious feeling.

"I need you," Mirek said as he pulled back. She opened her eyes to see him on his knees, sheathing himself. Then he guided himself into her in one fast, glorious thrust.

It was hard and fast as their lips crashed together. Her nails scratched down his back, and his fingers gripped her hips as he plunged into her again and again. Mirek had awakened every nerve in her body with a raw kind of pleasure she craved from him.

"I love you, Sam," Mirek said, his lips against her neck as he held himself deep inside her.

"I love... ah..." Her vocal cords ceased to work as Mirek drove into her again, hard and deep, and he called out her name as he took them both over the edge into ecstasy.

Hours later, they laid in bed, and Sam made a realization.

Both she and Mirek had admitted that they'd sacrificed themselves in the past, but neither of them had promised not to do it again.

It hadn't been an oversight—just something not brought up—because life-changing promises weren't new for them. Their promise twelve years ago proved that.

Twelve Years Ago

MIREK LISTENED to Rocky's soft breaths, not quite snores, from a few beds away, and wished he could fall asleep as easily as his cousin. They were the only two who used the male bunk room now; Eddie and Drew had rooms near the bosses.

Most nights, he enjoyed the quiet and the peace as it was hard to come by in the compound. But on nights when he'd been used and drained and pain ricocheted through his body, like tonight, he wished for distractions.

At twenty, and now a couple of inches over six feet, Mirek could hold his own in a fight and wasn't easily intimidated. And the bosses knew it. Keeping him drained of magic was one of two ways they could control him.

Threatening to hurt Sam, Morgana, and Rocky, or actually doing it, was the other way. Like they'd done with Taren. After that horrific day, he promised himself he would always show a neutral façade and never again allow his emotions to lead to someone else being hurt. Rocky didn't know he was used against Mirek too, and if Mirek had a say, he never would. His cousin already had enough guilt to carry. They all did.

Mirek heard soft footfalls, which could only belong to one person. He sat up quickly, threw his legs over the side of the bed, and winced against the pain.

"Sam, you shouldn't be here," he whispered.

When she sat on the bed beside him, he scooted over, putting a few inches between them. "I needed to see you."

After the trip to the worst parts of town and healing several people, Mirek had needed a shower. Rocky had given him a hand—they'd been through too much together to get embarrassed over their nakedness—with throwing on some pajama bottoms. Rocky helped him onto the bed, not bothering with a shirt. Now, he wished he had let Rocky put a shirt on him.

Sam had no idea what she did to him, and it was getting more and more difficult to control his reactions to her. He wanted to take her into his arms and hold her, but she was still too young.

"I like seeing you too, Sam, but you need to go back to your room. I need to sleep."

"Then why aren't you?" she whispered.

Using the bed as leverage, he pushed to his feet and grabbed the shirt he'd draped over the end of the bed. He managed to pull it on, and hoped she couldn't see his grimace in the dark. Ignoring her question, he stared down at her, and even knowing he would sound like a broken record, repeated his earlier words. "You shouldn't be here."

Sam stood. "I was worried. I overheard some of the guards say that something went wrong with one of the deliveries and you had to heal several people."

Closing his eyes, Mirek ran his hand along Sam's hair when she put her head back on his chest. He should force her to go back to her bunk room before they got caught, but he just wanted to enjoy the feel of her for a few more minutes.

"I'm okay, just a bit weak."

She took a step toward him. "You're not okay. I know that Zeus drained you earlier today because I didn't create his latest batch as fast as he wanted. It's my fault you're so weak."

Weak was his normal, and he hated that Sam had to see it. "It's not your fault; you can only work so fast. Plus, it doesn't matter what you do. Zeus gets a kick out of draining me. It makes him feel powerful."

"You seem stronger than I'd expected you to be. Did Rocky give you some of his power?"

"Yeah, and two of the guards." He gestured toward the door. "Come on, I'll walk you back to your room."

Sam put her hand on his arm, stalling him. "I love you, hero."

"I love you too, Sam." He gently pulled his arm out of her grip and took a step toward the door.

"I want to stay with you."

"We can't, Sam. You're only fifteen. It's not right."

"Not if I consent. I love you, Mirek."

He took her hand and tugged her along toward the exit.

"It doesn't matter if you consent. You're too young, and I'm five years older than you."

Sam stopped walking, jerking his arm so he'd turn and look at her.

"You're just saying that so you won't hurt my feelings. I know that I'm ugly. You can tell me you're not attracted to me, Mirek."

For the past ten years, Mirek had made sure to compliment Sam as often as he could—mentioning her intelligence, her kindness, her quick thinking, anything that came to mind—so she'd always know how amazing she was. It wasn't until this year that he realized he was attracted to her, but he hadn't told her because he wasn't going to act on them. He didn't want her to think she could have something he wasn't willing to give her.

"Sam, I think you're the most beautiful girl in the world."

"Don't lie to me. I'm not a kid. I can handle the truth."

"Have I ever lied to you, Sam?"

She was quiet for a moment and when he made his way toward the exit again, her hand still in his, she followed him.

"I don't think so, but maybe you have and I don't know."

"I've never lied to you." Using his free hand he pushed her hair away from the side of her face. "Don't ever hide. You're beautiful, Sam, just like Athena. Beautiful, strong, and wise. One day when you're old enough to make a decision about who you want to be with, we can talk again."

"If we lived in a different era, I'd be marrying age. Plus, I got my period two years ago, and that means I'm a woman."

Rarely could he ever win an argument against her, but he had to win this one. Chances were good that she had a case of hero worship for him—she even called him *hero*—but at some point, she might regret her actions. Not that he would have sex with a child, even though he loved Sam. "Not in the eyes of the law you're not."

She laughed as she pulled her hand from his and slapped it over her mouth. "That's funny, Mirek. You need to work on your debating skills. What has the law done for us in the last ten years?"

"I don't want you to have any regrets, Sam. We're going to wait until you're eighteen before we have this discussion again. It's not just your age; it's the age difference between us that's not right. If you still want me when you're eighteen, then I'd be honored to make love to you."

"That's three more years," she said quietly, a whine in her tone.

"Yes, and if you really love me, you'll still love me then."

They'd made it to her room. "From now on, we'll meet in the all-purpose room, okay?"

She nodded before going into her room.

He let out a large breath when she closed herself in the room. The next three years could be the death of him.

CHAPTER TEN

Present Day — December 1

"I'm going to disappoint everyone," Sam said to Mirek after dropping off her dirty dishes in the kitchen.

"You won't. The only person who expects you to solve all the problems is you."

"Not even Jack? He's depending on me to find a way to stop Maverick."

Mirek turned her in his arms, and her gaze met his. "No, he's not. He's hoping you'll find a way to capture the magic, but he's not expecting you to do everything on your own. You have everything in there to help you," he said, gesturing to the dining room with his chin. "Come on, let's sit down."

A few minutes later, Jack addressed the group. "Thanks for coming. I hope everyone had a good lunch." He paused and let out an uncharacteristic sigh. "We will defeat Maverick and make him pay for everything he's done. Then we'll get back to Meredith's big family dinners again."

Jack gave his wife a soft look before turning back to the

crowd, his expression stern and all business. "In the five days since Maverick attacked, there have been hundreds of reports of more people being 'zombified.' With the help of Ben and Frank's agents and a hell of a lot of volunteers, we've been putting these people into magic-induced comas."

Jack fielded the few offers to help, and then turned to her. "Sam, do you have a plan for us?"

No, not enough of one, she thought but didn't say. "I have a partial plan. I'm still not sure how to seal the box with the magic, but I know how we can extract it." She sought out Connor. "Do you have the original box the magic was held in?"

"No. Maverick took it with him after he consumed the magic."

"Okay, we'll have to work on that," she told him before addressing Jack again. "I've been overthinking this. We don't need as much of a plan as I'd originally thought. We need a spell to extract the magic from Maverick and then a way to funnel it into the box. Altering the extraction spell should work. The trickiest part will be getting to Maverick. But as long as we're within about ten feet of him, the spell should work if enough people say it simultaneously."

"Thanks, Sam." Jack gave her a nod and spoke to Reece. "Have you come across a spell like this?"

"I think so, but I can't be sure until I do some digging." He hesitated and looked at Sam. "Do you have a way to test it?"

"No, but I'll find a way." She just had no idea how.

After Jack answered a few more questions and said he would keep everyone updated, people prepared to leave.

"Wait!" Uncle Frank yelled as he held up his hand.

Everyone froze and turned in his direction. He had his phone at his ear and so did her dad.

Her dad hung up first and faced the group. "Maverick is

outside the FBI building demanding Frank, Jack, and I show up. And…"

Her dad's gaze locked on hers. "He wants us to bring you, Sam, but that's not happening!"

"I'll go." As her dad started to object, she held up her hand to stall him. "Dad, you don't know him like I do. If I don't comply, he'll hurt a lot of people. You'll all be there to protect me."

Before her dad could protest again, Jack spoke up. "Flash to the back of the FBI building where there's a covered space. I'm sending everyone the coordinates and a visual now."

As soon as Sam received the information, she turned to Mirek. "You're coming?"

"I'll go where you do. But…"

"What?" Sam asked when she realized that Mirek wanted to find to break something to her. "Just tell me."

"You know me so well," he said as if reading her mind. "But don't forget I know you too, Sam. Right now, you're all about the plan to stop Maverick and contain the magic, but you need to remember that you're not just dealing with science. Maverick is a narcissistic fuck who is now filled with evil. You can't predict what's going to happen. Please be careful."

"I will." She went up onto her toes and gave him a quick kiss feeling the connection between them. Then they flashed and arrived at the designated location as one person after another appeared.

"Listen up," Uncle Frank said. "I've been told that Maverick is out front and amassing a huge crowd. He's like an evangelical gathering his flock, and he's converting them fast."

"We'll split up and flash to the front and off to the side in groups," Jack said and separated people into groups. "Your group," he pointed to Meredith, Damon, Simon, Jo, and several magic FBI agents who had joined them, "will need to coral the non-magics and the unaffected magics and usher them into the building. Reece, your group will be inside the building, and once you've separated the non-magics and dealt with their memories, make sure the magics get the protection spell."

Jack directed the remaining groups to places surrounding Maverick. Sam and Mirek were to arrive on the left side of the building in Maverick's line of sight while Sam's dad, uncle, and Jack were going to flash right in front of Maverick.

"Now!" Jack barked, and everyone flashed.

Sam's feet touched down at almost the same time as everyone else's with Mirek right beside her.

"Welcome to the party!" Maverick bellowed when Jack, her dad, and her uncle flashed to a spot about fifteen feet in front of him.

"These people are innocent," Jack yelled over the noise of the crowd. "Leave them alone!"

"No! Everyone will report to me!" Maverick sneered like an evil caricature out of a cartoon movie. As Maverick traded insults with them, Sam watched his face. The movement was subtle at first, then the contortions became larger like they had the day in Isaac's shop.

Watching Maverick's face expand as if his cheeks were being poked from the inside, fascinated her. The contortions didn't seem to affect him. Perhaps he wasn't aware they were happening, but that seemed unlikely.

Like a thousand-watt lightbulb suddenly illuminating her thoughts, Sam realized what was happening. The magic inside Maverick was trying to escape. Every principle and theory of physics she'd ever read bounced in her mind as she calculated what would happen next.

Maverick's foot kicked out, like an uncontrollable twitch,

and Sam didn't wait. "Get down!" she yelled as she flashed in front of the others.

Flinging her arms to her sides, she pulled as much energy from her environment as she could and threw it all into a protection shield.

She erected it behind her just as Maverick exploded.

As blood, fluids, body parts, and magic erupted, Sam braced herself for the impact.

Mirek watched in horror as Sam took the brunt of the blast, rocketing her body backward. She landed on the pavement, her legs at odd angles.

He rushed to Sam's side and felt for a pulse. When he didn't find one, he wasn't surprised, but it didn't lessen his fear of what he'd find inside her. He hoped this wouldn't be the time that Sam's specialty failed her.

Jack and Ben knelt by his side just as the realization of what would happen next hit him.

Mirek jumped to his feet. "Get back!" he shouted. "Erect a shield! Now!"

He threw out his arms as Sam had done and created a shield around himself.

A second later, Sam's body rocked as the magic escaped looking for new hosts.

"Keep your shields up!" he screamed to those around him.

The magic smacked his shield, and he stumbled but stayed on his feet. He waited only a moment before dissolving his protection and ran to Sam's side.

He laid his hands on her torso and closed his eyes, but couldn't hold back a gasp as he got his first look at the devastation inside Sam. Every organ looked like it had ruptured, and blood pooled in an empty cavity where they used to reside.

He pushed a small amount of magic into Sam and waited. Mirek needed to see how it would react to the foreign magic before he added any more.

"Do you need more?" Jack asked.

Mirek could sense Jack kneeling on Sam's other side, but he didn't open his eyes, just shook his head. "Not yet."

What felt like a year later, although really only just a minute, Mirek saw a movement inside Sam. Fluids and tissue floated together, but he wasn't sure yet if his magic was helping. The tissues meshed for several moments and then stopped. Mirek pushed some more magic into Sam, and the tissues started to heal again.

He kept it up, pushing a little bit more of his magic into her each time. Mirek could feel the effects on himself as he began to drain his magic.

Opening his eyes, he looked at Jack. "I need to control this. Push your magic into me."

Jack nodded and disappeared, but a moment later, Mirek felt Jack's hands on his shoulders. "Ready?" Jack asked from behind him.

Mirek lifted his hands off Sam to avoid overloading her. "Yes," he told Jack, and almost fell forward as a blast of magic coursed through Mirek, reminding him of the speed of the cars in Formula One racing he'd once seen on TV.

Resuming, he pushed more magic in Sam at a slow pace, only giving her body the amount it needed to heal each organ. When he drained himself, he asked for more magic. He knew by the rate the magic hit him that it had been Jack the first few times. Then the hands were smaller, but the magic almost as fast—Meredith.

Sometime after first healing Taren and Sam so many years ago, Mirek had learned to detach himself from the healing. When he looked at organs and bones, he couldn't think of them as the person, only their body. If he didn't detach himself again now, he'd worry about Sam and the pain she must have felt. Realizing he was no longer detached, he stopped his train of thought and went back to seeing only tissue.

"More," Mirek said and felt hands on his shoulders again. This time they were man's hands, and although the magic was strong, it wasn't Jack. Not that it mattered.

By the time Sam's body healed the final organ, Mirek's legs were numb from kneeling on the concrete and his hands ached from pushing magic through his limbs. He pulled his hands into his lap and rotated his head and shoulders to bring some of the blood flow back.

"Why did you stop?" Stella asked. Lines etched her face and she looked like she'd aged a decade in the last... Mirek had no idea how long he'd been healing Sam's body.

"She's healed," he croaked, his throat almost too dry to speak.

A water bottle appeared in his line of vision. Mirek accepted it from Ben and drained the entire thing. "Thanks."

"Thank you, Mirek," Stella said with tears in her voice. "Will she wake up soon?"

"I don't know, but she'll be okay." He couldn't tell Stella how bad Sam's injuries had been because there'd be too many questions. No normal magic could have lived through what Sam had.

"Can we move her now?" Ben asked.

"Yes." Mirek looked up to see Jack and the rest of their families, as well as some of the FBI agents, sitting in lawn chairs around them. "How long?" he asked.

"Six hours," Jack answered. "We erected a shield to hide us and disguised it. Anyone passing by would see scaffolding and a couple of dumpsters and know to walk around."

Ben struggled to stand, and Nate helped him up before they both helped Stella. Mirek expected that Sam's parents had been kneeling as long as he had.

"Stella, can you give me your hand?" When she put her hand in Mirek's he pushed his magic into her, healed her stiffness, and removed her exhaustion. Then he did the same for Ben before once more turning to Jack.

"Can you flash Sam to the apartment we're using?"

"Of course," Jack said. He picked Sam up carefully, cradling her in his arms and then they were gone.

"I'm going to need an assist," Mirek said, and looked up at those still around.

"Let me," Simon said and helped him up. Mirek let Simon hold a lot of his weight, his legs too weak to fully support himself.

"Mirek, can I help you?" Meredith asked quietly as she came up beside him. When he nodded, she placed her hand on his cheek, and a cool breeze of magic flowed through him. It wasn't the racecar equivalent her and Jack had given him earlier, but it was enough.

"Thank you." He nodded at Meredith and then flashed to the apartment. The others could deal with the FBI building; Mirek just needed to get to Sam.

He landed in the foyer of the apartment. Jack and Ben were standing in the open-concept kitchen, each with a cup of coffee.

Ben handed Mirek another bottle of water and pointed to a large spread of sandwiches and fruit on the kitchen island. "Stella is with Sam for now, and she'll call when Sam wakes up. You need to eat and refuel."

As much as Mirek wanted to protest, he knew Ben was right. He downed the bottle of water, then sat on a stool at the island and grabbed a sandwich. When he'd finished his second one, he finally felt a bit more like himself.

"Tell us what happened," Jack demanded in a quiet voice.

"Sam must have figured out what was going on inside of Maverick. She'd told me that when she was in Isaac's shop, Maverick's face had contorted."

"Right," Ben said. "I'd forgotten all about that when Sam had been injured. Sam knew Maverick was going to explode?"

"I don't think so, but she must have figured it out just before it happened."

"When Sam flashed in front of Maverick and threw out her arms, she threw up a shield behind her, didn't she?" Jack asked.

"Yes. Well… at least that's my guess too. That she did it to prevent the evil that escaped Maverick from hitting everyone."

Ben frowned. "But I felt the magic bounce off me, like it was repelled by my spell protection. Others said they felt the same thing."

He would have to be careful how much to say. "Yes, and it may have bounced off Sam too, but the amount that hit her was likely more."

Jack conjured another coffee and directed his stare at Mirek. "How did you know we needed shields?"

"Because if the amount of magic that hit Sam hurt her, the magic wouldn't stay. It would still be looking for a viable host." Mirek hoped his answer would sound plausible. He didn't want to have to explain that Sam's body had been useless to the evil magic because Sam had died—again. That was the second time in a week, and he didn't know if her next death would be permanent. He would have to be ready for whatever came next, because he wouldn't let himself fail again.

Eleven Years Ago

Sam couldn't scream anymore, her throat too hoarse to utter a sound. Tears streamed down her face as she watched one of the guards beat on Mirek. Both Zeus and Snake stood off to the side as Maverick directed the guards. One of the men held Mirek up, one hand in his hair and the other clamped on his shoulder, while another guard belted Mirek in the face.

The force of the punch spun Mirek's head to the side, blood and saliva spraying from his mouth. The man with his hand in Mirek's hair used it to pull him upright, allowing the other guard to pound into Mirek's stomach again and again.

Rocky and Morgana had been taken from the room while Sam had a front-row seat to Mirek's beating. Guards on either side of her pressed down on her shoulders, keeping her in place. She could do nothing but watch the man she loved be brutally beaten. She'd learned a long time ago that using her magic was useless. They'd only hurt Mirek more. It was her fault—his beatings were always her fault.

"Enough," Maverick finally said, and the guards dropped Mirek. He hit the ground like dead weight.

Maverick stalked toward Sam. She had to force herself to cower, to pretend she was scared. If she stood up to the asshole for even a moment, he'd have Mirek beaten again. "Have you learned your lesson, Sam?"

She kept her head bowed. "Yes, sir. When you tell me to make a larger batch and have it ready by a particular time, I will."

Ever since Sam had been forced to work in the lab, she'd purposely worked slowly and claimed she could only make small batches of drugs. Although she wasn't slowing the production significantly, it still meant a few less batches of drugs out on the street. It wasn't until recently, when they'd brought in a new lab supervisor, that they'd discovered her deceit.

No matter what she did she couldn't win. She hated making drugs and was repulsed by the thought of people becoming addicted and possibly dying because of her actions. But if she didn't do what she was told, people she knew would suffer. Slowing the flow of drugs had at least made her feel like she wasn't just accepting her fate—she was trying to make a difference.

The new supervisor had been convinced she could make far bigger batches and work faster and told her to do so. She'd tried her usual excuses, but he decided to teach her a lesson by taking out a knife and slicing the cheeks of four of her young proteges. He told her she would remember her lesson every time she looked at them.

The next day he'd come in strung out on something, and in the afternoon when the young woman cleaning the lab had tripped and knocked product onto the floor, he'd killed her. Then the young woman's body disappeared, and her supervisor had gone to the bosses and blamed Sam for the mess.

Within minutes of her supervisor informing Maverick, they'd hauled Mirek into the lab. Sam had apologized profusely and sworn that if they left Mirek alone, she would do what they wanted. Maverick had become furious and slapped her across her good cheek before stating that she didn't get to dictate to them.

"Let her go," Zeus ordered as he and Maverick walked to the door, their goons trailing them. Sam dropped to her knees in front of Mirek with her hands hovering over him, unsure where she should touch.

"Oh, and Sam?" Maverick asked.

She looked toward the door. Zeus had already left, but Maverick stood in the doorway half-turned toward her.

"Even at sixteen, you're the smartest person I know, so if you do anything that stupid again, you'll regret it for the rest of your life, however long it is."

"Yes, sir," she said obediently.

As soon as Maverick and his remaining goons left, Sam turned back to Mirek. She was reaching for him again when someone gripped her shoulder and jerked her backward, knocking Sam onto her butt.

Her new supervisor crouched down next to her. "I'm the boss, and you will listen to me, or I'll make your life a living hell, even without Maverick or Zeus." His sneer matched Maverick's, but she wasn't afraid of the asshole. His days were numbered. She'd already figured out he was addicted to his own product, and it wasn't going to end well for him. Five Wednesdays from now would be a good day for him to die by his own hand. He was going to overdose. It would be far enough removed from today that no one would suspect her.

Never before had Sam planned someone's death, but she would make sure he never maimed or killed anyone again. Just as her plan solidified in her mind, he stood and kicked her hip before walking out of the room.

Once they were alone, Sam gently grasped Mirek's shoulder and eased him onto his back. She placed her hand over his face, healing the bruises and washing away the blood. He winced at the pain that came with healing, but she knew it was nothing compared to what he'd just been through.

Leaning over him, she kissed his lips softly. "I'm so sorry," she whispered. "I had no idea my supervisor would go to the bosses."

"Shhh," Mirek said, his finger coming up to her lips before he dropped his arms. "I'm okay."

"No, you're not. Let me heal you." She reached toward his waist.

He gripped her wrist. "No, I need you to be at full strength. If they see I'm strong, they'll drain me, and then we'll both be too weak to defend ourselves." His words were slurred from the swelling to his mouth, and hearing him sound so unlike himself was even worse than seeing the bruises.

"I will heal him," a woman's voice said.

Sam looked up as an older woman walked into the room and shut the door behind her. "You're the seer the bosses consult with?" she asked the woman.

The woman scoffed. "Consult? That is not the word I would use. Terrorize and threaten would be better, but yes, I am a seer. I can also heal."

Kneeling beside Mirek, the woman placed both her hands on his stomach. He winced again and then let out a slow breath.

A few minutes later, Sam helped Mirek sit up. "Thank you," he said to the seer.

When the woman struggled to her feet, Mirek helped her up while Sam pulled over some chairs. They sat close together with the woman and spoke in hushed tones.

"Maverick had asked me here to predict his *business* dealings." The seer scoffed when she emphasized the word *business*. "I finished telling him what I saw and left."

She looked at Mirek. "I was leaving and heard the guards in the hallway talking about you. I went back to Maverick and asked if I could help heal the young man. He knows your healing powers are far greater than any we have seen before. I told him you would be needed to heal soon and that you could not heal when you were hurt. As an older woman with ordinary powers except to see and heal, they do not consider me a threat."

"Thank you," Mirek said. "I appreciate you helping me, but please do not put yourself in danger for me."

The seer waved off Mirek's concern. "I am fine." Once more she struggled as she tried to stand. Sam lightly gripped her elbow to help.

The seer gasped and held out her hand to Sam. "Take my hand."

Sam hesitated for a moment, but curiosity got the better of her and she placed her hand in the seer's.

The woman's eyes closed for a moment. Then they popped open, and her expression changed to one of sorrow. "You are the half-dead one."

"What?" Sam yanked her hand back.

The seer sank back down to her chair. "I see many things." Her gaze volleyed between Mirek and Sam for a moment before it settled on Mirek. "You will be taken away from your young love, but you must not protest when it happens. It will be worse if you do."

Mirek reached over and took Sam's hand. He didn't let go as he looked at the seer. "Do you know when?"

"Not soon. Maybe in three or four years. It will be after they ask me to spellbind the other woman."

"They? You mean Zeus, Maverick, and Snake?" When the woman nodded, Mirek asked, "The other woman—is that Morgana?"

"The feisty one with long, wavy brown hair, only a year or two older than your young love here."

"Yes, that's Morgana. Is there anything we can do to stop you from spellbinding her?" Mirek asked.

"No. If you try to change the future, worse things could happen." The seer clasped Mirek's shoulder and used him as leverage to stand. "I must go now."

"Wait! You said I was the half-dead one, but what does that even mean? It's pretty obvious I'm alive." Sam waved her hand down her body as if pointing out her physical presence would make a difference in the woman's statement.

"You are half-alive and half-dead." The seer paused and gave Sam the kind of look only a mother could make that said, *use your brain.*

Something that she and Mirek had wondered about for years—but never had an answer for—suddenly made sense.

"It's why I survived the fire when I was five." Sam turned to Mirek as realization dawned. "Last year… you said you thought I was dead after I fell off the roof when I leaned over the side to fix the satellite dish."

"You *were* dead, Sam, at least for a moment. You didn't have a heartbeat."

Sam turned back to the seer. "Do you know why I'm like this? What caused it? Is this hereditary?" As questions popped into Sam's mind, sudden clarity hit her. "I'm immortal," she whispered.

"I do not have the answers to your questions." The seer let

out a breath and shook her head. "But, no, you are not immortal. I think it means you are not easy to kill. I…" She paused as if debating how much to tell Sam. "I believe I know your destiny. In the vision you were older than you are now… and I saw you die."

CHAPTER TWELVE

Present Day — December 8

Sam stared at the papers spread out on the kitchen island before her. There had to be an answer in them somewhere. Her previous plan to extract the evil from Maverick and funnel it into the box with a spell had been simple. Maybe that had been the problem all along—she should have known that nothing was ever that simple.

A knock interrupted her. Before she could answer it, Nate opened the door and walked in carrying a plastic food container.

"Hey, brought you some of Mom's cookies," he said, laying the container on the counter.

Sam wanted to stand and give him a hug but stayed seated and gestured to the stool beside her. "You going to stay?"

"Sure. I can for a bit." Nate moved the stool a few inches further away from hers, probably so they wouldn't touch, and sat.

"Did Mom really send you over here just to drop off cookies?"

Nate grinned. "That's what she said, but I expect I'll get an interrogation about how you looked when I get home. It's been a week since Maverick exploded…" He shivered like he was shaking ants off his skin. "It was disgusting. Anyway… it's been a week, and we've barely seen you now that you're pretty much living with Mirek."

"It's just easier being here in case I need to talk to someone."

"Yeah sure, you go with that," Nate teased.

She laughed and felt a lightness for the first time in a week. "Yep, that's what I'm going with."

"What's all this?" he asked, lifting his chin toward the papers. "You working on a new plan to contain the magic?"

Sam sighed. "Yes. I'm trying, but now there are so many new variables to consider."

"The new variables being the thousands, if not tens of thousands of people, who you now have to extract the magic from?"

"Yes, that. But let's not talk about that for a bit. How's your course going?"

Nate reached for the box of cookies and opened it, passing it to Sam before he took a cookie for himself. "Good. I'm almost finished it."

Sam was happy for her brother, but she envied him too. If her life had been different, she'd probably have a couple of PhDs by now. Instead, she had some online master's degrees under a fake name.

"Tell me about your degree," she said, "I don't know as much about criminology as I'd like to."

They chatted for a while and Sam mentally stored every tidbit of information about her brother, cherishing the time.

"I should get going," Nate said an hour later.

"Thanks for dropping by." Sam stood when Nate did but stepped back so she wouldn't be tempted to hug him.

"Sure. I'll stop by again. Ah…" Nate reached toward her and then dropped his hand. "I don't usually volunteer to touch someone, but I'm worried about you. Especially after last week."

"I'm good." Rubbing her pendant between her fingers, Sam took another step back. She didn't want to know what Nate might see.

Her hint wasn't subtle, but Nate didn't mention it. "Okay, see you later." He flashed as soon as his last words left his lips.

Back at the kitchen island, she pulled the papers toward her and wondered if she should have let Nate touch her. Then she would be prepared for what was to come. But she shook off the thought. No one could prepare for their death, especially when they weren't even thirty years old.

A few hours later she was still working on the plan when Mirek arrived home. She was in his arms in seconds. Their kiss was both sweet and passionate.

When they pulled apart, she truly looked at him. "You're exhausted. Did you heal too much?"

"I'm fine; Jack gave me some power."

Mirek excused himself to change into some sweatpants and a shirt that looked old and worn, like he'd had it since college, but she knew that wasn't possible. Although he'd gotten an online degree under a fake name too, he hadn't physically gone to school.

They fell into a comfortable routine of making dinner that they'd adopted over the last week. Conjuring was fine, but sometimes the act of cooking and all the smells it generated just felt right.

"Tell me about what happened?" she asked him quietly as the chicken cooked for their stir fry.

Mirek cut the veggies as he spoke. "With lots of people helping and supplying me power when I needed it, I never got too drained. I just... I think just seeing the sheer number of people lined up on cots, every one of them a victim of Maverick's... it got to me."

"We'll find a way to stop the magic," she whispered.

"I know... What I hadn't expected was the number of people coming in off the street because they'd been injured by someone attacking them or while escaping from someone. The magic is spreading fast, but luckily, word of where to go if you need help is too."

When their dinner was ready, they ate at the kitchen island and didn't speak until they were halfway through their meal.

"How is the... I don't know what to call it. Hospital? Triage area?"

"Everyone's calling it an infirmary. When you walk in, you'd never know that it was an empty floor in an apartment building a week ago. It looks like a highly equipped treatment center."

"Are the injuries so severe that people can't heal themselves or have someone else do it?"

"No, but I think fear is causing people to reach out. Fiona and your mom created a schedule for volunteers to sit and chat with people, so no one feels alone. It's becoming a community."

"If the building has another unused floor, Meredith should set that up for people to stay in if they're afraid to go home."

"She's already ahead of you and allocated two floors. Lots of volunteers conjured items to outfit the place." Mirek rotated on his stool and kissed her forehead. "You've always thought of others. You're a beautiful person, Sam."

"Don't put me on a pedestal. I've done some horrible

things. You're the one who heals people; I'm a killer. Whether directly or indirectly, it doesn't matter."

"I think you're wrong, but I know better than to try and win an argument with you on the fly. Let's clean up, and we can crawl into bed and talk."

"Or we could get into bed and watch a princess movie. All the apartments have access to All. The. Streaming. Services. I'm sure we could find a princess movie or two."

Mirek laughed as he hauled her off the stool. "For you, Sam, I'd watch *every* princess movie. Again. But maybe not tonight."

Less than a half hour later after teasing each other while they cleaned up and got ready for bed, they were snuggled in bed together. They laid on their sides and faced each other—something they'd started when Sam was seventeen.

During the years they'd been separated, she ran through so many of the conversations they'd had when they'd lain facing each other in the dark. They were her cherished times.

"Did you ever think we might never see each other again?" she whispered.

Mirek brushed her hair off her face and cupped her left cheek. A long time ago, she'd asked to swap sides with him so her left cheek was always face up. Not because she didn't want him to see the burns on her right side, but because he always laid his hand on her face and caressed her. The nerve endings on her right side were almost all dead and she couldn't feel much there. She didn't ever want to miss a moment of his touch.

He ran his thumb back and forth across her skin. "Not at first. They gave me frequent glimpses of you and it kept my hope alive."

When he paused, as if lost in thought, flashes of memories when she had only been given a quick look of him too, popped into her mind. Their situations had been horrible, but she always feared that Mirek's had been worse. He was the one who was taken away, drained, and abused. Sam got to work. The irony of it all was that she enjoyed working; if only she could have made something besides illegal drugs.

He closed his eyes while he thought

"I think at some point I lost hope. I don't know when it happened. Maybe it was gradual," he finally whispered, despair in his tone. "That I'd see you again became a pipe dream that I didn't think would ever happen. I would lie on my bed and remember what it was like to make love to you."

Sam closed the few inches between them and kissed him. There wasn't any reason to rush. The day after Maverick exploded and Mirek healed her, she'd felt as good as new, and they'd made love many times over the past week. Sometimes they came together in a wild frenzy of lust, and other times they made love slowly, like they had all the time in the world. They'd also taken the time to get to know each other again.

When they broke apart, she used the fingers on her free hand to run through the light smattering of hair on his chest. "Do you remember the first time we made love?"

"It's not something I'll ever forget. I waited years for you to be ready."

She lifted her chin to meet his eyes and grinned. "I didn't make it easy on you back then, did I?"

He barked a laugh. "No, you really didn't. I didn't think I was going to be able to hold out."

"But you did."

"And you were so worth it," he said as he moved over her, bringing his lips to hers.

Nine Years Ago

Mirek laid on his bed in the empty bunk room and waited, too hyped up to sleep.

Over the past three years, there had been times when he thought he wouldn't be able to stick to his resolve—to wait until Sam turned eighteen—to see if she still wanted to have the discussion about sex. For the first two years, she never brought it up, but she'd decided that seventeen was close enough to eighteen and wove the topic into their conversations many times. He began to question his own sanity with wanting to wait.

While he waited, Mirek sent silent thanks to his ancestors, grateful they had kept their magic strong, letting it pass down through the generations. His magic became a savior when cold showers, hand jobs, and distractions had only taken him so far. Sam had pushed him, testing his patience and igniting his lust. The ability to cool his body down—sometimes to the point of near-hypothermia—had saved him on more than one occasion.

Six months ago, he'd finally kissed her. Touching each other shirtless from the waist up had followed four months later.

While living in the compound, between reading encyclopedias and the porn mags the guards left around, Mirek figured out what was appropriate for a man of his age and what wasn't. With him being twenty-three and Sam not yet eighteen, he knew what they'd done wouldn't be considered right by some, but then, their situation wasn't normal. They'd continued to kiss and touch above the waist until a month ago.

One night, while they'd laid on the couch in the all-purpose room watching a movie, Mirek drained and so tired he could barely move, Sam had caressed his cock through his pants. For a moment, he thought he'd lose it right in his jeans. It felt like he'd been waiting forever.

When Sam had touched his dick and used the argument of fooling around to get ready for sex, he'd finally broken down. They'd moved to his bed in the bunk room.

Agreeing to use only their hands below the waist, they took their time learning each other's bodies. There had been laughs and a lot of awkward fumbling, but thanks to those porn mags, Mirek knew the basics. Listening to and watching Sam's reactions to see what she liked had enhanced his knowledge. The first time he'd brought her to orgasm with his fingers, he'd felt on top of the world.

Mirek heard the soft footfalls and rolled to see the digital clock by the bed. He couldn't help but smile. It was fifteen minutes past midnight, making it Sam's eighteenth birthday. She'd lasted longer than he'd expected; he wouldn't have been surprised if she'd shown up at one minute past twelve.

"Hero?" Sam whispered as she put her hands on the mattress before sliding onto it beside him.

He rolled toward her and placed a soft kiss on her lips. "Happy eighteenth birthday, Sam."

She chuckled quietly. "Since I'm way past sweet sixteen, no more *sweet* eighteen after tonight, right?"

"Are you sure?"

Mirek laughed softly when she huffed out a frustrated sigh. Every time they'd touched each other intimately over the past two months he asked her the same question.

"Please, hero, make love to me."

Her features were difficult to make out in the darkened room, but Mirek didn't want to miss a single expression on her face. Pushing some magic to his eyes, he heightened his vision to see her clearly. Then he threw up a protective bubble around them to blur them from sight and muffle any sound they made in case someone walked by.

Once more, like he'd done so many times over the years, Rocky had come through for Mirek, giving him some power. Otherwise, Mirek would have been too drained to do anything tonight. Rocky even declared it the perfect night to watch a *Rocky* movie-marathon in the all-purpose room. He wouldn't be back until morning.

Mirek wanted to make love as much as Sam did, maybe more, but he wanted the night to be special because it was her birthday. "Don't you want your present first?"

Sam's eyes widened. "I… um… I thought sex would be my present."

He cringed, hating that she would think that. He'd give her the world if he could. "Oh, Sam. I want to worship you every day for the rest of our lives. I want making love to you and cherishing your body to be something we do all the time. We will never need a special occasion for that, and birthdays should be about something more than I am already willing to give you."

Mirek knew every single one of Sam's expressions, and the way she scrunched her forehead, the scar tissue on her right temple not moving, meant she was weighing her options. She'd take the present before they made love, or at least he hoped she would. Then she'd know for sure that today was about more than sex.

"Okay, I'll take the present first," she said on a long sigh, as if it was a hardship to accept a gift. Her intelligence that warred with her innocence was just one of the many things he loved about her.

Mirek held out his hand, and a box floated from the nightstand onto his palm.

She took the small box and put it on the bed between

their bodies. After admiring it for a moment, she undid the ribbon and slipped off the lid.

Her excited gasp made every minute he'd toiled over making the gift worth it. She pulled out the gold chain and pendant, and instant understanding reflected in her eyes. "For Athena."

"I knew you'd get it." He'd fretted for months about what to get her before he'd seen a picture of the gold pendant. Shaped into the outline of an owl, it perfectly represented Athena's sacred animal.

"The source of her wisdom and judgment," Sam said more to herself than him.

"I saw an ad for the owl with it nestled in the company's blue box. I thought it was perfect, but I couldn't... Well... I'd never conjured gold before, so I had to practice. Rocky practiced too, and our first attempts were horrible." He was babbling—not something he normally did—but he'd been so nervous for weeks as he'd practiced over and over again. First, to conjure gold, and then to shape the owl. Years ago, he'd stopped wishing to be normal—to have a job and independence, to be able to buy things—because it only led to frustration. Yet wanting to do something special for Sam brought back all those yearnings.

"It's beautiful." She sat up and handed it to him. "Will you help me put it on?"

He pushed himself up and took the necklace from her. When she turned her back to him and lifted her hair, he fastened the tiny clasp with the ease of practice.

He kissed the back of her neck, just above where the chain rested. "It took me eighteen tries to get it just right," he said softly. "It had to be a sign."

They laid down again, facing each other, and she fingered the owl. "Eighteen tries to get it perfect for my eighteenth birthday... Thank you, hero. I love it."

"I'd do anything for you, Sam. Do anything and sacrifice anything. I love you."

Her lip quivered as she met his gaze. "I love you too."

Mirek stretched his arm under her shoulders, cradling her as he leaned over and pressed his lips to hers. She opened for him right away with none of the awkwardness of two months ago. They came together like they were made for each other.

Kissing Sam was the best feeling in the entire world. Every time their lips met, the world fell away, and all he could think about was the softness of her lips and tongue against his.

"No magic tonight," he whispered against her lips after they'd kissed for what felt like hours. "I want to undress you because you're my gift." Her lips were swollen from his kisses and parted with her aroused breathing. Her auburn hair fanned around her shoulders as if framing her body like she was a gift solely for him. Desire hummed through his veins along with anticipation, knowing they were going to give themselves to each other for the first time.

Pressing his body to hers, he rolled her onto her back and shimmied down the bed several inches. He lifted the hem of her shirt and tugged it up before trailing his lips along her soft skin as he exposed it inch by inch. Pushing her shirt above her breasts, he heard her sharp inhale as he kissed the top of each one, just above her bra.

He couldn't get enough of her. He spent time lavishing her skin before making his way lower. Cupping her breasts in his hands, he sucked one of her nipples into his mouth.

The first time he had tongued her nipples, he'd been nervous and worried about hurting her, but she had giggled at the light touch. Since then they'd come to learn how much pressure the other liked and he used that knowledge now to heighten her pleasure.

Mirek toyed with one of Sam's nipples, using his fingers to pinch and tug, while he sucked the other. Her soft moans reassured him he had the pressure hard enough to please her, but not too hard.

Sam threaded her fingers into his hair, her grasp almost painful, igniting a flame deep in his groin. The more he pleasured her, the harder her fingers pulled his hair and scraped along his scalp, and the harder he became.

The soft sounds Sam made as his hands and mouth made love to her spurred him on. He kissed her stomach, and it was then he realized there was a flaw in his plan—removing her shirt without magic meant they would both need to sit up. He looked up and saw her smirk.

"Need some help?" she asked. Before he could nod, she used her magic to remove her clothes and then his. He had wanted to peel her panties off himself—thinking it would be romantic and sexy—but maybe it was better this way. Maybe Sam just needed him to love her.

Back on track, he brought his body over hers. When their lower bodies connected, they both groaned. He felt like he was in a dream—he'd fantasized about this moment for years and now it was becoming a reality.

He moved down the twin bed and kneeled on the floor. Threading his hands under her legs, he cupped her ass and pulled her down the bed. She moaned as she planted her feet on the bed and opened herself to him.

He kissed one of her inner thighs, and then the other, moving up her legs to her heat. Leaning over, he trailed his lips across her stomach and moved back down. He smiled against her skin when she groaned and pushed up.

Placing one hand on her stomach, he used the other to open her with his fingers. He blew on her lightly before licking her. She bucked up, and he sucked her clit into his mouth. Writhing beneath him, her sounds of pleasure spurred him on. Alternating between licking and sucking, he eased two fingers into her and curled them up. Her response was almost instant as she cried out, her body clenching around his fingers as her orgasm flooded her.

Seeing and hearing Sam take pleasure from him made him feel ten feet tall.

He moved up her body and reached for the condom he'd placed on the nightstand earlier. After sheathing himself, he hovered over her and waited until she opened her eyes. Her smile was pure bliss.

Leaning down, he kissed her and then paused.

"I can taste myself on you," she whispered. "Kiss me and make love to me, Mirek."

Knowing she understood why he paused, he no longer hesitated and kissed her; his lower body pressed against hers.

After a few moments, Sam pulled her lips away from his and arched up. "Please, Mirek."

"Are you sure?" Mirek couldn't help but ask again; it was just part of who he was.

Sam threaded her fingers through his hair and tugged. "Now, hero. I need you."

"Look at me, Athena," he said softly.

She met his gaze, and he reached between them and guided himself into her heat. When she fully enveloped him, they both moaned. Feeling her around him was the most intense and glorious thing he'd ever felt. He didn't know how long he'd last, but he'd do his damn best.

He kissed her softly and began to move, slowly at first, reveling in the friction their bodies created.

"More, Mirek. I need more."

Rocking back onto his knees, he grasped behind her thighs and pushed her legs forward. Keeping his gaze on her expressions, he pumped into her harder, and then faster. Sam gripped his forearms and threw her head back

"Yes!" she whisper-yelled as her body tightened around him and she flung her head back as her release claimed her.

Mirek didn't hold back any longer and thrust into Sam's heat several more times. His own body rocketed with the greatest orgasm of his life, complete with the feeling of stars exploding behind his eyelids.

It took a moment for him to come back down to earth, and when he looked down at her, she smiled, slow and wicked.

"I love you, Sam."

"I love you too."

She pulled him down for another kiss, and he knew he'd love her forever.

CHAPTER THIRTEEN

Present Day — December 9

Sam pulled her hair forward to frame her face and watched everyone file into the boardroom as she prepared herself to disappoint them. They were coming to hear her plan. And while she had one, it was missing a critical step.

Mirek bumped her shoulder lightly. "You'll figure it out," he whispered.

"I don't know how."

He gently clasped her shoulders and turned her toward him. "You're beautiful. You don't need to hide." He pushed her hair back from her face. "And don't stress about the plan. It will come. I have faith in you."

"Sam?"

At Jack's call, she and Mirek straightened and faced him.

"Are you ready to explain the plan?" he asked.

She nodded, her throat suddenly too dry for her to speak. Mirek handed her a glass of water, and she gave him a small smile before taking a drink and handing the glass back. Not only was he always in tune with her, he sacrificed himself for her, and now she was about to let him and everyone else down.

"Yes," she said, looking at Jack and scanning the others in the room. Her parents smiled at her, and Nate gave her a thumbs up that had her lips twitching into a smile.

Everyone was sitting, except Jack, her dad, and her uncles, who stood behind the others gathered around. She focused on her dad as she spoke.

"I believe that when Maverick consumed the magic, escaping was its intention all along—*it* meaning the ancient magic's. It needed to break free of its host—Maverick—because he was confining it. The evil magic's best chance of survival—and perhaps growth—was to become ubiquitous. By destroying its host and spreading to other individuals, it can do just that. Two things tell me that: quantum entanglement and chaos theory."

"You're going to explain those big words for us simple folk, right?" Reece called out.

Sam laughed along with everyone else and felt herself relax.

She nodded. "Quantum entanglement is a phenomenon that occurs when a duet of particles is generated, interact, or share spatial proximity in such a way that the quantum state of each particle of the group cannot be described independently of the state of the others, including when the particles are separated by a large distance."

"Uh, Sam?" Reece called out, raising his hand like he was a student in school. "Simple?"

"I'm getting there," she said with a chuckle. "Meaning… particles can influence each other even at a distance. For us, that means that regardless of where the evil magic particles are, they are going to influence each other. *They* need to be disentangled from each other to separate them from the human bodies and then be captured. Quantum disentanglement."

"Sam?" Uncle Joel asked. "You're saying that you believe the magic will be able to use someone in... let's say... Vancouver... to influence someone in Mexico City?"

"Yes, exactly. The magic in one person will easily be able to influence someone three countries over and more than three thousand miles away. And it will be able to do it over even greater distances than that." Sam hated being the bearer of bad news, but on the other hand, she liked knowing and giving facts, and everyone needed to know what they were dealing with.

"How does chaos theory play into this? It is still just a theory, isn't it?" her dad asked, raising his eyebrows comically. "I could be wrong since I've been out of school for a while."

"A while? Is that like saying the Rocky Mountains aren't very tall?" Reece asked.

"Or Babe Ruth was just an okay player?" Jack said, getting in on the teasing.

"No, it's like saying the pyramids are kind of old," Simon said.

Her dad held up his hands. "Okay, okay," he said, grinning. "Let's go with a long while." When the laughter died down, he turned back to her. "As Reece said earlier, how about a simple explanation, sweetheart?"

Sam loved that this group could joke with each other amid the doom and gloom she was forecasting. She just hoped they'd still be joking by the time she finished explaining her plan. "Yes, it's still a theory. But it's a theory that's stood the test of time—even if it can't be proven—because it seems extremely plausible."

She conjured a glass of water and took a large gulp

needing to center herself before delivering bad news. She disappeared the glass and looked back at the group.

"Chaos theory teaches us to expect the unexpected, and it's made up of six principles. I believe two of them may be in effect in this case. The first principle—the butterfly effect—says that small changes in the initial conditioning can lead to drastic changes in the results. Maverick absorbed the magic, which was a change in the condition of this volatile magic after likely hundreds or thousands of years of being dormant.

"The second principle we need to consider is mixing. Turbulence ensures that two adjacent points in a complex system will eventually end up in very different positions after some time has elapsed. For example, two neighboring water molecules may end up in different parts of the ocean or even in different oceans. Which means, if we don't contain the magic now, it could spread to the entire world, and quantum entanglement says that the magic particles will influence each other. We will have another controlling Maverick on our hands, but he will be ubiquitous, with no one source of control we could stop."

"By that theory, the magic could eventually inhabit non-magics as well," Uncle Joel said.

He hadn't posed it as a question, but Sam answered anyway. "Yes, I believe so. There will be nothing to stop the spread. Eventually, the magic could control the world's entire population."

Silence descended upon the room, and Sam began to question whether she should have given so much information.

Mirek wrapped his arm around her shoulders and pulled her against his side, his warmth sinking into her.

"That was worst-case scenario," Mirek said, his tone light, not matching the tension she felt in his body where it rested against hers. "And Sam has a plan. It still needs some work, but she's going to tell us where to begin."

He dropped his arm and stepped back, gesturing for her to take over. As she had so many times in the past, she thanked the universe for giving her Mirek.

She gave him a small smile and faced the group again, still nervous, but with more resolve. "Yes, I have a plan. Creating it, explaining it, and getting your agreement was step one." Sam panned the faces in the room and settled her gaze on Jo. "Jo and Simon, you'll be step two."

"Yes!" Jo said, rubbing her hands together. "Let me have it."

After explaining each step, Sam grew more confident. It would work—if only she could find a way around Kate and Isaac's role in step six of a nine step-plan.

For now, she'd focus on the steps that could be completed, starting with Jo.

December 12

Jo PUSHED the book away and sat back in the chair. "I'm getting déjà vu, and not in a good way."

Isabella barked a short laugh. "I'm pretty sure I said that after we found the mirrors and then had to figure out why they didn't work."

Reece reached over, and Isabella let out a squeak when he pulled her into his lap. "You didn't expect finding a quantum disentanglement spell would be easy, did you?" He gave her a loud and wet kiss on the cheek.

She playfully shoved him and moved back onto her chair. "No. Well... maybe. Since we've all been through something similar before, I thought it might be a little bit easier. I guess I didn't think we'd still be here on day three."

Simon placed his forearms on the table and leaned forward. Jo knew that look. "What are you thinking, Superman?"

"I wonder if we're being too clinical."

"How so?" Reece asked.

Simon gestured to the books in the middle of the table. "These books are all ancient. Quantum entanglement didn't exist when they were written."

Reece laughed. "No shit. I wasn't looking for the actual words."

"Then what *were* you looking for?" Simon asked.

Jo snapped her fingers. "I get where you're going. We haven't really defined what we're looking for. And if we do…" Jo looked over at Isabella with her pierced brow raised in question.

"Oh damn." Isabella's eyes widened. "If we know what we're looking for I might be able to find it, instead of us just looking through book after book without any real direction."

Reece said, "Okay, Professor Williams, define it for us."

Jo strode to the end of the table and conjured a whiteboard on a stand so the writing surface was at eye level. Well… her eye level. She held out her hand and grinned when she conjured a dry erase marker.

With the fun part over, she faced the whiteboard and spoke as she wrote the words *Quantum Entanglement*. "Sam said that particles will influence each other, regardless of distance between them."

Jo drew a dozen small circles on the board, taking up half the space. Then she connected the circles with arrows going in both directions before turning back to her *class*. Most days, she didn't miss teaching, but she was enjoying this.

Simon strode over to the other side of the whiteboard so

they flanked it. He held up a whiteboard eraser as if he was a magician showing his audience the tools of his trade.

"Okay, Merlin," Reece said with a laugh. "What have you got?"

Simon erased the middle portion of each arrow. "That's what we're looking for," he said, using the eraser to point at the spaces between the lines. "We need a spell that can separate hundreds or thousands of things at once without destroying the host."

Jo looked at the drawing and realization dawned. "I've been thinking about disentanglement as separating things." She pointed at the board. "Just like you've drawn, but what we really need is a spell to *extract* the magic. You mentioning not destroying the host is what clicked with me."

"Would the word *extract* have been used when these books were written?" Isabella asked.

Simon disappeared the eraser and whiteboard and took Jo's hand, tugging her back to their seats.

"I don't think we need to worry about that," he said. "When Jo and I were looking for spells, the books translated them into English."

"Right." After three days of frustration, Jo felt excitement that Simon was closing in on what they needed. "If we keep the word extract—or a visual of the magic releasing from people—in our minds, the books will know what we need."

Isabella walked to one side of the shelving at the back of the room and raised her hand to the top shelf. Starting with the first book, she dragged her fingers along lightly over the spines as she walked.

"Hey, cupcake, let me make this easier on you," Reece said while making his way to Isabella.

Reece stood several feet away from the shelves and an entire row of books floated in the air, their bindings still perfectly aligned. Raising the books to waist level, he rotated them all at once so their spines faced up.

"Wow," Jo quietly breathed out. She knew Reece didn't have to direct his magic with his hands, like most of them did, but she'd never seen him in action like this before.

Simon lifted Jo's hand and brought it over to his lap. They held hands and watched as Isabella moved along the books, one row at a time. When she was done, Reece would direct the books back to their shelf and pull out another row. Not one book fell to the floor.

After nothing on the back shelves stuck out to Isabella, she and Reece moved over to the shelving on the side wall. They were on the second row from the top when Isabella stopped.

"That one has something," Isabella said, pointing to a book bound in dark leather.

"Okay, give me a second, cupcake." Reece levitated the books back to the shelf and the book Isabella had indicated floated into her hands.

An hour later, they'd all taken a look at the book but none of them had found a spell that spoke to them.

Isabella pushed the book away, a look of dejection on her face. "I was so sure this book meant something."

"I think it does," Simon said. "I feel something in the book calling to me, I'm just not sure why."

The door to the room opened, light and noise spilling in from the main part of the library. Jo turned in her seat to see if Viktor was coming to join them, but it wasn't just him.

"Catherine," Jo shouted as she jumped from her chair and pulled the woman into a hug.

They held onto each other for over a minute before Jo finally stepped back. "I'm sorry we haven't seen you since we got back from Budapest this last time. It's been a bit crazy."

"That's alright, my dear." Catherine patted her arm and

turned to Simon where he came up beside them. He embraced the woman who had become like a mother to him. Each time Jo saw them together, her heart melted a little.

"Are you here visiting Viktor?" Jo asked, leaning around Catherine to wink at Viktor.

"I'll get to spend time with him at home," Catherine said and gave Jo a wink before she held both her hands in front of her, palms up. An old, weathered book landed on her hands, and she passed it to Simon. "I was upstairs in Oliver's old office. I was… well, I'm not sure what I was doing there. I just knew I needed to be there, and then a book fell off the shelf right into my hands. It doesn't look familiar to me but I'm guessing it's important."

Simon moved over to the table and sat with the book in front of him, the pages flipping back and forth.

Catherine put a hand on Simon's shoulder, leaning over to look at the book. "What do you hope to accomplish by flipping them so quickly, dear?"

"I'm not doing it, the book is doing it all on its own." He looked up at Catherine. "Speaking of the book… was there a particular reason why you had to retrieve the book instead of flashing here with it? It's light enough. I'm guessing you flashed here?"

Moving around the table, Viktor pulled out a chair for Catherine and they both sat. Jo took her chair beside Simon.

"That's because one of the strangest things happened… I've seen a lot of different magic specialties," she said, smiling at Simon, "but I don't think I've ever seen an object possess the magic that this book does."

Jo frowned. "We've seen several books turn the pages on their own."

"Yes, dear, but have you seen a book refuse to go inside a bag?"

"What?" Jo waited for Catherine to say something more. A punchline perhaps.

"I tried to put the book in a reusable cloth bag, but as long as my hand was holding the book, I couldn't reach inside the bag. It was like there was a force holding my hand steady. I even tried a different bag and a backpack. Nothing worked. I even held it in my hand and tried to flash but couldn't."

"How did you know you'd be able to retrieve the book by calling it to you once you got here?

"I didn't know for sure, but I had a sense, just like I had a sense that I had to go up to Oliver's old office."

"Simon, may I see it?" Isabella asked, holding out her hand for the book. The pages had stopped turning and the cover had closed on its own while they'd been talking.

Simon passed the book over. Jo felt her breath hitch, as if everything was riding on the next moment.

Isabella put the book on the table in front of her, laid her hand on the cover, and closed her eyes. A moment later, her eyes popped open. "It's here," she said as she opened the cover.

The pages turned on their own once more, as they had for Simon, but after less than ten seconds, they stopped.

Isabella glanced down at the open pages, and then lifted her head and grinned. "It's not in English, but I know this is it. I can feel it."

Jo felt an adrenaline rush, mixed with a bit of trepidation, like she had when she and Simon had found the book to save Reece. Excitement, but also a bit of wariness, wondering if everything would work out. "Woo hoo, step two is complete. Who do we pass the baton onto for step three?" Jo asked, looking at the others.

CHAPTER FOURTEEN

December 13

Flashing directly into their living room, Mirek's feet touched down softly on the carpet. Sam sat at the kitchen island, books and papers strewn over the marble surface.

He stayed still, enjoying watching her while she was immersed in work. Past memories of her excitement as she soaked up knowledge from encyclopedias, or helping her study, flooded into him. It didn't matter how many years had passed, his favorite and most vivid memories were always of Sam.

Pulling his phone out of his pocket, something that still felt strange, he noticed the time. Almost midnight. He'd been at the infirmary, and things hadn't gone well.

Beyond tired and drained, Mirek needed Sam.

"Hey," he said softly, not wanting to frighten her as he covered the short distance between them.

Sam flung her head up and her tired gaze met his. "How'd it go?" she asked as she stood and walked right into his arms, the light scents of honeysuckle and orange drifting up to him.

Shifting her in his arms, he brought his lips to hers and their kiss exploded with a passion that belied their exhaustion. With one arm around her back, he reached under her legs, lifted, and cradled her.

She snickered as they kissed while he walked them to the bathroom. "Turn on the shower," he said against her lips.

Lost in the feel of her, he barely registered her fingers pulling out from between the buttons of his long-sleeved Henley. The sound of the shower filled the bathroom. Steam drifted over them, and he still didn't want to pull away from her. Perching her butt on the bathroom counter, he used one hand to direct his magic and removed their clothing, sending the pile to the clothes hamper in the corner.

She threaded her fingers through his hair and chuckled, finally pulling her lips from his. "I like the way you think."

"Good." He picked her up again, and she wrapped her legs around his waist. Supporting her with one hand under her butt, he opened the stall door and shut it behind them before walking them both under the spray.

"You can put me down now."

"No."

She laughed at him, then gripped his face between her hands and tilted his head to look him in the eyes. "I love having you against me all slick and muscly, but... usually you're a little more talkative. Is something wrong?" Sam flattened her palms on his chest and pushed back, releasing her legs and lowering herself to her feet.

That was a good question. Besides being tired... he'd dealt with injuries and sorrow all day. Every time Jack and Meredith had to put another person in a magically induced coma, or Mirek had to heal injuries on someone who was hurt by an infected person, it ate at him a little more. It felt like death by a thousand cuts—no one big thing—just hundreds of smaller ones.

"I think seeing so many people injured is taking its toll on me."

"I wish I could help."

"You being here is helping." His thoughts kept going back to how close he'd come to losing Sam just under two weeks ago. Rationally, he knew she was safe—for now—but what would happen if she had to use her specialty to close the magic box?

Picking up her shampoo, he poured some into his hand and turned her around. "I missed you today," he whispered as he washed her hair.

"I missed you too."

Mirek finished washing Sam's hair, loving her moans as he massaged her scalp. Neither of them spoke as he rinsed her hair and then applied the conditioner and rinsed once more. They washed each other's bodies, all slippery hands and suds. It wasn't sexual, but a caring and tenderness they'd both had so little of in the last several years.

A little while later, they lay in bed facing each other. Sam laid her hand on his cheek. "Now will you tell me what's really wrong? It's more than just the injuries, isn't it?" she asked quietly.

"I told you… I missed you today." It was the truth, just not the complete truth.

"I know, and I missed you." She pressed a light kiss to his lips. "What else, hero? Please don't hide from me."

Mirek curved his arm under Sam and pulled her against his side. She rested her head on his shoulder and her hand on his chest.

"Seeing all those people today… more suffering that Maverick caused… it just got to me," he whispered, and threaded his fingers with hers.

"It gets to me too. I… I wonder if I'll find a way to close the box without Kate and Isaac."

"You will. I believe in you…"

Sam pushed up on her elbow and met his gaze. "I sense a 'but'."

"Less than two weeks ago, I worried that I wasn't going to be able to bring you back. Sam… it was worse than anything I've ever seen before." He closed his eyes, took a breath, and looked at her. "What I saw inside you was even worse than when Taren died."

She put her head back on his shoulder and what felt like a long time passed before she spoke. "I… I didn't know what else to do. I didn't realize until the last second what was going to happen. I needed to protect everyone."

Mirek tilted her chin up to look at him. "That's just it, Sam. *You* didn't need to protect everyone," he said. "The seer who spoke to us years ago said you're not immortal. You *can* die. What if it's the next time you decide to save everyone?"

Sam flattened her hand on his chest. "And what about you? What happens when you try to heal one too many people? What if no amount of Jack or Meredith's power will be enough then?"

She was right. They'd both been trying so hard to do the right thing. To make up for past mistakes that were out of their control.

He brushed her hair off her face and cupped her cheek. "I love you, Sam. You mean more to me than anyone or anything else and I want a future with you."

"I want that too… I… I sense another 'but'."

"No, not a 'but'. I want to have forever with you, and in order for us to have that we have to stop putting ourselves in harm's way."

"Like everyone keeps saying… spell it out for me. What are you saying?"

"No more unnecessary sacrifices. You can't try and save the world all by yourself, and I'll make sure I never harm myself trying to heal someone. We have to come first in each other's lives." Mirek watched Sam's closely, looking for her agreement.

"Okay. No more unnecessary sacrifices."

"So…" He gave her a sly smile. "What about that future? We used to talk about kids, and we can even think about careers."

"I've always wanted kids with you—that hasn't changed—but let's wait until we seal the magic away."

He was surprised that she wanted to wait, but it was late, and they were both exhausted, so he didn't push. Hopefully soon, they would start to plan a life together.

December 14

THE NEXT NIGHT, Sam let her gaze slowly pan over everyone chatting in hushed tones as Mirek sat beside her talking with Simon.

Although the tone of the conversation tended toward jovial, a blanket of sadness hung over the group.

Meredith had called earlier in the afternoon, asking everyone to meet at The Magic Plate for dinner. The restaurant was still closed to the public, as were all the businesses in the Williams's buildings due to the risk posed by the evil magic spreading.

According to Meredith and Jack, the gathering's main purpose was to brainstorm ideas for ways to lock the box. But Sam expected they had another reason in mind—connection. They'd lost two of their own and Sam bet she wasn't the only one wanting to keep those she cared about close.

You okay?

Sam jerked her chin up, surprised to hear her mom's voice in her mind. Since she'd been back home, her mom had only spoken telepathically to her two or three times.

She looked across at her mom and smiled. *I'm fine.* Her mom didn't look convinced. Even after all their time apart, her mom still had maternal intuition, because Sam wasn't really fine. Jo and the others had located the book two days ago, and Sam still didn't have an answer for what to do next.

There were days when she got mired in memories of the past and everything she'd done for Maverick and his greedy band of not-so-merry men. If someone needed her to make some illegal street drugs, she could get right on that, but find a way to get onto the next step of her plan? She was stumped. Even in death, Maverick was defeating her.

Mirek bumped her shoulder. "Hmmm?" she asked, her brows raised in question.

"Deep in thought?" He nodded down at her hand.

Looking down, she realized she was playing with her owl pendant. So often she wasn't even cognizant of what she was doing, but somewhere deep inside her, she felt the reassurance from holding it.

"I'm frustrated."

"I know." He leaned forward and kissed her softly. "You may be the smartest person in this room, but that doesn't mean you can't ask for help. We're not alone anymore."

"I need to do this. You know why," she whispered, suddenly aware of the lack of conversations around them.

Mirek took her hands in his. "I know you think that, Athena, but you have nothing to prove. Nothing you did in the past was done voluntarily. And the same is true for me.

We'll help because it's the right thing to do, not because we need to make up for anything."

"Are you two alright?"

Mirek dropped her hands and she turned to face her dad. "Yeah, we're fine."

"Actually…" Mirek said as he pulled one of her hands into his lap. "Sam needs some help."

Sam wanted to cringe, but maybe Mirek was right. Not in that she didn't have anything to make up for, but she could get some help.

"What can we do to help?" her dad asked

Everyone looked to Sam for direction.

"I don't know what to do next…" Feelings of failure threatened to overwhelm her, and she felt the tensions around her rise. So many more people were going to die if they couldn't contain the magic, and Sam had promised them she'd come up with a plan to do just that. She fiddled with her pendant, gaining some strength from it, and pushed on. "Jo and Simon found the spell, but—"

"Hey, what are we? Chopped liver?" Reece called from down the table and his joking cut the tension in the room faster than a hot knife through warm butter.

When the laughter died, Sam smiled at Reece, and then her gaze landed on her parents. Her dad gave her a small nod.

"Contain the problem and start small, sweetheart," her mom said. "It could be as simple as pepper."

"Pepper?" Jack asked with a laugh in his voice. "I feel like there's a story that goes along with that that I'd like to hear."

"Me too," Morgana said, along with others.

Her mom beamed. "When Sam was just three years old…"

Mirek put his arm around Sam's shoulders, and she relaxed into his side as her mom regaled the group with the story of how three-year-old Sam took down a thug who was after them, by throwing a small handful of pepper at him. The pepper didn't take the guy out, but it was just enough to cause him to fall backward and hit his head on the ground.

There were so many questions that her mom then launched into the story of how they had first escaped from her brother's house.

Sam didn't remember any of the stories her mom told, and hearing them made her feel closer to her mom.

"You're amazing, Sam," Morgana said above the light din in the room. "You always have been. So… as Stella said, let's start small. What's our pepper in this situation?"

Sam looked at her friend and saw the difference the last four months had made in her life. Besides her transformation, Morgana had bloomed with Damon's love and shed the insecurities from their time in captivity. She'd embraced her amazing innate qualities—passion, courage, and bravery. If Morgana could and wasn't holding onto the guilt from their time in captivity, then Sam could as well.

What was their pepper? Was it really that simple?

"Okay… we have the spell…" She smiled at Reece and then let her gaze wander across the many faces in the group. "I thought it would tell us how to contain the magic. Since it's no longer just a matter of putting the evil back in the box, we need to extract it from hundreds, if not thousands, of people and then contain it."

She had already memorized the spell and was running it through her mind again when she felt Mirek put an arm around her and give her a light squeeze. Looking up, she realized she'd been lost in thought. Everyone was staring at her expectantly.

Always there for her, Mirek took over. "Sam figures the spell can extract the magic, but we'll need two things. First, a way to cast the spell on everyone at once, and second, a way to funnel the spell back into the box."

"Did you recover the box?" Damon asked Jack.

Jack stood and walked to the head of the table. "Not yet, but we're working on it."

Sam wished she had confidence like Jack—he looked self-assured, like he never had to worry about compensating for anything in his past. She wished that, one day, she wouldn't either. Unfortunately, she'd learned a long time ago that wishes didn't always come true.

"We need to brainstorm," Jack told the group. "As Mirek said, we need two things—a way to extract the magic from everyone who is contaminated and a way to funnel it into the box... Reece, can you go through the list of spells you've collected and see if any of them will help?"

"I've already been doing that, but I'll keep going," Reece said, not sounding quite as jovial as usual. Sam knew the tremendous amount of effort it would take to comb through every spell from the ancient books they'd uncovered and she didn't envy Reece his task.

"Fiona," Jack said, looking over at her where she sat between Damon and Morgana. "Have you had any visions that might help? I've only continued to have the same one as before. I think it has something to do with this, but I haven't been able to connect the dots yet."

"No, no visions," Fiona said softly. She cleared her throat, and Sam thought she suddenly looked visibly refreshed, as if she'd given herself an instant glamour. "I think those of us in this room have enough experience that if we start throwing out ideas of where to look, we'll find the answer," she told Jack, sounding stronger this time.

"Alright, everyone, you heard Fiona. Let's start bouncing ideas around." Jack turned to the side and a large, freestanding whiteboard appeared beside him.

Several people laughed and a few groaned. Then someone

threw a whiteboard marker at Jack. He caught it above his head, and the corners of his lips twitched.

"Frank. You want to do the honors?" Jack asked, holding up the marker.

"Why, because I'm the oldest or because I have the neatest penmanship?" her uncle Frank asked as he walked over to Jack.

"Let's go with penmanship," Meredith called out, and garnered a few more laughs.

Sam listened to people throwing out ideas, such as creating a spell to funnel the magic into the box. No one hesitated to offer a suggestion, and they worked as a group expanding on each other's ideas. They supported each other like one big family—whether by blood or love or caring—it didn't matter.

It drove home the enormity of what she and Mirek had missed out on by not growing up surrounded by these people. If they had, she and Mirek might not be where they are right now and she wouldn't give that up for everything.

"Wait," she called to Meredith, as something she said caught Sam's attention. "What did you say?"

"I said, I thought maybe we could create a containment area like some magics did in the twelfth century."

"How do you know that's what they did in that century?"

Meredith nodded at her husband. Still standing by the whiteboard, Jack took over. "When Meredith and I became co-leaders of the North American council, we went through a ceremony. Each council member goes through a small ceremony and gains some extra skills," he said, lifting his chin toward several of the couples, "but, Meredith and I obtained some extreme powers and skills, along with all the knowledge of past council members from over the centuries. It's…"

"Overwhelming to sort through," Meredith said.

"Yes. We need to compartmentalize it, or it could drive us insane," Jack continued. "I'm not even sure how much knowledge we possess, but when we need something, we have to think of something specific and rapidly go through thousands of memories and thoughts to extract a specific piece of information. We discovered the containment from the twelfth century by accident when looking for something else."

Sam leaned forward and tried to contain her excitement. "I think you just found the answer."

Jack didn't look as convinced. "We'd need to know what to look for."

"No, you just need to know *who* to look for. If you can sift through your memories to find someone who was around during the time the box was created, they'll be able to tell you what to do since they were likely involved with the creation of the spell we found."

Sam's hope continued to swell, and she tried to tamp it down as she turned to Connor and Rowena. "If Jack and Meredith found someone to talk to, could you reach out to them?"

Rowena looked at Connor for several seconds, possibly speaking to him telepathically, before she turned to Sam. "It's possible, but we'll need to figure out who can assist us." She chuckled. "Reaching out to a ghost in the beyond isn't as easy as filling out a form on a website's contact page."

"But it's possible?" Sam asked.

"Yes," Connor said. "It's possible."

Finally, Sam let her hope off its leash as she looked at Meredith and then Jack. "Could you do it right away?"

Jack blew out a breath. "You make it sound easy, but okay... Let's say we find the person and Connor and Rowena can reach them. Then what?"

Sam turned to Rowena. "You ask for a way to funnel the magic once we've extracted it from everyone."

"What about extracting it from thousands of people?" Jack asked, a frown marring his features. "And then what about locking the box? We still don't have a way to forge the sword into a lock."

The mention of the lock reminded Sam of Kate and Isaac. She looked around the room and realized by the saddened expressions that she wasn't the only one who was thinking of them right now.

"Pepper, Jack," Fiona said, her tone strong, but her eyes held a glassy sheen. "Let's not get ahead of ourselves. Finding our ancestor is our small handful of pepper. We'll start there."

Fiona waved her hand in front of her face, her eyes dry as she looked around the room. "We will put an end to this. We will not lose a single more loved one."

Sam sat back and turned into Mirek's embrace to hide her own tears. She hoped Fiona would understand when Sam had to make the ultimate sacrifice. Regardless of what she'd promised Mirek, if it was the only option, Sam would use her magic to end the evil.

CHAPTER FIFTEEN

$\mathcal{M}$eredith reached for the counter when a sudden dizziness swamped her.

"Too much?" Jack asked as he wrapped his arm around her shoulders to steady her.

"Yeah." She huffed out a breath and pushed off the stool. "Maybe we should move over to the couch and get comfortable, so I don't fall and do something dumb like hit my head."

"Good idea. I wish I'd thought of that."

Meredith thwacked Jack's arm with the back of her hand. She hadn't missed the playful sarcasm in her husband's tone. "Okay, fine. You were right. I just hadn't expected we'd be at this for so long."

Jack sat in the corner of the couch with his legs stretched over the cushions and pulled Meredith between them.

"How long has it been?" she asked as she leaned back against Jack's muscular chest and picked up his wrist in her lap to look at the time, having forgotten to put her own watch on.

She groaned. They'd been searching their memories for three hours already.

"Let's relax for a few minutes." Jack conjured a glass of wine and handed it to her before conjuring a high-ball glass filled with amber liquid.

"Mmmm, delicious."

They sipped their drinks and enjoyed the quiet for several minutes, until Jack broke the silence.

"I'm worried about you, Bubbles."

She turned in his lap when he placed a kiss on her cheek and met his lips. They kissed slowly for a moment as she held her wine out to the side.

When they settled back into their positions, she took another sip. "I'm okay, just tired."

"Are you sure that's all it is?"

She heard the worry in his softly spoken words.

"I want it all to be over. Like Fiona said earlier today, we can't lose anyone else." She choked on the last word as her throat tightened at the thought of all the loss they'd suffered.

Her glass disappeared, and Jack turned her so she straddled his lap as he tightened his arms around her.

"I can't promise you that, Bubbles." He dried her tears with his magic and looked into her eyes. "But I can promise that we *will* defeat this evil. I want a family with you, and I want our kids to grow up without the fear and loss that we did."

"There are never any guarantees, Jack. We don't know what will happen, even if we stop the evil."

"True, but we can give our kids the best chance at a normal life."

"Kids… hmm… plural?" she teased, hoping to lighten the mood. "We've always said we wanted kids, but we never talked numbers. How many are you thinking? Two?"

Meredith saw a glimpse of rare mischief in his smile and knew he was going to mention twins.

"Since we're both twins, there's a good likelihood that we'll have twins, so three sets would be good. Or maybe four."

"F… four?" She choked on the word. "You want eight kids?"

"Or six."

She searched his expression to see if he was teasing, but he looked serious.

Flipping back around in his arms, she leaned against his chest again and he wrapped his arms around her.

"Okay."

"O…okay?"

Meredith grinned when Jack choked this time on speaking a single word. Keeping her husband on his toes was one of her tiny little joys in life. "Well… we can't control the twins part… or can we?" She twisted to look at him over her shoulder.

He shrugged. "Maybe," he said, looking serious once more.

That was a new one. Even with all her power gifted from the council, Meredith could still be surprised by magic.

She settled against him. The thought of children warmed her soul, but they wanted to bring kids into a safe world. "I guess we should get back to work," she said with a sigh.

"We should, but maybe we can narrow things down. Instead of looking for memories connected to the magic box or even a time period, I think we should each pick one ancestor and see if we can isolate their memories."

"Okay. How should we do that?"

An image of an old man formed in her mind. "Did you just give me that?"

"Yes. I came across him and a few people who were

mentioned with the magic box when I was searching in the archived memories. We'll go through them one at a time."

Meredith wiggled her butt to get a bit more comfortable on the cushion and closed her eyes. Holding the image of the man in her mind, she went back in his memories.

Two hours later, after stopping for a bathroom break and a snack, Meredith had become discouraged. There were hundreds of years of memories to sift through. Instead of going through each one—which would be impossible—they were looking through ones that matched an ancestor and keywords, such as magic box.

"Maybe we need a new plan."

"Not yet. I think I found something," Jack said.

She twisted around and pulled up on her knees facing Jack. "What?"

"Silas, Divit, and Hiro. Those are the names of three magics who foresaw the destruction that the box could bring and did something to counter it. At least I think they were. It's a start. And if it's not them, maybe they'll know who else we can contact."

"Contact," Meredith huffed out a humorless laugh. "Rowena and Connor said it wasn't that easy. How are they going to find them?"

Jack stood and lifted Meredith into his arms. "I have no idea. But we've done our part for now, so we're going to pass the baton."

When he carried her toward their bedroom, she snuggled into him and couldn't hold back a yawn.

"Exactly. We're both tired." He yawned too as they reached their bedroom. "We'll get a hold of Rowena and Connor in the morning."

"Ok—" Her words were cut off as she yawned again. She hoped her cousin could find some answers, because if she couldn't… Meredith shut down her thoughts, not willing to think of losing anyone else she loved.

December 15

ROWENA TOOK in Mirek's appearance as he chatted with Connor about their favorite books. Her brother looked better than he had when he'd been rescued a month ago. With the help from magic, no longer having his own siphoned, and good food and rest, he had filled out and wasn't gaunt anymore. Working outdoors had probably helped too.

The last time Rowena had seen him, he'd been ten years old. She hadn't known what to expect when she'd laid eyes on him again. Their father had been a tall, muscular man, and Mirek reminded her so much of him. It used to hurt so much to think of her parents, but the last couple of months had done a lot to help with her healing. Speaking with Taren had opened old wounds, but she was more at peace about him now too.

She could see the similarities in her brothers. Their eye and hair color were the same. Mirek's hair was shorter than it'd been when he was rescued. As a kid, he used to complain about the curls they'd all inherited from their mom.

Seeing him now was bittersweet, but not painful like it would have been only a few months ago. It made her more wistful for what they used to have.

"Rowena, stop staring. You're going to give me a complex," Mirek said as he rubbed his scarred cheek.

She blinked at her brother. "Oh, sorry. Just wool gathering."

"Wool gathering," Mirek whispered, more to himself than her. "I had forgotten that phrase."

"Taren said the same thing."

Mirek's eyes looked like he had just closed off, and she wanted to kick herself for mentioning Taren. They still needed to talk about his death, because until they did, Mirek wouldn't be able to move on. She just hadn't found the right time to bring it up.

"Hey," Meredith said in greeting and thankfully lightening the atmosphere.

Rowena twisted in her seat on the couch to see the foyer. "Hi, come on in. We're just chatting."

Meredith chuckled as Jack sat in a loveseat and pulled her down almost on top of him. "Sorry we're so late. I thought we'd be here first thing this morning, but I was exhausted after searching through memories last night."

"You don't have to apologize, Bubbles," Jack said quietly.

"I know. I just… Anyway, we found something."

"Should I get Sam?" Mirek asked. "She's visiting her parents, but I'm sure they'd understand if you need her."

Meredith waved her hand, as if to brush off the comment. "No, it's okay. Sam deserves to relax, and we've got this." She patted Jack's leg. "You want to take over?"

"We believe we've uncovered the names of the three people the seer told us about before you found the key," he said, looking at Connor and Rowena.

Mirek sat forward on his chair, rubbing his palms on his jeans. "Can you catch me up? I know about Connor finding the key and Drew stealing it since he bragged about it," Mirek said with a disgusted sneer. "Then Maverick stole the box from you and consumed the magic. But I don't know who you're referring to?"

Jack nodded at Rowena, so she picked up the story.

"Taren helped us contact a seer, Helen, who Connor's dad had known. She told—"

Mirek held a hand up in a gesture to stop. "If Taren helped you, then the seer is dead?"

"Oh, sorry." Talking to the ghosts wasn't an everyday occurrence for most people.

Mirek leaned back in the chair and laid one foot on his other knee. It was a move she remembered her dad doing all the time. "You don't need to apologize, Ro. I've been gone a long time," he said softly.

"Right." She gave him a smile, and this time, tears didn't threaten at the reminder of someone they'd lost. "Anyway... Taren contacted Helen, and she told us that when the box was created by those that desired more power, there was nothing that could be done to reverse its creation. But some powerful magics who foresaw the destruction that the box could bring about decided to do something to counter it. That's where the key came in. They couldn't destroy the box or the map to locate it, but they were able to create a key to make it more difficult to find. They also created an object, that when forged, will permanently close the box."

"The sword," Mirek said.

"Yes. And if the names that Jack and Meredith found are who Helen was referring to, maybe they can help us."

Connor turned on the couch toward her and clasped her hands. Their knees touched, just like they did the very first time they combined their magic so they could see Taren. That moment had led to events that changed her life—having closure with her brother and falling in love.

"Jack, what's one of the names?" Connor asked.

"Silas."

"Can you send me his image?" Rowena asked.

"Sure," Jack answered and a second later a picture of a man appeared in Rowena's mind.

"Got it."

Connor looked into her eyes. "Since we don't have a connection to this person, like we did through Taren, do you have a way to contact him?"

"Yes. I'm going to think the words to a spell that Reece found and then say the name of the man we'd like to contact in my mind while I picture him. It's supposed to channel the ghost, but it will take a connection between us to summon him. What I don't know, is if it's an immediate thing or not."

"Well, let's try." Connor gave her hands a small squeeze. "You ready?"

"Yes." This was the easy part, unlike talking to Taren had been at first, because this ghost meant nothing to her. It was funny, in a weird way, that contacting ghosts was becoming second nature.

Rowena closed her eyes and recited the words of the spell and then the man's name. She popped her eyes open and looked around. Nothing.

"It's okay," Connor said quietly. "Just keep trying."

On the fifth try, Rowena heard Meredith gasp, and she popped her eyes open again. A man, wearing long, white robes, hovered in the middle of the living room. So startled by his appearance—even though his arriving was what she hoped for—she would have broken the connection with Connor's if he hadn't been holding onto her tightly.

He looked old and not pleased to have been summoned.

Looking directly at Rowena, he spoke in a language she didn't understand.

"I'm sorry, I don't—" Before she could finish her sentence he waved his hand across his throat and then cleared it.

"English is not my language, but I should have been prepared. This calling is not unexpected," he said, his tone wary. "I am far older than the seer you spoke with so I cannot stay in this realm long. Say your peace."

"Are you the one who hid the magic box and created the key and map to find it?"

He nodded, and although he didn't move otherwise, he reminded Rowena of an old college professor who would gesture for students to get to the point.

"The box was opened, and one man consumed the evil magic, but the magic burst out of him and is spreading to other magics. People are dying. We have a spell to extract the magic from everyone, but we don't have a way to funnel the magic from thousands of people into the box."

The man nodded again, and his form wavered in and out of focus, like Helen's had.

"You will need to find an ancient symbol and manipulate it to act as a funnel." An image appeared in the air, floating in front of the man's chest. "This is it."

"That's in my vision," Jack said, his tone full of awe as he walked around to face the image. He held out his hands, and a piece of parchment landed on his palms. Then Jack muttered a few words too quiet for Rowena to hear and the image floated onto the parchment, embedding itself into it, like ink. "Thank you," he said to the man with a slight bow.

An idea occurred to Rowena as the man started to fade. "Wait! Please, I have one more request."

"I am not your servant. I will grant you one request if I can, but only because I did not stop the evil during my lifetime. I regret that something I failed to prevent has harmed so many generations after my own. State your request."

"Can you contact my brother? Taren Williams. He's twelve years old. I've spoken to him before, but I'm unable to contact him anymore. I need him to help someone—he's the only one who can."

"That is not a simple request, but I will do my best," he said and then was gone.

"Rowena? What are you doing?" Mirek asked, his voice huskier than usual.

"I'm trying to—"

"Sorry to interrupt, but Meredith and I are still tired. We'll catch up later." Jack held his hand out for Meredith, and they both flashed away.

"Rowena, I think you're playing with fire." Mirek frowned at her, and she almost laughed because it was such a big brother thing to do. She'd missed that.

Ro? Taren said in her mind, and she scrambled to grasp Connor's hands.

CHAPTER SIXTEEN

The image of Taren on the floor, blood pouring from his chest, popped into Mirek's mind like a visceral punch to his gut.

Mirek had often felt like a failure—each time he was unable to stop their captors from torturing Sam or his cousins—but Taren's death was all his failures multiplied by infinity.

He'd gone over it in his mind more times than he could count. Sam had been right that Taren's death was physically Eddie's fault, and Drew's, since he'd pushed Eddie. But Mirek's lack of emotional control—him taunting Drew—is why he needs to take the ultimate blame for Taren's death.

"Mirek?"

He would never forget his brother's voice. It hadn't changed at all, but then, why would it? Taren would forever be twelve years old.

Mirek took a deep breath and slowly turned around. From a glance, Taren appeared corporeal, but his feet were floating several inches off the ground.

Taren's shirt was the same one he'd had on the day he

died, but it was fresh and clean with no giant tear over his heart or blood stains. His hair was also the same as it had been the day he died—a mess of wild curls with a few falling over his forehead.

Mirek had always been the one to make sure they had new clothes and shoes when they'd grown out of their old ones, whether he had the strength to conjure them or not. And haircuts had been his responsibility too. Taren had been due for one.

Now his appearance was set for eternity because Mirek hadn't taken the time to give his brother one last haircut.

"Wow. You've gotten old," Taren laughed. "You're almost as old as Dad was."

"Not quite," he said and smiled at his little brother. Even if Mirek couldn't make himself outright grin, he didn't have to force it either. Taren had always been able to bring that out in people.

"Dad was in his forties when…" Mirek swallowed the lump in his throat. It didn't seem to matter that his dad had died twenty-two years ago; being home and seeing Taren's ghost brought all his guilt and grief to the forefront.

Taren laughed again and pointed at him. "Yeah, yeah, but you're close."

"I love you," Mirek said, not caring that he'd gotten serious when Taren had kept things light. He needed Taren to know how he felt, knowing this would be his only chance.

Seeing his brother now—looking the same as he had all those years ago—didn't seem right.

He thought he'd at least accepted Taren's death, even if he would never make peace with it. Now he knew that he hadn't. He'd only buried it.

The love for his brother and feeling his loss all over again threatened to break Mirek. Taren would never get to grow old. He'd never be part of the family reunion as he and the others were. Never get to experience all the rights of passage that a young man should. Never fall in love and have a family of his own.

Mirek pushed his magic through his body to cool himself off. He didn't want to cry in front of his brother, but not because he thought crying was unmanly. He didn't want him crying to be the last image Taren had of him.

"I love you too," Taren said, his tone more serious. He didn't cry, and Mirek expected he probably couldn't. His image wavered, just as the ancestor's form had.

"I can't stay long," Taren said, and turned to Rowena. "And this is the last time," he said, imitating a high-pitched woman's voice and wagging his pointer finger up and down as if scolding someone. "You do not get to pop back and forth between realms, boy. You tell your family that. Blah, blah, blah..." he said with a laugh.

Rowena chuckled, and Mirek expected Taren had rolled his eyes, something he'd done often when he'd reached his tween years.

Taren turned back to Mirek, but he wasn't laughing anymore. His expression was one of sadness Mirek had seen so many times in the early days of their captivity before they'd become resigned to their fate.

"Mirek, you are not responsible for my death," Taren told him with an authority in his voice Mirek hadn't heard before.

"I know it was Eddie who held the knife and..." Mirek pushed the images aside and focused only on Taren. "But I taunted Drew. If I hadn't lost control—"

"No. Stop. You couldn't do anything more. You did more for me than anyone. You were the best big brother I ever could have hoped for. It wasn't your fault, and you need to accept that."

Taren waved his hand at Mirek's face. "You got that scar

because of me. Every time you look in the mirror, I want you to see that scar as a badge of honor because you stood up for me and Sam. And Morgana and Rocky. They all survived because of you." Taren's image wavered again. "I've got to go, and I won't be able to see you again, so this is really goodbye."

He turned to Rowena and Connor. "I won't see anyone again, but I want you to know that love you."

Taren's image faded, and a dam of emotions broke inside Mirek.

He fell into the nearest loveseat as tears streamed down his face. Leaning forward, he put his face in his hands and let out everything he'd been holding in for years about Taren's death.

A moment later, he felt his sister wrap her arms around his shoulders as she perched on the edge of the loveseat with him. He turned into her and sobbed like he'd never done before.

It felt like all his failures for the last twenty-two years had come to the surface, and each one had to get out.

A tissue appeared in front of his face. Taking it, he wiped his eyes, then used his magic to mop up what one tissue couldn't even begin to.

After he disappeared the tissue and felt a bit more in control, he looked at Rowena. "Thanks."

She gave him a watery smile and kissed his scarred cheek before she moved over to sit next to Connor on the couch.

"For over twenty years, I blamed myself for Sam's death, before I knew she was still alive," Connor said quietly. "We were kids dealing with magic and evil beyond our control."

Mirek wasn't sure what to say. He got that Connor had similar guilt, but there was a difference he couldn't fully understand because Sam was alive, and Taren wasn't.

"It's because of you, you know?" Connor said.

"What is?"

"That Sam's alive."

"Yeah, but—"

Connor held up his hand to stop Mirek's protesting. "No buts. I've talked to Sam, and I know what you did for her and Taren and your cousins. You were only ten years old when you were taken. You did the best you could."

Mirek wanted to believe that, but seeing Taren again made his old guilt over Taren's death feel like it was brand new all over again.

"I lived with guilt too," Rowena said quietly. "I felt guilty for years because I had survived and I thought none of you did. I tried to be helpful in any way that I could, to give to others and lead a good life. To make sure I was worthy of being alive when you weren't."

"Like *Saving Private Ryan?*"

She laughed. "Yes, exactly like that. I'm surprised you figured that out."

"We watched a lot of movies. That's how Rocky—er—Dylan got his name."

Rowena grinned and he saw the young sister he remembered.

"Taren told us, and so did Morgana, when she remembered. She said she drove you crazy watching princess movies and when Sam arrived, she backed up her choices. Taren liked the *Land Before Time* movies until he got older and Rocky liked... well... *Rocky* movies and other action movies."

Mirek felt a weight lift off his shoulders as he remembered all those times watching movies. Their lives weren't ideal, but they made the best of them and had some good memories. "Yeah," he groaned around a smile. "I think I can recite every Disney princess movie by heart. And when the younger kids went to bed, Rocky and I watched action movies and war movies. The scene at the end of *Saving Private Ryan* got to me because I'd learned from Sam that our dad had died, and even though we'd been taken, I was still alive, and like you, I wanted to live the best life I could."

Rowena let out a cry and launched herself into his arms. "We did," she said, her words muffled in his shoulder as he held her. "We did the best we could."

When they pulled back and dried their tears again, he realized that maybe he had. Now there were new dangers, and he still needed to protect Sam, even if it was from herself. He needed to be strong enough to do it—seeing Taren showed him that.

It might take him a while to truly digest it, but Mirek knows his emotions aren't to blame. Nor should he fear they'll get in the way of him keeping Sam, and all those he loved, safe. To do that they needed to complete the next step in the plan.

December 18

"It's getting so bad. Even in my craziest of nightmares, I never would have imagined it'd get this bad," Isabella said.

Reece could hear the anguish in her voice, even over the phone. "We're going to fix this, cupcake. We'll find the symbol tonight, and then we'll almost be ready." He didn't feel as optimistic as he sounded, but doom and gloom was everywhere lately, so he didn't need to add to it.

He listened as Isabella told him about her day and how she had helped outfit two more floors above the existing one in his bakery building for people to stay. If they needed any more, they'd have to start using the empty floors above the apartments in the same building as Isaac's tattoo shop. Could they still call it Isaac's tattoo shop now that he was gone? As part owner of the buildings, he knew that eventually they'd fill the space with a new business, but for now he couldn't think about it.

A light breeze hit as he stood on the balcony of his hotel room and continued to listen to Isabella.

"Anyway…" she said. "It's all set up. Now, tell me again where you are and where you're going. I swear I wasn't awake when you told me before you left this morning."

"That's because I kept you up late last night." He couldn't help but smile as he vividly remembered why they'd lost sleep the night before.

She chuckled. "Yes, you did, and you're welcome to anytime. But I know you have to go soon, so tell me again where you are."

Reece pulled his phone away to check the time—fifteen minutes before eleven p.m.; he still had time. "We're in the city of Nova Sintra, which is in southwestern Cape Verde. Pretty much in the middle of the Atlantic Ocean between the US and the African continent."

"And that's halfway to Johannesburg, South Africa… ah… you said that's where you're going, right?"

"Close enough. We're going to the Sudwala Caves, which is a couple of hours away from Johannesburg and another five thousand miles from here."

"How was it flashing five thousand miles?"

"Okay, I guess. When I got here, all I could think about was food. But that makes sense since I used more energy."

They talked for a few more minutes and then Reece told Isabella he loved her before they said their goodbyes. What he didn't say was that he might not live through the night.

The day before, Jack had pulled him aside after another group dinner and planning session.

"I know from my vision that you have to be one of the ones to go with us, but it could be dangerous," Jack said, stress lines that hadn't been there before around his mouth.

"I'm in, no matter what we face. But how dangerous do you think it's going to be? And is there anything we can do to prepare?"

Jack ran his hand through his hair and let out a sigh. "I don't know how dangerous it'll be, but you're going to have to manipulate part of a cave wall, and we'll have to replace it. It's about 500 feet underground in one of the oldest caves in the world. I still can't tell in my vision what Morgana is needed for, but since she can hold back fire and gravity, that must mean something involving one of those elements is going to happen. And as for preparing for that... I don't know how we would."

Reece looked over at Isabella as she chatted with his cousins. He wanted a life with her—to grow old together and watch their kids grow up, and hopefully grandkids. Maybe because he'd almost faced death once, he knew how truly precious life was, and that's where the catch lay. If they didn't capture the evil magic and lock it away, none of them might grow old.

He looked back at Jack. "Can we bring more help?"

"We could if we needed to, but I'm not sure we should. Most magics would take several days to get there by plane or flashing with multiple stops, and then they'd have to deal with jet lag. That would all take extra time I'm not sure we have."

Reece agreed, even as he worked to come up with alternatives and play a bit of devil's advocate. "Anyone who is already a council member has the extra power to flash at least halfway there in one trip, same as me."

"Yeah, and I've thought about that. But in my vision, I only saw the four of us."

Since they needed to travel ten thousand miles to get to the caves the ancestor had told them about, they had to make the trip in two parts. Now that he had some extra magic from becoming a council member, he was able to flash half the distance at once. Going twice as far would have been impossible, although Jack and Meredith didn't have any trouble, even with another person.

Meredith transported Morgana in her flash, and Jack brought Mirek and then went back for Sam. Although only four of them were going into the caves, as per Jack's vision, Reece felt some reassurance with Sam and Mirek standing by ready to help if necessary.

Because of the time difference, they left Blue Mountain at eight in the morning and a few minutes later arrived on the island of Brave at two p.m. local time. They'd timed it right for check in.

Reece checked the time again—it wasn't yet six p.m. in Blue Mountain, but almost eleven p.m. local time. He turned off his phone, tossed it on the bed since he wouldn't be needing it, and left his hotel room.

After knocking on Jack and Meredith's door, two rooms down, he waited until he heard Meredith call out to enter. Although the suite wasn't large by US standards, it had a small sitting area with a couch and a few chairs.

Jack was typing on his phone, Sam, Mirek, and Morgana were already there. He greeted them and Meredith shoved a cup of coffee at him. "Hi, here's some caffeine, just in case," she said, smiling at him. "It's still early back home, but you don't want to get sleepy where we're going."

"Thanks." He leaned down and gave Morgana a kiss on the cheek as he used his magic to call over one of the chairs by a small table. "I don't suppose anyone slept?" he asked before taking a sip of his coffee.

"Meredith and I had lunch and chatted," Morgana said. "I just want to get on with this and get back home. I think I've had enough adventures for this year."

"I hear you," Meredith said, giving her sister a small smile.

They'd all had too many adventures this year, and not the

good kind. In only two weeks, it would be the new year. Reece wanted to ring it in with Isabella and his family while knowing that the evil was locked away and everyone was safe.

"I wanted to see inside the caves," Sam said. "But we'll be waiting outside for you. Did you know that the Sudwala Caves are one of the oldest known caves in the world, and began to form around 240 million years ago? Their formation was caused when natural acid in the groundwater seeped through the faults and joints of the Precambrian dolomite rock."

Reece bit the inside of his cheek to stop from smiling when Sam took a breath and kept on going. She was such a wealth of knowledge that he'd have to remember to consult with her the next time he needed to know something, instead of Googling it.

"While there are not many signs of life inside the cave," Sam continued, "the discovery of primitive stone tools indicate that early humans may have inhabited the cave from as far back as the early Stone Age era—2.5 million years ago."

"Jack said it's a tourist attraction now," Meredith said.

"Yes, and a huge one. There are even concerts performed there. I'm not sure what part Jack is taking you to, but even the tourists go 600 meters into the caves and 150 meters underground. They use meters in this part of the world. A yard is only slightly longer than a meter."

Sam paused as she'd almost spit that information out in one breath. Reece didn't need to hear everything about the caves, but he figured providing information was Sam's way of protecting them. He liked that about her.

"You won't feel claustrophobic because the central chamber of the cavern complex is as big as a 500-seater concert hall and thirty-seven meters high. And there is a steady stream of fresh air that keeps the chamber's temperature at a constant seventeen degrees Celsius—that's sixty-three degrees Fahrenheit—but no one knows where it comes from. The caves became accessible to the public in—"

Sam cut herself off when Mirek leaned over and whispered something in her ear.

"Sorry," she said as a blush crawled up her neck.

"It's okay, Athena," Mirek said. "I only cut you off because Jack is ready now."

"I've missed my walking, talking encyclopedia," Morgana said wistfully.

Sometimes Reece forgot his cousins and Sam had over twenty years of history together that the rest of them hadn't been a part of.

"Hey, Reece," Jack said and gave him a single nod. "Before we head out, I got some news from the Emissary."

"Sam, Mirek. Have you been brought up to speed on the Emissary?" When they shook their heads, Jack launched into an explanation. "The Emissary is the appointed leader of all seven magic councils and she and her co-leader are also the leaders for the European council. Council leaders cannot interfere with matters of another council, but we help each other out from time to time. Anyway... I reached out to her because she was looking for other magic blacksmiths who would be capable of forging the lock."

"And?" Sam asked, sitting forward.

Jack shook his head. "Two tried and both went into trances like Kate did."

"But what about another tattoo artist who can do what Isaac was going to do?" Just like thinking about Isaac's shop, Reece hated asking about replacements for Kate and Isaac—it seemed wrong. Yet they needed to proceed with the plan, and no one would fault them for that.

Huffing out a mirthless laugh, Jack shook his head again. "The sword has clocked a lot of miles recently. Mary—the

Emissary—and I have been sending the sword back and forth between Colorado and London to try different things, but so far, no luck. That's how the swordsmiths in Europe were able to try. And two of the tattoo artists Mary spoke with said they weren't skilled enough because embedding magic in memorial tattoos is a lot simpler. The third artist said he'd give it a try, but neither of the swordsmiths are willing to risk it."

"I'll come up with something else," Sam said, a steely determination in her tone.

Jack's expression softened. "I know you're working hard, Sam."

"And it doesn't all rest on your shoulders," Mirek whispered to her, but in the quiet room, everyone heard him.

"Mirek's right; we're a team," Jack told her. "And I didn't mean to put so much pressure on you. And... Kate and Isaac... we're still all grieving their loss and..." Jack's voice sounded hoarse. He cleared his throat. "I don't want to replace them, but they can't be the only two people on the planet who can help with the sword. There's got to be others who can help."

Meredith stood and walked over to sit on the arm of Jack's chair. He took her hand in his lap, and they exchanged a look that spoke of the love they had for each other. Reece recognized it because it was how he felt about Isabella.

He pushed thoughts of her from his mind to focus on the task at hand.

Reece met Jack's gaze. "It's now eleven-fifteen p.m.; you ready to go?"

"Right." Jack stood, and the others followed. "I scoped out the cave earlier in the evening, and there's a viewing deck outside the caves, so I'll flash there first with Mirek. Meredith will bring Morgana, and I'll come back for Sam. Once we're all there, we'll flash inside the cave to where I think the symbol is. As Sam said, the caves are massive and well-traveled, but not where we're going... Reece and Meredith, I'm sending everyone the coordinates to the spot outside the cave now."

An image, along with numbers, appeared in Reece's mind. Somehow, he knew exactly where to go, just not what he would find.

CHAPTER SEVENTEEN

*E*ven with the possibility of danger, Reece could feel his adrenaline pumping as they stood outside the caves.

"Here's where I think we need to start our search," Jack said as another image and group of numbers appeared in Reece's mind.

"This area is deep inside the cave and still receives fresh air, but the ceilings aren't as high. It's also separate from the usual tourist areas, so we should wear headlamps."

It didn't take long to outfit themselves with headlamps and say goodbye to Mirek and Sam who would wait outside on the viewing platform.

Reece flashed to Jack's coordinates and as soon as his feet touched the earth something smacked into his arm. Then his back.

"What the hell?" Morgana yelled as Meredith shrieked.

Reece stood still, looking through his headlamp's beam to see what was hitting them. A swirling mass of blackness moved around them.

"Bats!" Jack yelled. "Hold still!"

The last thing Reece wanted to do was hold still, but he did as instructed.

"Okay, you can move. I've erected a thin barrier. It'll be just enough to keep out the bats, and it will move with us as we walk, keeping us protected." Jack said.

"Morgana?" Meredith asked, walking in front of her sister. "Morgana, can you hear me?"

Reece wanted to ask Jack how he'd erected such a malleable protection, but his cousin was a priority.

Meredith was talking softly to her sister, but she still seemed to be in a panic.

He wrapped his arms around Morgana's shoulders and whispered into her ear. "Hey, beautiful, it's Reece. You're safe. You're with us. Open your eyes, beautiful."

Morgana jolted out of his embrace and looked around. "Reece? Oh shit… I freaked, didn't I?"

Meredith pulled her sister into a hug. "It's okay."

"I've got the bearings. Morgana, you okay to keep going?" Jack asked. At her nod they began working their way through the cave.

The first few times the bats hit the bubble, Morgana flinched, but now, two hours and hundreds of bats later, she ignored them. They all did.

"Let's stop," Jack said. "We need to get a better idea of where we are."

Reece could hear the frustration in Jack's voice. Since he'd already scoped out the area, he had thought he knew where to go. But they hadn't seen anything that resembled the map at all, and no symbols.

"I don't want to be a Debbie Downer," Meredith said. "But is it possible, that because Silas, the ancestor, embedded the symbol so long ago, it doesn't exist anymore?"

Jack held the parchment under the light from his lamp and studied the map. "It's possible. But see this?" The paper floated in the air as Jack pointed to an outcropping on the map. "I think we just passed something that looks like that."

Reece leaned in to get a better look. "The sketch is rough, but I agree, I think it's maybe five or ten minutes back."

"Meredith? Morgana? You okay to backtrack?" Jack asked both women.

"Sure," Meredith said.

"Yeah, I'm game, but could you flash us there?" Morgana said and shivered. "I've had enough of this cave—it brings back a few too many memories. I mean… I know, it's not claustrophobic in this section…."

"Good idea. I've had enough too," Jack said with a smirk and clasped his hand around Morgana's upper arm. "Let's flash two hundred feet at a time."

Meredith followed them and Reece brought up the rear. Three stops later they decided that the area looked enough like the spot on the map to explore it further.

"I get that Silas wanted to hide his symbol, but couldn't he have just put it in another dimension with a spell? Like where Jo and Simon found the book? Do we really have to go in there?" Meredith asked, her tone laced with trepidation.

Reece hadn't noticed the narrow crevice until Meredith pointed it out; he didn't like the look of it any more than she did. His excitement about being in the cave had worn off ages ago. "Hopefully, we won't have far to go," he said, then stepped into the tight space.

Less than ten feet inside the tunnel, he had to turn his shoulders sideways as the crevice narrowed even further. Luckily, he didn't need to duck as well since the ceiling was high enough for him to walk upright.

Reece stopped when a wall blocked his path. "Maybe this wasn't the way," he said, looking over his shoulder at the others.

Jack was in the rear of the line, studying the map. "I don't think that's real." He looked up at Reece. "Try a simple unlocking spell."

Reece turned back around and propelled his magic toward the wall. He jerked back in surprise when the wall disappeared like it had never existed. "That's a good sign," he whispered to himself and walked forward into a space that looked about the same size as The Magic Plate.

There weren't any waterfalls or crypts like the movies always depicted. Just an open space. Reece walked over to the wall on his right, hoping to see something etched into the stone, but couldn't find anything.

"Anyone see a symbol?" Jack asked from the other side of the room.

"No," Reece said, along with Morgana and Meredith as they all met in the middle of the room.

Meredith slumped against Jack, and he wrapped his arms around her shoulders. "I guess we shouldn't have expected it to be so easy," she said.

"We'll find it. This is the room from my vision," Jack said, looking around. He waved his hand toward the entrance and a stone door appeared, identical to the one that had just disappeared. With a scraping sound and a small clunk, the door settled into place. "And if it's not here, then it's probably gone. I doubt it would be anywhere else. We'll flash out from here, and no one will know we were ever here."

"Oh, thank goodness," Morgana said as she walked over to one of the walls and flattened her palm along it before walking forward. "Let's get this over with. Feel the walls."

Reece wasn't sure why a hidden wall would be inside a hidden room, unless it was a precaution to avoid someone accidentally stumbling upon the symbol. A room within a room made him sure they were in the right place.

Walking over to the last wall, he started on the far-right side and flattened his palm against the rough stone. The surface was warmer than he'd expected it, considering the cool temperatures of the caves they'd walked through so far.

Halfway across the wall, Reece felt a pulse under his palm. "I think I've found something," he yelled over his shoulder.

Tilting his head downward, he shone his lamp's light on the spot where he'd felt the movement.

"What'd you find?" Jack asked from beside him.

Reece pointed to the spot. "Feel there."

Jack pressed his palm against the stone and held it there for several seconds. When he dropped his hand, he took a step back, and the corners of his lips tipped up. "I think you found it."

Reece rubbed his hands together and looked at the wall as if it had the answers. "It couldn't be as simple as using the same unlocking spell that worked on the door, could it?"

"I have no idea, but my concern is that the wrong spell could lock it," Jack told him.

"Don't be so negative," Meredith whispered as if he could jinx something. "The ghost didn't warn us about anything."

"I'm with Meredith," Morgana said coming up behind them. "Why would he mess with a good thing? Try it."

Reece backed up a couple of fee and propelled his magic forward, like he'd done on the door, but with less force. Within seconds, a thin layer on the wall wavered, like a gentle breeze hitting a curtain, then it disappeared. In its place was a large picture, not really a symbol at all, barely bigger than a shoe box.

"That looks like a conch shell, just wider at both ends," Morgana said.

"Agreed," Jack said. "And nothing like the symbol I was expecting."

Reece tilted his head, trying to look at the drawing from a different angle. "You said the ancestor's original language wasn't English... Maybe the symbol was the best interpretation of whatever word he'd said."

Meredith stepped around Jack, coming up to the wall. "It doesn't matter what it's called. The important question is... how do we get it off the wall?"

Reece turned away from the wall to face everyone. "Jack?"

"In my vision, you manipulated it," Jack told him. "After that the vision cuts out every time I wanted to see more... I'm not sure we have any other options, and I know you and Morgana had to be here. So you must have something to do with how we get it off the wall. Want to give it a try?"

"It might be all we've got." Reece faced the wall, unsure how close to stand. Too far away and he wouldn't catch the shell if he managed to free it from the wall, and too close could bring the wall down on top of him.

Choosing what he thought was the middle ground, Reece stood back about five feet. Rarely did he use his hands to direct his magic anymore, but he'd never manipulated a picture off the surface of a wall before.

He held out his hand, then took another step back, so his palms weren't too close to the image. Gathering his magic, he let it trickle outward while he envisioned the conch coming off the wall and materializing in his hands.

Ten seconds went by, then twenty, but nothing happened. Reece sent more magic toward the wall, then a little more.

A crack thundered in the cave-like room and the floor shook. He shifted his hips, trying to stay on his feet, when Morgana's shout tore through the room.

"Look out!"

MIREK WATCHED the group disappear with a flash and wondered if he should have gone with them.

"You wished you were going down there with them, don't you?" Sam asked quietly.

He wrapped his arm around her and led them over to a bench on the raised, wooden viewing platform, nestled among trees surrounding the cave's entrance.

They leaned back against the bench, their legs touching, and Mirek reached for Sam's hand. "A part of me does, maybe… I looked out for you and Morgana for so long that it's second nature."

"I hear a 'but'."

"No… not really." He chuckled at his own thoughts, because Sam was almost right. "I didn't *wish* to go with them, just wondered if I should have."

"If something happens, you'll be of more use to them up here. But I don't expect anything will. Those caves have been around for millennia, and tourists traipse through them three hundred and sixty-five days a year. I didn't read about anything ever happening. They're safe."

Mirek looked out into the darkness, only the silhouette of trees visible with the sun still hours away from rising. The comfortable temperature felt like it was in the low seventies, not too much lower than what they'd arrived to in Nova Sintra that afternoon, yet so different from the single digits they'd left in Colorado that morning.

"What are you thinking about?" Sam whispered, just like they used to do at night when alone in the bunk room.

"The weather."

"Really?" She sounded incredulous, like the weather was

an inane thing to think of when they always had so many enormous problems.

"Sure," he said, tilting his head to look down at her. "It's simple, and although it can cause destruction, right now it's nice."

Sam shifted, bringing her knee up onto the bench so she could face him, keeping her hand in his. "You were always able to pull me away from huge thoughts..."

Her voice trailed off, and Mirek feared those big thoughts of hers were going somewhere deep. Since he'd been back, they'd spent a lot of time talking, but they'd yet to talk about one of the most important moments in their lives.

Sam was right; he had been the one to pull her out of her thoughts that could lead to a downward spiral. Even if his own thoughts took him places he feared he would never climb out of. He'd always done his best to remain positive for her.

If they were truly to move on with their lives and stop trying to make up for past mistakes, they had one last thing to talk about.

He ran his thumb over the back of her hand. The hand of a woman now, not even the young adult she'd been when he'd last seen her before they were separated years ago.

Lifting his eyes to hers, he saw her fiddling with her owl pendant with her free hand as her eyes roamed his face.

"I've thought a lot about the last time we saw each other... before this year, I mean." In deference to the quiet night, Mirek spoke softly.

"I was twenty-two and so dumb."

He heard the self-depreciation in her tone, and it brought his feelings of failure to the surface. Over the years, he'd tried to stop her from feeling that way, but it wasn't lost on him that he felt the same way about himself. It was time for them both to stop.

Letting go of her hand, he used his left hand to cup her right cheek, feeling the burn scars slide under his palm. "No. You are not dumb," he said, emphasizing each word. "You're my Athena—beautiful and strong. The goddess of wisdom and battle strategy. You were—"

"But I did—"

Mirek shook his head as he slid his thumb over her lips, cutting off her words. "No, Sam. You're not dumb. You've always been the smartest person I know, and not just book smarts. You always doubted your EQ, but it's high too. You're kind and empathetic and even at five, you absorbed the emotions around you and responded to them with empathy and tenderness."

Dropping his hand from her cheek, he took hold of both her hands in her lap and continued to meet her gaze. "We spent years being emotionally and psychologically tortured."

He closed his eyes for a moment and let himself absorb his own words. If he wanted Sam to accept that what had been done to them wasn't her fault and she had done the best she could in horrendous situations, then he would need to accept it too.

Opening his eyes, he saw hesitation in hers. "None of it was our fault, and it's time we stopped trying to make up for things other people did. The other night, we promised we wouldn't unnecessarily sacrifice ourselves, and now I think we need to do something else. We need to accept that we have nothing to apologize or make up for."

Sam lifted a hand out of his grasp and cupped his left cheek. He didn't feel her entire palm, but what he felt was enough. *They* were enough. He brushed her hair away from her face.

"Do you really believe that?" she asked so softly he almost didn't hear her.

"I know it's true, even though a part of me always thought

I could have done more. But we couldn't. We were just kids, Sam."

He felt his throat tighten like it had when Taren showed himself the other day. Calling up his magic, he cooled off his throat so he could continue. They both needed this talk. "It's just going to take a while for us to stop the self-depreciation talk, but it's time."

Mirek leaned forward, and Sam dropped her hand. He pressed a soft kiss to her lips. "I love you, Athena."

He felt her smile against his lips. "I love you too, hero."

They wouldn't change overnight, but it was a start. When Mirek straightened, he grasped her hands in her lap again. "Sam, we still need to talk about that day. When you were twenty-two, but not dumb," he said and smirked at her.

She chuckled, and it was exactly what they needed to lift some of the tension.

"Even if I wasn't dumb, my actions still caused you to be tortured," she said as tears welled in her eyes.

Using his magic, he dried her tears and then cupped her right cheek again.

"No, they didn't," he said more harshly than he'd spoken before. He needed her to truly absorb his words this time. "You didn't *cause* it, Sam. You chose to make a stand and tried to stop the manufacturing of those drugs. The fact that the assholes tortured me is on them, not you."

She sucked in a small breath. "But when they dragged you into the room covered in blood and continued to beat you…"

Sam's words died off, and he reached for her. She turned so he could pull her onto his lap, sitting sideways with her legs extended along the bench. He cradled her back and kissed her temple, breathing in her scent of honeysuckle and orange.

"It wouldn't have mattered what you'd done, Athena. You could have made double the batch they wanted, and the assholes would have still done the same thing. It was their way of making sure you never stepped out of line."

With his free hand, he turned her face so he could look into her eyes. "They may have physically tortured me, Sam, but they tortured you too. Everything they did was psychological torture."

"We'd been separated for two years when they brought you in... I missed you so much. I didn't think..."

Her eyes filled with more tears, and her lip trembled before a sob tore from her throat. Mirek let go of her face and pulled her against him, wrapping one arm around her back and the other around her head to hold her to him.

The sound of her sobs made his chest physically ache, but Sam needed this. It was time for them both to let go of the pain and move on.

When she finally cried herself out, she conjured some tissues and two bottles of water. Then they talked quietly about some of the other things they'd been through in the seven years they were separated.

"Hero, I need to tell you something."

Mirek had heard Sam start other conversations that way, and it usually meant bad news. He braced himself for the worst while also promising himself they would get through whatever it was. "Tell me," he whispered.

She fingered her necklace, her brows narrowed in a frown. "When Kate and Isaac... when I was in their shop, you know I got hurt..."

He squeezed her hand, hoping to give her the courage to continue.

"Well... I told you that Dad had Nate come to be with me while he and Jack went to talk to Fiona..." She took a deep breath and leaned back against his arm, looking him in the eyes. "Ah... Nate saw my death."

It took everything Mirek had to stay calm. He wasn't mad

at Sam for not telling him earlier, only their situation. "Was it what happened at the FBI building when Maverick exploded?"

She shook her head and dropped her gaze. "No, I don't think so."

"Sam, look at me, please." He waited until she looked him in the eyes. "We can't stop the future, but we can be safe, okay? No more unnecessary sacrifices, right?"

"Right." She cuddled back against his chest.

For two hours after Sam's confession, they held each other and talked. They had just finished disappearing their second lot of tissues and water bottles when the bench shook.

Mirek tightened his arms around Sam before she toppled off his lap.

"That came from the caves," she whispered, then lifted up to get off his lap, but he tightened his hold on her.

"Mirek, we need to go to them. They could be hurt," she said, her eyes wide and he could hear the panic in her voice.

Pushing down his own worry, he kept his voice calm when he spoke. "And us getting hurt in the process won't help them. No more sacrifices, remember? We'll wait to see if they reach out."

Sam settled back onto his lap, and Mirek had to force himself not to hold his breath as he hoped he made the right decision.

CHAPTER EIGHTEEN

*W*hen Morgana shouted, Jack threw his arms up, erecting a bubble above the four of them. It wouldn't be strong enough to hold up the roof of a cave, but maybe it would buy them some time.

Dusted floated around them. He blinked to clear his vision and choked back a cough to stop his arms from trembling. He might need all his power to get them out of the cave, and he wasn't willing to waste any on getting rid of dust.

"Meredith?"

"I'm here," she said, coming up beside him. "Jack, help Morgana."

"Reece, hurry," Morgana shouted, sounding out of breath.

Jack turned only his head to get a good look at his sister-in-law and almost dropped his jaw. He'd heard all about her magic specialties and had been outside the compound in Mexico when she'd apparently levitated boulders, but to see her powers firsthand was something else.

She stood with her arms extended, locked tight, and her head tipped back. Completely covered in dust, her brown hair almost white in the light from his headlamp, she made an imposing figure. What looked like tons of rock hovered inches above her head.

He dropped his hands, realizing if Morgana let go, a protection bubble wasn't going to do them a damn bit of good. Stepping over debris, he moved close to Morgana but was careful not to touch her. "How can I help?"

"Fuuuuuck. I never thought... I'd be here... again... This... is the... worst... déjà vu ever," she said as she took a breath every few words. "Just get... Reece to... hurry."

Jack could hear the strain in her voice and wanted to take the weight from her, but even with all his power, he couldn't resist gravity the way she could. He feared trying to help her could bring the weight down on all of them.

"Okay, I will," he told her, hoping he could keep that promise. Her eyes fluttered closed, and then she opened them again and gave him an almost imperceptible nod.

Worried he could do damage if he flashed and overshot by even a couple of inches, Jack hurried over to Reece and crouched next to him. At first glance, he thought Reece was pushing on the wall, but when he looked closer, he felt his eyebrows climb into his hairline in shock.

Reece wasn't holding up the piece of wall—his hands were embedded in the rock.

"What can I do?" he asked, hoping that this time he could help.

Reece kept his gaze straight ahead as he spoke. "I've got a grip on the conch, but I fear that as soon as I pull it out, everything will collapse."

"Jack, hurry!" Meredith shouted from behind him. "Morgana can't hold it much longer. Her arms are wobbling."

Every day, Jack made split-second decisions, but he was chalking this one up as the worst of his life. If he got this one wrong, there would be no do-over.

He stood and faced his wife, who was standing next to Morgana, sweat pouring off her face. It was now or never. "Meredith, switch places with me."

She moved as quickly as she could among the rocks, and he did the same. When their gazes met, he could see the trust she had in him and he hoped he would prove himself worthy of that trust.

"Press yourself against Reece's back and wrap your arms around him and ready yourself to flash. Morgana, I'm going to do the same to you," he said as he positioned himself behind her.

"As soon as I wrap my arms around Morgana, I'll count down. Meredith, you need to flash on one. Got it?"

"Yes," she said, her voice steady, her arms around Reece.

"Morgana, I'm wrapping my—"

"I can't hold it much—"

Jack flung his arms around Morgana and counted down. "Three, two, one!" he yelled.

He waited only a split second to make sure Meredith had flashed with Reece.

The wall Reece had been embedded in began falling forward, huge chunks crashing to the floor.

He flashed up to the surface with Morgana.

Jack's feet touched the wood planks on the platform, and he let out the breath he didn't know he'd been holding. For the first time in his life, his legs felt unsteady after a flash, but it had nothing to do with the transportation.

Once he was sure Morgana could stand on her own, he looked around until his gaze locked on his wife. She was already walking toward him, and he opened his arms. "Bubbles," he breathed into her hair. Only when she was safe against him did he let go of the fear that had threatened to consume him.

She tilted her head up and pressed her lips to his, parting

them for him. It wasn't a long kiss, but one that said, *we're alive.* They held each other for a moment more, before pulling back. He took her hand in his, still needing to touch her.

"Everyone okay?" he asked, looking at each person. Reece was sitting on a bench, Mirek crouched in front of him, his hands on Reece's arm.

"What happened?" Jack asked Reece as he walked over to him, Meredith's hand still in his.

"I think the wall was offended," Reece said with a small smile, but it didn't hide the lines of pain etched around his mouth. "I hadn't felt it when my hands were inside the wall, but a chunk of stone crushed my forearm." He grimaced and flinched, looking down at Mirek. "Hey, man, easy," he said to him.

"You'll be fine," Mirek said as he stood. "The rock may have felt like it crushed your arm, but it was only broken in about six places. It's as good as new now."

"*Only six?*" Reece looked up at him. "Well, then, no problem." Gingerly, Reece stood. "Only six," he muttered to himself.

Jack heard some snickers behind him, and knew they'd be fine. "But you got the conch?" he asked Reece before noticing it was on the bench beside him. "Sorry, just saw it."

Reece picked it up off the bench. "I don't know for sure, but it looks alright to me—no cracks or anything."

"Good. Sam, you can take a look at it when we get back to Blue Mountain. Speaking of that… what time is it?"

"It's five here," Sam said, looking at her phone. "Which means it'll be two in the morning in Nova Sintra. It's December nineteenth."

Jack got Sam's subtle message loud and clear—another day had passed and the evil was still spreading. As a magic person, he felt the fear and the loss of everyone around him, but as co-leader of the council, it weighed on him, heavier than the stone Morgana levitated. And he knew Meredith felt the same.

There was nothing they could do at the moment but get some sleep. "Let's flash back there. Reece, you going to be okay?"

"Yeah, I feel really good," he said. Jack knew that meant Mirek had likely given Reece more of his power than he'd needed to, but Mirek didn't need to flash, so he could afford to.

Jack nodded at Reece in acknowledgment and looked at the group. "I'll take Morgana and Meredith can take Sam. Then, Mirek, I'll come back for you. That work?"

"Wait," Morgana said. "What about the cave? Won't the people in charge wonder what happened?"

"I don't think they'll even know. I put the doorway back, and I didn't see any cameras, so I doubt there was anything to register motion. Everything should be contained in the room."

"Are you kidding me? The ceiling came crashing down," Morgana said, rolling her eyes, and he almost laughed at her implied "idiot" at the end.

"That room was closed off. There could be some settling and dust around the area, but it's so far inside the tunnel we went through, it should be hidden."

"I'll watch the news, just in case," Sam said.

Morgana nodded at Sam, as if her reassurance was enough.

"We'll flash back to the hotel suite, and everyone try to get some rest. We can meet up for breakfast at ten and then flash to Blue Mountain. It'll only be five in the morning there, but you'll probably need to rest again. Meredith and I will." She squeezed his hand she was still holding, and he looked down at her.

"Okay, let's get back to the hotel."

Meredith took hold of Sam's hand, and they were gone. "I'll be back soon," he said to Mirek, took Morgana's hand, and flashed back to the hotel.

A half-hour later, cuddled up next to Meredith in bed and everyone else in their rooms, he went over the events of the last several hours. Step five of Sam's plan was complete, but without Kate and Isaac, they had no way to complete step six.

All he could do was hope that they'd find a way.

December 21

SAM REACHED across the kitchen island for one of the spells Simon had translated from a book Reece found. Everyone had been helping out where they could, whether that was in the infirmary or searching for whatever she might need, as they waited for her to figure out the next step in the plan.

She looked down at the spell, her other hand poised to add to the notes on the pad of paper beside her. The words swam in front of her eyes. She blinked, hoping to clear her vision, but the words were still blurry.

Grabbing the coffee mug beside her, she looked into it, then shrugged. Clean enough. She conjured a full cup and took a sip. If the caffeine didn't help, she'd use magic to make her vision clearer.

"Duh," she muttered to herself, and sent magic to her eyes. Putting down the mug and picking up her pen again, she glanced at the spell. Better.

An hour later, she tossed her pen on the counter. There hadn't been anything in any of the spells that gave her a clue as to what to do with the sword without Kate and Isaac. Something was missing, but she'd run out of places to look.

Sam picked up the parchment Jack had imbued the map onto. The original map would have been made thousands of years ago. If the originator had created the sword and needed it to be forged into a lock, then he would have assumed there would be enough skilled people available to perform the task. She refused to believe that the fate of the evil magic could rest on one person.

"Evil magic." She snorted as she said the words. It sounded like a villain out of a comic action movie. Thanks to Rocky and Mirek, she'd seen every comic movie ever made. At least until the last three years.

Lifting her necklace, her fingers played with the owl, and she used her other hand to rub the sudden tightness in her chest. Just the thought of those three years and why she'd stopped watching movies still pained her.

Pushing the thought aside, as she'd done so many times over the years, she concentrated on the patterns in the movies themselves. Since she'd run out of places to look for an answer, she was desperate enough to look at comic book heroes for clues.

The good guys always won—though maybe not every hero survived—but the group in general defeated the bad guy and the evil. In their case, the chances of them all getting out of this alive looked a lot grimmer than any action movie she'd seen, but Sam was going to hold herself and Mirek to their promise of no unnecessary sacrifices. To do that, she needed to figure out the next step. Even running through every comic movie through her mind on fast forward, she couldn't find an answer.

For the past three days she'd been trying to figure out what to do about the sword and locking the box. A check with Rowena and Connor confirmed that the last time they saw the magic box was after Maverick had consumed the magic. They said he'd picked up the box and disappeared.

Assuming Maverick hadn't destroyed the box to prevent the magic from being locked away again, Sam held out hope they would find it. When they used the spell to extract the magic from everyone, they'd funnel it into the box. The lock was the piece they were still missing.

She picked up her coffee mug and took a sip. "Ugh." Cradling her mug in both hands, she sent magic through her palms and warmed the coffee just enough to be bearable so she could gulp down the rest.

When she lifted the mug to her lips, her eyes landed on her plan. While drinking her coffee, she went over the steps. Maybe there was a way to change it.

Step one: make a plan.

She chuckled to herself because as silly as it was, she'd always loved that step. Check—they had a plan.

Step two: Find a quantum disentanglement spell.

Complete. They had the spell and a book, but Sam hadn't figured out where the book fit in yet. It was too much of a coincidence that the book showed itself to Jo and the others while they were looking for the spell for it not to be needed somewhere.

Lines and notes in the margins covered the paper where she'd crossed out steps and added new ones as she adjusted steps.

In the beginning, she'd planned to find the spell and then use it on Maverick. That step morphed into Jack and Meredith looking back in their memory to find an ancestor.

Which led to step four: Rowena and Connor contacting the ancestor—now a ghost. Looking at it now, Sam realized they'd had some luck on their side for all the pieces to be falling into place.

Though she didn't know if it was luck or Jack's quick

thinking to flash out of the cave during step five that saved them. Whatever it had been, they now had the funnel and step five was complete.

Sam stared at the words she had written for step six. *Isaac tattoos Kate so she can forge the sword.*

It was as if the words were taunting her. But she *would* find an answer.

"UH." She jumped when a hand landed on her shoulder, feeling like her heart had jumped to her throat.

"Sorry," Mirek said softly. He took her hand and pulled her off the stool. "Come on, it's after one in the morning and you need to get some sleep."

Sam looked at her hand in his as he gently tugged her and then back at the papers. "I have to keep working. I don't—"

With another tug, Mirek brought her against him and kissed her gently. "You're exhausted, Sam. You've been at this since the moment we got back. That's almost forty-eight hours and you've barely slept. You need sleep to have energy to keep going."

A yawn so big it threatened to crack her jaw took over Sam. The mention of sleep could have triggered it, but Mirek was right. She let him lead her into the bathroom off their bedroom and she got ready for bed.

In bed, already naked, they came together without words, reaching for each other. He hovered over her, and she guided him into her heat, looking into his eyes until he picked up his pace. She threw her head back and thrust her hips up.

She gripped his shoulders, her nails biting into flesh, as he drove into her again and again. There weren't any words of love or tenderness, because in that moment they didn't need them, only each other. It was a claiming, a possession by both of them.

It took only minutes before she was breaking apart in his arms, and then he joined her.

When their breathing had slowed down, they turned on their sides, her on her right and him on his left. He ran his fingers along her cheek and absently pushed her hair off her face.

These quiet moments were some of her favorites. And as much as she didn't want anything to intrude on it, there was something she still hadn't shared with Mirek. At first, she didn't tell him because she worried he wasn't emotionally prepared to hear it. Only after they were at the caves did she realize he was ready.

In the two days since, she feared telling him may be selfish on her part because it wouldn't change their relationship. Then she'd think of Rocky and knew that Mirek needed to know how much his cousin had done for them. She'd be forever grateful for the small glimpses of news of Mirek that Rocky had given her.

If all her planning failed and something happened to her, Sam wanted to share everything she could with Mirek while she still had the chance.

"I saw you once," she whispered. "Three years ago."

"Where were we?"

"At the compound. I didn't even know you'd been there."

He leaned forward and kissed her forehead softly. "I'm sorry, Sam. I don't remember much of that time."

"It's okay. It was two years after they brought you into the lab and beat you." She shuddered. "It wasn't long after my twenty-fourth birthday. Rocky came into the lab and spoke with my supervisor. Then my supervisor said the bosses needed something and gestured for me to go with Rocky.

"Rocky must have lied because he didn't take me to any of the bosses, but instead he led me to a window in a room on the other side of the hall."

As she told Mirek the story, she could see it in her mind as clear as if it had happened the day before.

Rocky used the side of his closed fist to clean away some of the dirt and grime on the window. Then he pointed outside toward where vehicles were usually parked. "Look."

Sam did as he said, and her breath hitched. "Mirek." She turned, needing to get to him, but Rocky gently grabbed both her upper arms, holding her in place.

"You can't go out there, Sam. It's not safe. They already know how much you love him, but when it's not front and center, I think... well... maybe they forget."

She turned back to the window and touched it with her fingertips as if she could touch Mirek. He leaned against a vehicle. His hair was longer than it had been when he'd been brought into her lab two years earlier, and his clothes hung on him like he'd lost so much weight that they were now several sizes too big.

"Why did you let me see him? Did you want to torture me?" she asked quietly. Her heart felt like it was shriveling up while her gaze remained glued on Mirek.

Rocky laid his hand on her back and rubbed awkwardly, as if offering someone comfort had become foreign to him over the years.

"I'd never do anything to hurt you, Sam. I just wanted you to see Mirek. To know that he's alive and okay... well...okay as he can be. He's too skinny because they're still siphoning his magic and it makes him too weak to eat and..."

His voice trailed off, but Sam didn't need to hear the words; she knew what they did to Mirek.

"I'm not sure if they'll ever bring him back here, so I wanted you to see him. He loves you so much."

Someone helped Mirek around to the other side of the vehicle, and he disappeared from view, as if he'd maybe gotten into the backseat.

She turned to Rocky. "I love him too. I—"

Rocky jerked her forward and wrapped his arms around her. "He knows, Sam. He knows."

Just as quickly as he'd hauled her against his chest, Rocky pulled back, holding her upper arms again. When he looked into her eyes, she saw the love he had for Mirek too. "I can't promise you that they'll stop hurting him, but I promise you two will be together again. I will do whatever is needed to keep him alive."

"He never told me," Mirek whispered when she finished.

His thumb swept under her eye, and then she felt a cool breeze, as if he used it to dry her tears. Sam hadn't even realized she'd been crying.

When she focused on Mirek's eyes in the darkened room, she saw they were glassy. "It kept me going. I never saw you again while you were there, but five times during those three years, Rocky got word to me that you were okay."

Mirek rolled on his back and pulled her to him so she was half-draped over his chest. His hands roamed her back as she wrapped her arm over him.

"You're going to figure everything out and we're going to have the life we always talked about," Mirek said softly against her hair.

Sam wished that were true. The problem was that it didn't account for the fact that Nate had already seen her death.

CHAPTER NINETEEN

December 22

An update. Jack's message popped into Mirek's mind jarring him awake. He sat up, and Sam did the same from beside him.

"What time is—" Her words were cut off by her yawn as she slapped her hand across her open mouth.

Mirek looked out the window. Seeing only black in the slit between the two curtains, he looked at the digital clock on his side of the bed.

Groaning, he flopped back on the bed and pulled Sam against him. "It's only six fifteen. The last time I noticed before we fell asleep was two thirty."

He heard her yawn against his chest.

"Wanna just lie here until Jack gets back to us?" she asked.

"Sure." It wouldn't be long, but there wasn't any point in rushing until they knew what they had to do.

Less than a minute later, Jack messaged them telepathically again.

The Magic Plate. Seven for breakfast. We have news.

Sam flopped onto her back. "Has Jack ever given us good news in an update?"

"I don't think so, but there's a first time for everything." He rolled over and got out of bed. "Let's have a shower and wake each other up."

Sam hopped out of bed like she'd just had a full eight hours of restful sleep. "Yes, but you'll have to catch me," she said, laughing as she ran to the bathroom.

Mirek joined Sam in the shower, and they used each other for a little stress relief before the meeting.

At exactly seven a.m., they walked into The Magic Plate to see people loading up their plates from platters of food laid out on a side table.

He and Sam got in the line for food, and with full plates, sat in the next empty chairs at the line of tables that had been pushed together. Connor and Rowena sat across from them.

"Good morning, sweetheart," Stella said as she and Ben then took the chairs next to Sam. Nate went to the other side of the tables and sat beside Rowena.

It didn't take long for the chairs to fill up and everyone to start eating.

Mirek concentrated on his food but half-listened to the idle chitchat around him. Conversation centered mostly around the weather and speculation about if they'd get another dump of snow before Christmas, which was only three days away.

With everything going on and Kate and Isaac's deaths being so recent, it seemed strange to think about celebrating a holiday. But it was Fiona who had announced to the group the week before that life must go on. Then she passed around a Christmas stocking filled with everyone's names. Mirek had to buy for Reece and Sam had to get a gift for her youngest brother, Travis.

Instead of conjuring gifts he and Sam decided to get into

the holiday spirit by shopping. The day before their adventure in South Africa they'd gone to the largest shopping mall in the city. Mirek hadn't been to a mall since he was a kid and tried his best to enjoy the experience, but he failed miserably.

Everything was too much—the piped music pouring from speakers every few feet, the decorations plastered on shop windows, the people pushing to get to their next purchase, and stores overcrowded with merchandise.

The only way to describe a mall at holiday time was uncontrolled and overwhelming.

In the end, they'd gone back to the apartment, opened a bottle of wine, played Christmas music quietly in the background, and conjured gifts. Before deciding on each gift, they brainstormed ideas. Despite Fiona's best intentions, they ended up getting a gift for each person. This was their first Christmas back home in over twenty years and he and Sam agreed to give to everyone in their family-friend circle because they'd never gotten to do that before.

It was a memory Mirek would cherish for as long as he lived.

"Good morning," Jack greeted everyone, pulling Mirek out of reminiscing. He turned toward Jack and scooted his chair closer to Sam's, snugging up beside her. Resting his hand on top of hers on the table, Sam flipped hers over and laced their fingers together.

Jack stood at the head of the line of tables and a sudden, heavy silence blanketed the room. They didn't need any more bad news, but Mirek braced himself for some anyway.

"What? No whiteboard?" Reece called out, breaking the tension in the room and garnering laughs.

"Not yet. Maybe later," Jack said, and the corners of his lips twitched up in an almost smile. "I have a feeling some brainstorming will be needed, but first... some good news."

He turned to Fiona, who was walking toward him. "Will you do the honors?"

She nodded and turned to face the group. Her eyes were glassy with unshed tears, as she smiled. "Kate and Isaac are alive!"

Sam's fingers gripped his tighter as the chatter increased around them. This wasn't the place to pull Sam aside to talk, but he knew her—instant self-loathing would have sprung up inside her for telling everyone Kate and Isaac were dead. He ran his thumb along the outside of hers, offering the only comfort he could for the time being.

Fiona waited until the shocked comments died down and waved her hand in front of her face. Now dry-eyed, she smiled at the group.

"A few months ago, I started having a vision—more like just a flash of an image—of Kate lying on the floor in a white room. I'm not a gifted seer like some, but what I see usually comes to fruition. When Kate and Isaac di—"

She waved her hand in front of her face again and cleared her throat. "When they disappeared, the vision came to me more often. Sometimes five or six times a day. I still had no idea what it meant... Then last night, it stopped. I was exhausted and went to bed early... About two in the morning, another vision came to me. My visions feel different than dreams, so a part of me was awake, watching it play out... I saw my grandson. He was about two years old—and he was Kate and Isaac's son."

Damon got up and walked over to his mom. He turned her toward him, and although his voice was soft, it carried to everyone at the tables.

"Mom, I want Kate and Isaac to be alive too, but are you sure that's what you saw? How can you be sure that the little boy you saw wasn't *my* son?"

Fiona took a step back and patted Damon's chest like she

was placating a small child, even though he towered over her, both in height and breadth.

"I know what I saw, Damon. It was a vision of the future. That means she's alive and she's pregnant. I can't tell you how I know she's pregnant now and not months or a year from now, but like with all my visions, I just know. We need to find them," Fiona said and looked toward them. "Sam?"

Sam pulled her hand from his. "I'm… I'm so sorry. It's my fault you thought they were dead."

In seconds, Mirek was out of his chair and kneeling in front of Sam. Damn the people in the room hearing what he had to say. One of her hands gripped the owl on her pendant, but he took the other in both of his. Her hand was freezing cold. Using his magic, he pushed some warmth into her.

"Sam. Sam… Athena, look at me," he said quietly but with strength behind his words.

Their eyes met, and all he could see was anguish; it made his heart hurt for her. For so long she'd struggled with doing the right thing and berated herself for the terror her work had caused others. It didn't matter that she'd had no choice in making the drugs.

Only three days ago they'd sat on the bench in South Africa and purged so much of what they'd gone through during the years they'd been apart. Then they'd talked more over the last couple of days. Mirek hoped they could start to move on. That maybe Sam would begin to forgive herself.

Now, she thought she had caused more people she cared about to suffer. With everyone thinking Kate and Isaac were dead, that meant no one was looking for them. She would blame herself for that too.

Squeezing her hand softly, he locked his gaze with hers. "Sam, this is not your fault. You had no way of knowing Kate and Isaac were still alive."

"He's right, honey," Fiona said. Mirek looked up to see

Fiona standing by their sides. She cupped Sam's cheek and gently turned her head so she could look into Fiona's eyes. "You couldn't have known. Maverick tricked you into thinking they were dead. Even your dad and Jack thought they were dead."

"I know, but…" Sam choked on the last word but didn't look away.

"No, honey. No 'buts'." Fiona tugged her up into a hug, her hand pulling away from Mirek's. He stood just as Stella and Ben came over, each also giving Sam a hug.

Quiet conversations sprang up as Sam hugged her parents, but Mirek could still feel a new level of tension in the room. Maybe one day they could all meet for meals and there'd be only joy in the room. It was one of his many wishes for the future.

"Okay, Jack," Reece called out with a raised voice. "Conjure the whiteboard. We've got some brainstorming to do. Let's bring Kate and Isaac home."

Once more, Reece's comments broke the tension in the room. Reece had been six, four years younger than Mirek and Rocky, when they'd been taken into captivity. Even back then, Reece had been a jokester and never shy. Mirek looked forward to spending more time with him and the rest of his family. Another wish for the future, they were piling up.

No matter what the next few days brought, Mirek was determined to contribute however he could so they'd all have a future worth looking forward to and that all their wishes would have the chance to come true.

December 24

SAM STOOD at the head of the line of tables, waiting for everyone to arrive. December ninth had been the first time she'd formally addressed the group. Now it was December twenty-fourth—Christmas Eve morning—barely two weeks later and yet so much had happened.

At least she had a full plan this time. They would find Kate and Isaac, who would forge the blade, and then they would capture the evil magic and trap it away forever. It sounded so simple, and she could only hope that it would be.

She smiled at people as they took their seats, determined that tonight Kate and Isaac would be home safely.

Mirek walked toward her with a worried look on his face.

"You okay?" she asked as he came up beside her.

He leaned down and gave her a brief kiss. "I'm fine. It's you I'm worried about."

She took a step back and looked up at Mirek to reassure him. Her vision faltered, and she threw out her arms as she pitched sideways.

Mirek's hands wrapped around her arms as he steadied her.

"Jack!" Mirek yelled, his face turned away from her.

"It's… I'm okay, Mirek," she told him, but she knew it was a lie. The world around her appeared blurry and her legs buckled.

"I've got you," Mirek said against her hair as he picked her up, one arm under her legs.

"What's wrong?" Jack asked, appearing beside them as Mirek eased her into a chair. The heat of embarrassment climbed her neck and face.

"I just got a bit dizzy. I'm fine," she protested, but it sounded weak even to her own ears.

"You're not fine," Mirek said, his tone quiet but firm—a tone she'd heard a lot from him over the last several days.

"Sam's been burning the candle at both ends, and while she's been figuring out how to find Kate and Isaac, she's barely slept. Maybe five or six hours in the last fifty."

Jack pulled over a chair and sat in front of her. Tilting his head toward her, he kept his voice low. "We all appreciate how much you're doing, but you can't kill yourself in the process. Can I give you some power, at least enough for now to refuel you?"

If Jack could shore her up, she might not need to sleep until after they found Kate and Isaac. "Yes. Thank you."

The infusion of power was subtle at first, only a slight tingle. Within a minute, she could feel Jack's power mingling with her own. She sat up straighter, feeling more awake than she'd felt in weeks.

"How's that?" he asked.

Pushing the chair back, Sam stood and took a deep breath. "I feel great. Thanks, Jack."

"Don't let the power fool you, Sam. It's only temporary and it won't replace you getting food and sleep."

He paused; the lines around his mouth deepened as his expression became more serious. "I've relied on you a lot, Sam, and I know how hard you've worked. But—and I need you to really hear me, Sam—you don't have a single thing to prove. Morgana told me and Meredith so much of what happened in that compound in Mexico, and none of it was your fault. You have nothing to make up for. This family is a team, and you are just one part of it. We will find Kate and Isaac with your help, but the task doesn't rest completely on your shoulders." Jack nodded at her and Mirek before moving over to where Sam had stood previously.

She suddenly found herself in Mirek's arms, her head against his chest. Breathing in his familiar scent, she felt better than she had in days.

He's right, Mirek said, speaking to her telepathically. *If you won't believe me, please believe Jack.*

I'm really trying to. She pulled back and smiled at him.

"Sam? You ready?" Jack asked.

Mirek squeezed her hand, then took his seat next to the end of the table.

Covering the few feet to stand beside Jack felt almost monumental. She may be just one part of the team, as Jack said, but she wanted to do her part to help them find Kate and Isaac. They wouldn't blame her if she couldn't, but she didn't want to let them down.

You've got this. Mirek said into her mind, as if he could sense her doubts. She gave him a small smile.

"'At first, I thought I'd just kill Curtis's daughter, but now I think I'll add a twist to it.' Those were Maverick's words just before he shot his magic at Kate."

Sam glanced at Fiona, having heard her soft gasp. She hadn't meant to cause Kate's mom even more pain, but Fiona just flicked her hand twice at Sam in a gesture that said for her to continue.

"It was those words and his next that finally clued me in to what he'd done," she told the group. "My theory is that Maverick sent Kate, with Isaac tagging along unplanned, somewhere for... well... for safekeeping. I think he wanted to have Kate out of the way so she couldn't forge the sword, but not get rid of her in case he needed her skillset later."

"What were his next words?" Jack asked.

"He told me to look down and asked if I liked his little twist." Sam let her gaze wander over the different faces in the group. "I think his *twist* was not killing her, but he wanted me

—and Dad—to believe they'd died. That's why he told me to look down. There was a pile of ashes at my feet."

Her dad stood and walked over to her. Sam had the feeling he was too restless to stay still, remembering that day and what Maverick had then done to her.

"I accused Maverick of incinerating Kate and Isaac," he said. "Then Maverick told me it needed to be done."

"And that was my next clue." Going over Maverick's words again for the group reinforced her belief that she was right. Her hope that they'd find Kate and Isaac today became a belief.

"Maverick didn't say 'they needed to die' or 'she was in my way, and I had to dispose of her' or anything like that. He said, 'it needed to be done,' and that was his twist. Once I realized that, I figured he had sent Kate—and by default, Isaac—some place for safekeeping." She winced as she said the word again, but she didn't have a better description for it.

Sam glanced over at her uncle Joel, who didn't always come to all the family dinners, but he'd been coming since the evil had been unleashed, perhaps for safety in numbers. Brainstorming with him had helped her figure out where Kate and Isaac were. Her uncle smiled in encouragement.

"Now that I know Kate and Isaac didn't die—and I had already eliminated the possibility of them flashing away—the only other explanation is that they went through the wall and are hidden. I believe the magic Maverick used created a temporary rift or distortion in the fabric of reality, and that's why they appeared dead. Well... that and he obviously created a pile of ash. Maverick effectively trapped them in an alternate space."

Sam paused for a moment to let that sink in. Mirek handed her a bottle of water, and she took a big gulp before she dropped the next bomb.

"I also believe that because Maverick created the rift and

now that he's dead, the dimension Kate and Isaac are trapped in will collapse. It's probably already started to deteriorate."

Sam heard the gasps and a few choice curses but didn't respond because false platitudes wouldn't help them.

"How long do they have?" Fiona asked in a flat tone, none of her excitement from two days ago, or even an hour ago, evident.

Sam wanted to lie and tell Fiona her daughter still had lots of time, but she couldn't. "I don't know. Since you had the vision recently, I believe they're still in the dimension." At least she hoped they were… and they were still alive.

"The magic Maverick used to create the other dimension still exists," Jack said loud enough to stop the murmuring that had started after she'd delivered the bad news. "It's just divided. So, why would the dimension collapse if the magic that made it still exists, even if it's not inside Maverick?"

She glanced at her uncle again, and this time he held up his finger to stall her answering.

"We believe that the magic used to create the rift wouldn't have immediately disappeared upon Maverick's death," her uncle told the group. "But it could be slowly dissipating now because he's no longer controlling it. It's being spread through who knows how many people. According to quantum entanglement, the magic will eventually influence everyone it is inside of—as Sam has said—but for now, the magic is like hundreds, or even thousands, of children let loose at Disneyland with no supervision. Eventually they'll all be corralled, but it will take some time. Until then, the molecules of magic don't know what the others are doing and wouldn't be aware of the dimension Maverick created. Which means they wouldn't be able to support it."

"Then what's next?" Jack asked looking at her uncle and then her.

When her uncle nodded at her, Sam answered the

question. "Well… quantum entanglement—which is a problem because the magic particles will eventually influence each other—could help us in this case. I believe that Kate and Isaac are entangled with specific energy signatures related to the evil magic. By identifying and tracing these unique energy patterns, we can locate where Kate and Isaac are."

"How?" Fiona asked, her voice stronger this time.

With each answer, Sam felt a little more like she was on stable ground. "We do two things. First, we use a locator spell to detect Kate and Isaac's energy frequencies. Then…" Sam moved her gaze to encompass Jo, Simon, and Reece.

"We—well… you three, since you're the spell experts, create a spell inspired by quantum entanglement principles. It needs to lock onto the residual energy left by the evil magic. Although magic energy usually dissipates quickly, I don't think this will have. Because of the enormous amount that would have been needed to create the dimension, the residual energy will have a far longer half-life.

"You'll have to go to Isaac's shop to pick it up. And you'll need to make sure the spell isolates only the original energy so it doesn't pick up the evil energy that's now in so many magics. The spell must create a compass to guide us toward the location where the dimensional distortion occurred."

"Wow, is that all?" Reece asked, his tone laced with humor, before looking at his sister and Simon. "You two up for the challenge?"

"You're damn right we are," Jo said as she stood and then turned toward Fiona. "We're going to bring them home."

Fiona only nodded. Then everyone else stood and began cleaning up from their late breakfast, or early lunch, since it was now almost noon.

As her friends and family said their goodbyes to each other, Sam realized a fundamental fact about all humans. It didn't matter who they were or what they were—magic or not—they were creatures of habit. Sam could tell herself over and over again that she had nothing to make up for—that she was part of a team and she'd just passed on the baton, as she'd done before—and she had nothing left to prove. And maybe that truth was slowly sinking into her consciousness, but no one could make a quantum leap in personality overnight. Accepting that something you believed was wrong wouldn't happen in an instant. Change took time. And understanding her new truth—that she had nothing to prove —didn't mean she would suddenly stop trying to make things better.

And that thought led her back to thinking of all humans being creatures of habit. Sam wouldn't be able to stop herself from using her unique magic specialty if it meant she could save those she loved, no matter what it did to her. Nor could she let Mirek know, regardless of what she'd promised.

CHAPTER TWENTY

"We kept running up against a wall," Simon said. "It actually felt like a literal one every time we tried something different."

Reece nodded before replying. "It wasn't until we went back to Isaac's shop for the third time that we started to get some success."

They were all back in the restaurant and everyone had their winter gear in preparation for heading outside into the cold night air. Mirek's coat was open, as he leaned against the wall, and Sam leaned against him, her back to his front.

"You could have been picking up the evil magic's energy instead of the residue," Sam said.

Simon nodded. "That's what we figured. We had to use a spell to block the evil's current energy before we could isolate the residue from when Kate and Isaac went through the wall."

Jo stepped forward and clapped her gloved hands together. "Enough talking. Let's head outside."

As everyone bundled up in their outerwear, Reece explained that when they used the locator spell in Isaac's shop to detect the energy frequencies, they got a buzz, like they were close.

Once outside, Mirek zipped his coat right to the top as the frigid cold bit wrapped its icy fingers around his neck.

"I was excited when it first snowed," Sam said, sounding wistful. "Then it warmed up so much it all melted. Maybe it will snow again for Christmas." Sam gave his shoulder a friendly bump. "Not used to the weather yet?"

He could see their breaths in the glow from the streetlights. "No. Even though I've been back here for a couple of years, I never went outside."

Sam's expression changed from teasing to sad, and Mirek could have kicked himself for reminding her that even though he hadn't been in the compound in Mexico, he had still been a prisoner. "What about you? You came right here from Mexico at the end of September. What did that feel like?"

She chuckled. "It was a shock, but I wanted Colorado to feel like home, so every time I stepped outside, I would stop and breathe in the crisp air, willing myself to get used to it."

Mirek tried to remember if he'd seen Sam do that and realized the only times they'd been outside together were going to the mall and when they'd flashed to a back alley.

"On December thirty-first, let's stand outside and welcome in the New Year in the fresh air under the stars."

She went up on her tiptoes and pressed her lips to his in a quick kiss. "Okay," she said quietly.

It wasn't a promise, and he feared she didn't make one because she didn't know if she'd be able to keep it. New Year's Eve was six days away, and he was going to do whatever he needed to make sure they welcomed it together.

Mirek hadn't been paying much attention to where they'd walked, just followed the person in front of him as Jo led the group to the far side of the next building, the one that housed Isaac's shop and all their apartments.

When Jo stopped, she looked both ways before stepping onto the street. "Ben. Frank," she called. "Can you conjure some pylons or a spell or something so we can direct traffic away from here?"

"Sure, give us a minute," Frank said, and he and Ben were gone in a flash.

Less than two minutes later, they were back. "All good," Ben said. "We won't be getting any traffic down this way."

Jo stepped onto the street. "Everyone, spread out in the middle of the street in a wide semi-circle starting about twenty feet in that direction," she said, pointing past the last building. "And going to the bakery building. Face the buildings."

Mirek moved into the line, with Sam at his side. Everyone looked to be about two or three feet apart, putting him and Sam roughly in the middle, facing the restaurant.

Once everyone had settled into position, Simon stepped forward. "Jack," Simon shouted to him at the far end, closest to the bakery. "Turn and face the street, and then every second person do the same."

They were so close to finding Kate and Isaac that no one wasted any time doing as instructed. Sam stood on one side of Mirek and Morgana on the other, and both turned toward the street. There was a bit more shuffling before everyone grew quiet and waited for further instructions.

"We don't know if the dimension will stay visible once we use the spell or if we'll have to continue repeating it," Reece said loudly. "We'll count down before we recite the spell. It's only six sentences and won't take long to say, so keep your eyes peeled."

"What are we looking for?" Meredith asked.

"That's just it," Jo said. "We don't know. In the spell, we've asked for the dimension to be revealed, but if that's a door, or a wall, or something else… We don't know. Just look for anything out of the ordinary."

Jo walked over to Simon, holding a piece of paper, and Reece joined them. "Ready?" Simon asked.

A chorus of "ready," answered him and Reece counted down.

Simon, Jo, and Reece recited the spell as one, their voices projecting into the night.

Mirek scanned the buildings and street around him. Nothing seemed out of place.

"There!" Sam shouted, and he felt her take off at a run.

He turned and followed, along with everyone else. Sam led them across the street to the park that ran perpendicular to the sidewalk for several miles. A running path cut through the narrow strip of park and benches dotted the path every few hundred yards.

Sam stood on the grass on the far side of the path, looking up.

At first Mirek couldn't tell what she was looking at. Then he noticed a small light about ten feet off the ground. It looked like someone had left a door open a small crack and they were seeing the light coming from the other side.

"That's the rift," Sam said. "That's where Kate and Isaac are."

Mirek stayed back, not needing to get in the way as Jack and Ben walked over and flanked her sides.

"Any idea how we get in there?" Jack asked.

Sam shook her head. "No. I thought the spell would reveal more of it."

"Can we pry it open?" Ben asked.

Again, Sam shook her head. "I'm worried that if we do that, we could crack whatever is holding Kate and Isaac up."

Everyone closed in; Mirek guessed they wanted to be in on the conversation without yelling into the night.

"What if we recited the spell again?" Simon asked. "Could it open the crack some more?"

Sam shrugged. "Sure, it's worth a try."

Jo and Reece went to Simon and all three of them repeated the spell.

Mirek kept his eyes on the crack of light, but nothing changed.

Sam slowly rotated in a circle, and he knew his Athena was calculating her battle strategy. They might not be in a war against a rival clan or god, but they were in a battle against time.

"Dad," Sam said. "We're going to need some volunteers. Probably fifty to a hundred."

"We'll get however many people you need," Ben said, his trust in his daughter evident. "What skills will they need to have? What will they be doing?"

"You want a perimeter," Jack said.

"Yes. We need to protect the area and make sure that no one comes near here." She explained her idea for a ring around the dimension, with each person holding a blocking spell that would give the illusion of the area being blocked off, perhaps with tarps and scaffolding, as if something was being built in the park.

"We'll get started on it," Ben said as he scanned the group. "Simon, Jo, Connor, Rowena, Nate, Joel, Frank, and Damon. All of you come with me. We're going to call in an army to help."

Without another word, Ben headed toward The Magic Plate with his group.

"Now what?" Fiona asked.

Morgana wrapped her arm around her future mother-in-law's shoulder. "Can't we just physically pry it open? I can hold it if something threatens to fall."

Mirek walked over to Sam to lend his support, but he didn't pull her into his arms, even though he wanted to. If she needed him, she'd let him know. At least, he hoped she would.

Sam looked up at the crack of light. "The crack in the dimension may mean that magic can penetrate inside," she said almost to herself before turning around. "Jack, you're the strongest telepath here. Well… you and Meredith… can you try reaching out to Isaac? And Meredith, can you reach out to Kate?"

"Sure," Meredith said, and Jack nodded.

"Nothing," Jack spit out a moment later.

"I'm sorry, I didn't…" Sam said, her gloved hand wrapping around her pendant.

"No, Sam. I'm sorry. Yes, I'm frustrated, but it's not aimed at you."

"Okay."

Mirek wasn't so sure Sam was convinced. Either that or she was taking this setback personally, as if this, like so many other failures in their lives, were her fault.

Sam looked utterly defeated and this time, Mirek wasn't about to wait for her to ask for support. He figured sometimes you knew when someone you loved needed support, even before they did.

He wrapped his arm around her waist and pulled her to his side. "Okay, let's brainstorm. Isn't that what this group does? There's got to be another way to reach them."

As if he had just given the motivational speech of a lifetime, everyone gathered closer, ready for some ideas. There weren't many tossed out—a spell to widen the crack, a spell to stabilize the dimension while they manually pried open the space, and trying again to reach Kate and Isaac, hoping the repetition would get through to them if they were sleeping.

A few hours and lots of conjured mugs of hot coffee later, Ben and his team had returned with scores of volunteers, but they were no closer to reaching Kate and Isaac.

"Jack, the perimeter is set up and Ben and Simon have an agent in charge of a schedule for spelling people off," Damon said as he walked up.

Mirek looked out toward the street. A line of people stood on the sidewalk, evenly spaced apart like trinkets on a shelf. Each person held their hands in front of them, but their hands were empty. Many of them were talking and laughing. He'd been so absorbed with trying to find a way inside the dimension, like everyone else in their group, he hadn't noticed the volunteers arrive and set up.

Damon went to Morgana and wrapped his arm around her. She slouched against him but didn't utter a word, and Mirek was reminded of the stoic seven-year-old she'd been when they'd first been kidnapped.

"Jack, are you going to keep trying all night?" Damon asked. "It's already three in the morning and everyone is exhausted."

Jack didn't respond but looked around as if assessing the situation. Mirek would give him a few moments to decide what to do next, and if he didn't, Mirek would step in.

A born leader, it didn't even take a minute for Jack to turn to Fiona. "I can't imagine what you're feeling, Fiona, but Damon is right, we need to take a break so everyone can get some sleep and refuel or someone could make a critical mistake. The volunteers will ensure that no one who happens upon the area will see the dimension."

Fiona glanced at the crack of light hovering above the ground before she nodded. "Agreed."

"Let's all meet back out here at ten in the morning," Jack

said, projecting his voice to be heard by everyone. "It will give us all a chance to catch at least a few hours of sleep and to eat."

Mirek expected Sam to protest, and when she didn't, he knew she was more exhausted than she'd let on. He dropped his arm from her waist and took her gloved hand as they followed everyone toward the buildings.

"It's snowing," Sam whispered as she pointed up at a streetlamp.

A few flurries were visible in the glow cast by the lamp.

Tugging on Sam's hand, Mirek halted them in the middle of the park path and pulled Sam against him. He tipped her chin up to look into her eyes. "Merry Christmas, Athena."

Smiling wide, Sam wrapped her arms around his neck. "Merry Christmas, hero."

Their breaths were like little clouds in the low light as a few snowflakes fell between them. Mirek kissed her softly and slowly, but not for long, knowing they had to get inside.

A short while later, they were tucked in bed with Sam in his arms, already asleep. As he drifted off to sleep, he wished for the evil magic to be trapped and Sam to be safe so he could share a first Christmas morning kiss with her for many years to come.

December 25

WATCHING FROM AFAR, Sam couldn't help but smile as Kate played with the little boy in the tall grass. They looked so happy, as if the only thing in the world that mattered at that moment was having fun during the beautiful fall morning.

Sam shot upright in bed, the adrenaline of her dream still

coursing through her. She took deep breaths to calm her breathing and racing heart, which was pounding so hard it felt like it was trying to break out of her rib cage.

"What's wrong?" Mirek mumbled, half-awake as he pushed up onto his elbow beside her.

"I had a dream," she whispered.

"A bad one?"

She shook her head as the vision continued to play in her mind. Pushing it aside, she shifted to lean back against the headboard. "No… It was… good."

As the true realization of the dream's meaning registered with her, she scrambled out of bed. "Hurry, we've got to go," she said and hurried to the bathroom.

She grabbed her toothbrush, doing a rush job, and then flipped on the shower.

"It's only eight," Mirek called from the bedroom. "Come back to bed, we've got another two hours."

Sam grabbed the soap and was just about to reach out to Jack when she looked down at herself. She wondered if telepathically contacting Jack while she was naked in the shower was the same as texting while sitting on the toilet. "Nope, can't do it," she muttered to herself.

Cool air hit her back just as she was rinsing off. She turned in the large stall to see Mirek gloriously naked. He shut the stall door and flattened his chest against her back.

He lifted her wet hair off her neck and kissed her in the hollow between her neck and shoulder. She tilted her head to the side, giving him better access as she groaned and rocked her hips back against him.

Then she remembered the dream Mirek had momentarily pushed from her thoughts. "No, we can't."

She spun around to face him, went up on her toes, and gave him a quick kiss before reaching for the door handle. "Hurry."

Laughing at Mirek's exaggerated groan, she stepped into the bathroom's steamy air and quickly dried herself off. In the bedroom, she rummaged through her dresser, looking for a warm pair of leggings. When she didn't find any, she conjured a pair and pulled them on before donning warm socks and a long sweater.

"Presentable," she mumbled as she looked at herself in the full-length mirror on the closet door.

Picturing Jack in her mind, she reached out to him. *I have the answer.*

What do you need?

Good question. She probably should have thought of that first, but too late now; she thought back to her dream. *Reece, Simon, Jo, and Fiona at least.*

Eight thirty. The Magic Plate.

Thank you.

Her adrenaline had spiked again in anticipation of what was to come and now she needed to keep herself busy for a moment. She pulled on her magic and straightened the covers.

"I just got an update from Jack," Mirek said as he walked in.

Her adrenaline rocketed up again, but this time for a completely different reason as she took in Mirek's lean muscles. "Put some clothes on, please," she told him, her voice sounding breathless.

"Oh, am I a temptation?" He stalked toward her with a predatory smile.

Laughing, she held up her hand and took a step back. "No, we have to hurry."

He stuck out his bottom lip, like a little boy pouting. "Fine."

She laughed again, his mock huff so adorable.

"So… the update," he said as he sat on the bed and pulled on a pair of socks. "That was about whatever woke you up?"

Sam couldn't hold back her grin. "Yes." Her excitement felt like a tangible thing bouncing around inside of her. She knew for sure they would rescue Kate and Isaac today. It would be the perfect Christmas present for everyone.

When Mirek was fully dressed, she gave him a quick kiss. "I know what we need. See you in The Magic Plate." Mirek's eyes widened just before she flashed.

Sam smiled as she landed in the restaurant portion of The Magic Plate. Since the restaurant was closed for the indefinite future and all the non-magic staff had been given time off with pay, not having to flash into the back hallway was one less thing to worry about with everything else going on.

"Good morning, honey," Fiona greeted her from her seat at the end of the table.

"Morning." Sam conjured a cup of coffee as she walked over. Fiona looked perfectly made up in an effortlessly casual way that some women had a knack of pulling off. There weren't any visible lines of strain on her face, unlike the other day.

She pulled up a chair across from Fiona just as Mirek and her parents appeared. Within a few minutes, everyone else had arrived and the level of chatter in the room rose. But as Sam looked around, she noticed that most people were a little more subdued than usual.It could have been the lack of sleep or the grave task they had in front of them.

"Good morning," Jack said, projecting his voice across the group. "If you'd like food, you can conjure it today because you're on your own."

He looked over at Sam, and his eyebrows rose as if asking if she was ready. She nodded and hoped she had the right answer this time.

"Sam has a plan for us, so I'll turn the floor over to her, but…"

He paused and one corner of his mouth popped up in a lopsided smile, as if he couldn't make up his mind whether to smile or not.

"Let's make this the best Christmas ever and bring Kate and Isaac home. Merry Christmas."

A chorus of "Merry Christmases" followed, and then all eyes turned to her.

Sam stood and walked to the end of the tables to give herself a clear view of the group. As everyone stared at her in anticipation, she felt her palms grow damp and her breathing increase.

You've got this. Mirek said into her mind, just like he'd done the day before.

She smiled at him and stood a bit straighter. "This morning, my dream woke me up…"

"Hey!" Simon called. "Make sure you keep it PG."

"You stole my line," Reece said and crossed his arms across his muscular chest pretending to pout.

There seemed to be a lot of that going on this morning, but things were about to get serious. Not only did they need to rescue Kate and Isaac, but the threat of the magic evil was also never far from Sam's mind.

She looked over at the two jokesters. "Be quiet and pay attention," she told them. As a second round of chuckles and ribbing ensued, Sam scanned the group and Christmas decorations hanging on the wall caught her eye.

They'd been up for over a week, she'd seen them plenty of times, but now that it was Christmas day, her brother's prediction of her death during Christmas felt more real than ever.

Sam gave Fiona a quick glance.

"Say what you have to, honey."

"As I was saying…" She said, no longer able to joke with Simon and Reece about interrupting as the seriousness of her situation was driven home by the decorations. "This morning, my dream woke me up. But… it wasn't really my dream… well…" She stopped, unsure how to explain herself.

"It's okay, Sam," her dad said. "Just get it out, and we'll ask questions if we need to."

Sam smiled at her dad and started again. The support in the room was overwhelming—something she had never had before.

"It was my dream, but I dreamed of Fiona's vision… or at least how my mind interpreted what she'd explained. And that got me thinking that since we can't reach Kate and Isaac, maybe we can reach them in their dreams. Through your vision."

She turned to Fiona. "Can you call up your vision at will?"

"No. Well… I don't know. I'm not sure I've ever really tried," she said, frowning.

"If you can, then I think you could pull Kate or Isaac into the vision and talk to them."

"How?" Fiona asked.

"With a spell," Reece said and met Sam's gaze. "As soon as you mentioned reaching someone in a memory or vision, it made me think about a spell I'd seen. It referred to pulling a dreamer into a vision. I catalogued it in my database, but… honestly… I had no idea why there would be a need for it, unless someone just wanted to show off a vision."

"Will you be able to use the spell if Fiona can't call up the vision at will?" Jack asked.

"Believe it or not,"—Reece grinned—"I have a spell for that."

Sam laughed with the others. Once more, Reece broke the growing tension. Too bad she was going to bring it back.

"I'm worried Isaac and Kate could be running out of time.

Maverick died twenty-four days ago, and Uncle Joel and I tried to calculate how long his magic would hold out... We could only really hypothesize, and we think it could be in the next few days."

Reece pushed back his chair and stood. "I'll get right on it," he said, then he was gone.

Jack stood as well. "Get something to eat if you need it and we'll meet out at the dimension."

With her lingering adrenaline and the thought of Nate's prediction swimming in her mind, Sam wasn't hungry. She pulled on her magic to retrieve her coat from her apartment. As soon as it landed in her hand, she stuck her arm in one sleeve.

Mirek put his hand on hers. "Wait. It's going to take Reece at least a few minutes to find the spell. Let's eat something."

"I'm not—"

"Sit and eat," her mom and Fiona both said at the same time.

Mirek pulled her coat off her arm and put it on the back of the chair. "It must be a mom thing... Come on, please, Sam, you've had almost no sleep in the last six days, and you've barely eaten."

With a sigh, Sam sat down, and two plates of eggs and bacon appeared in front of her. Laughing, she looked up at her mom and Fiona.

Her dad waved his hand, and one plate moved over to Mirek. "Mirek will eat one of those," he said. "Now eat."

She shoved a forkful of eggs in her mouth to hide her grin as she complied with the order.

"And while you're eating, I can regale you with stories about Trudy," her mom said. "Do you remember her? She owned the bakery where we stayed for a bit. She created your love of cinnamon buns. Anyway... we see each other every few months. She got married..."

Sam listened as her mom told her stories and although she didn't remember the woman, she looked forward to meeting her again. After years of only surviving, there were a plethora of things for her to look forward to.

Less than twenty minutes later she was outside in the park—fueled up with both food and good stories—and felt pretty good. She wondered if she'd be as smart—and as bossy—as her mom when she became a parent. *When.* She used to think *if,* but… Knowing Nate's prediction, *when* was probably a pipe dream, but it's what she would have liked.

After that, the only thing she could do was wait. Periodically, Jack and Meredith tried reaching out to Kate and Isaac telepathically, but without any luck.

"We've got it. Well… them," Reece said when he flashed to them, along with Jo and Simon, a little after noon. "Sorry it took so long. The spell I mentioned this morning wasn't quite right. Simon and Jo gave me a hand altering it and now it should work."

"This spell will help you step right into your vision," Jo said, handing Fiona a piece of paper. "You don't need to be lying down, but we should probably get you a chair."

"Thank you, honey." Fiona looked down at the paper. "Can I recite this one in my mind, or do I need to say it out loud?"

Reece and Jo both turned to Simon. "You can say it in your mind," Simon told her before he conjured her a folding chair and set it on the grass.

"Once you're inside the vision, you'll need to recite the second spell, which will pull Kate into your vision," Reece said, handing her another piece of paper.

"I guess I'm going to have to memorize the second one since I'll already be in my vision?"

"Ah… I hadn't thought of that," Reece said, frowning.

"This spell is twelve stanzas. It will probably take you some time to memorize it."

"Can I see it?" Jack asked, holding out his hand to Reece. Jack took the paper and looked down at it. "Fiona, I think I can read the spell into your mind once you're in your vision. Then you'll just have to repeat each stanza after me."

"Thank you, Jack." Fiona sat down and looked at the first spell for several long moments before she closed her eyes.

When Fiona's body relaxed, Jack focused on the spell in his hand.

After a couple of minutes Jack lifted his head, not looking quite as relieved as Sam had expected he would if the spell had worked.

"Fiona was able to hear me and repeat the spell from inside her vision," Jack said. "But I couldn't see what she did, so I don't know if it worked."

"It didn't work," Fiona said when she finally opened her eyes. Crestfallen, her hand holding the paper lay limp in her lap. "Should I try again?"

"Maybe it's not the right spell," Jo said. "How will we know if it is?" she asked the group.

Jo's question was so similar to her one the night before, Sam worried they'd go in circles trying different spells and she wasn't even sure the spell was the problem. Kate and Isaac didn't have time for them to play around and figure it out.

Sam looked at the crack of light in the air. She wasn't an expert on spells, but she knew that most of them didn't have to be exact. Something else was preventing Fiona from getting through to Kate. Still staring at the light, Sam hypothesized possible barriers to reaching Kate. Without numerous calculations and testing—which they didn't have time for—Sam's best guess was that the outer shell of the dimension was the problem. "I think we need to widen the crack in the dimension."

Jack frowned. "Yesterday you were worried if we did, we could crack whatever is holding Kate and Isaac up."

"I know… But I'm worried that whatever is holding Kate and Isaac in the dimension is probably too thick to be penetrated. If that's the case, we'll never reach them… I've been doing some theorizing, and I think the only reason we were able to find the dimension, is because it's secured somehow. Maverick would have had difficulty locating it when he needed to if it was free floating, so he must have fixed it in place. Like some kind of a box inside the dimension."

Sam looked at the light again. "If we can peel away some of the layers, like with an artichoke, we can get to the center —in this case, the box Kate and Isaac are in. Then Fiona might have a better chance of reaching them."

More than six hours later, the sun that had melted yesterday's few flurries away had long since set, and Sam watched Kate and Isaac being helped to the Williams's buildings. It had been touch and go for a while.

Once they had peeled back some of the dimension's outer layer with help from Reece's ability to manipulate objects, Fiona had tried reaching Kate again. She finally got through to Isaac. Then Jack had taken over, and even that had been harrowing.

Isaac had been the linchpin by helping them from the inside.

When Kate and Isaac were safely inside the building, Sam turned toward what was left of the room the two had spent a month trapped in.

Under Jack's supervision, volunteers destroyed the room's contents while shifts continued around the perimeter, blocking the site from passersby.

From her position—leaning against a tree to stay out of the way for the last hour—Sam watched as Mirek walked toward her. His face appeared gaunt, and his coat was looser than it had been earlier in the day. From the snippets of conversation she'd heard, Kate had been on death's door, and it had taken Mirek's full powers, with help from Jack, to bring her back.

Sam headed to Mirek, meeting him in the middle, and grasped the hand he held out. She hated that he had to suffer to help Kate, but she would have done the same thing. With Jack by his side, Sam wouldn't consider what Mirek did this time self-sacrifice, but it still took a toll on him.

There weren't any kisses on the path that night, but she had Mirek at her side and that was good enough.

Once they reached the apartment, they had a quick bite to eat and crawled into bed. Beyond exhausted, Mirek pulled Sam against him, spooning her from behind.

Within seconds, Mirek's breathing evened out in sleep, while Sam ran her plan to close the box through her mind. When Kate and Isaac recovered, they'd be able to complete step six. It was step nine—the final step to trap the evil magic —that Sam feared. As sleep pulled her under, Sam hoped that when it came time to do what needed to be done, her magic would protect her.

CHAPTER TWENTY-ONE

December 27

$\mathcal{M}$irek took a sip of his coffee as he listened to Sam and others chat around him. He and Sam were up late the night before, first talking and then making love. It had been their reprieve in the middle of the storm.

Kate and Isaac's rescue and the gathering yesterday to hear their story and fill them in on what they'd missed, brought both relief and increased tension. There was not time to wait to move onto part six of the plan.

To do that, by eight in the morning, Mirek and Sam were at Kate's shop and not still in bed. Standing just inside the shop's open, large double doors, Mirek listened to Sam and the others, prepared to help Kate if needed.

"Sam," Isaac said laying his hand on her arm. "I know I said it yesterday... but... I just want you to know how thankful Kate and I are for everything you did." Isaac looked at Damon, Morgana, Jo, and Simon, who had come to Kate's as a precaution. "All of you—thank you." He gave them a single nod and walked into the shop toward Kate and her mom.

"I didn't do it alone," Sam protested, although Isaac was likely out of earshot.

Mirek disappeared his coffee mug and walked over to Sam, wrapping his arm around her waist. "You're welcome," he whispered to her.

"What?" Sam asked, tilting her head to look at him.

"*You're welcome.* When someone says *thank you,* you're supposed to say *you're welcome.* Isaac and Kate know that it took a group effort to find them; they're still thankful for everything you did."

"Right. So…" she said to the others. "If any of Maverick's minions show up, we should use them as a test run."

Mirek knew a change of topic when he heard one, but he didn't mind. Change didn't happen overnight. Eventually, Sam would learn to accept others' gratitude and offer help because she wanted to, not because she felt a sense of misplaced duty due to her past.

"We'd need the conch shell… er… symbol… you know," Morgana said with a smirk. "That thing we found in South Africa."

Damon leaned down and placed a kiss on top of Morgana's head. "We understood, angel."

"I asked Reece to be on standby, just in case," Sam said. "How's the other part of the plan coming?"

Simon grimaced. "I had a few moments where I thought I might have blown it, but—"

Jo elbowed Simon in the side. "You were fine, Superman. I already told you I didn't notice anything. We're our own worst critics, you know."

Damon gave Simon a nod. "Agreed. I didn't notice anything either."

Mirek thought Sam's plan was genius, and as Jack had

told Kate and Isaac yesterday, thanks to Simon, no one but their group knew that Maverick was dead.

"There's Jack with the sword," Sam said and Mirek looked into the shop. Jack laid a wrapped package on Kate's workbench and disappeared.

Mirek lifted his chin toward the inside of the workshop. "I'm going to head inside so I'm closer in case Sam needs me."

Morgana wrapped her arms around herself and rubbed her parka-covered arms. "Good idea. It'll be warmer in there."

"Hey, you've been here longer than us," Sam teased as they walked inside, "Shouldn't you be acclimatized by now?"

"Nope," Morgana said, popping the p. "I never liked the cold." She stopped and turned back to the door. "Oh… is it okay for all of us to go inside? Do we need to stand watch?"

Damon grasped Morgana's hand and propelled her forward. "No, the six agents that Jack and Ben pulled in for this will be enough. They'll alert us if anyone shows."

Mirek waited with the rest of the group in the middle of Kate's shop as she stood in front of her bench. Isaac stood behind her with his arms wrapped around her. He'd explained earlier that his tattoo had forged a bond between him and Kate, and if she needed him or the sword pulled her into a trance, he'd know.

Fiona hovered nearby, but Mirek couldn't blame her. For almost a month, Fiona thought Kate was dead. He couldn't imagine what it felt like to believe you'd lost a child. Though he'd tried to for years, knowing his mom, aunts, and Sam's parents thought their children were dead. For so long—when he had thoughts of his parents—he berated himself for not doing more to escape. He was learning to let that go, but like Sam, he couldn't change overnight.

Sam lifted her chin toward Kate's workbench. "Kate's

finished… well… she's stopped. And I think her kissing Isaac is probably a good sign."

"Unless she's consoling herself," Morgana said dryly.

Mirek and the group met Isaac and Kate halfway as they came toward them. Judging by the grin Kate sported, no consoling would be needed.

"We were wrong," she said, grinning from ear to ear. "We don't need a lock."

"Then what do we need?" Sam asked.

"The sword, which we have." Kate's grin morphed into a frown. "Unfortunately, we need an ancient spellbook too. I can sketch some details of it because I saw it in my mind, but I don't know where it is."

"Well, that's handy," Simon said. "We found a spellbook and didn't know what it was for, only that a spell we were using said we would need it."

Mirek turned to Kate, a small smile on his face. "I'm glad you didn't need my services today."

A laugh of relief burst from Kate. "Me too. Now, we—"

"Protect yourselves!" someone bellowed from behind Mirek. "We're under attack!"

Mirek spun around, looking toward the shop's open door. An FBI agent landed inside the workshop less than five feet away from them.

"I need to get the sword," Kate said, sounding panicked as she turned toward her workbench.

The large workshop doors ripped from their hinges and flew through the air before landing on the shop's concrete floor, bringing with it the ear-splitting sound of metal on metal. The doors rocked back and forth on the floor, the hinges dangling from the frame.

The average magic wouldn't have had enough power to pull the doors off. Mirek took a step toward Sam just as men stormed inside. The fifteen or twenty of them outnumbered their group, even with the FBI agents who flashed inside to join them.

"I've contacted Jack," Damon shouted over the sound of stomping boots.

"Throw up shields," Jack commanded as he landed amongst them, and Mirek wasted no time.

"We need Reece too," Sam called out, her voice echoing through her shield.

"Here," Reece declared from where he landed beside Jack.

"Kate, get the sword and leave," Isaac yelled at her.

Mirek kept his gaze on the group in front of him, knowing enough people would have eyes on Kate.

"Look who we have here," an unfamiliar voice bellowed from the front of her shop.

"It's the bitch from the restaurant," the man said.

A hush fell over the room like the calm before a storm. Both groups stood, facing off, like in an old-fashioned western.

"I'm leaving," Kate said loudly from behind him.

"Good, you're useless to us," Jack said equally as loud.

Sam flinched, frowning at Jack.

He doesn't mean it, Mirek said into Sam's mind. *He's giving her a way out.*

I know.

Sam's words contradicted her reaction. Mirek expected that intellectually, Sam knew Jack hadn't meant what he'd said, but the words were too close to ones Maverick and the others had said to Sam again and again. Even when she was the genius behind their business.

"Kate," Isaac said, as if in warning.

Mirek turned to get a look at Kate while keeping his protection around him.

"Fuck you, I'm leaving!" Kate screamed, her tone full of defiance.

As she reached for the sword, the guy who seemed to know Kate landed right behind her in a flash. He yanked her hair, cranking her head backward.

The guy looked down at his hold on Kate's hair and didn't see her grip the sword.

She pivoted on her heels, adopting a fighting stance, and forced the guy to release his grip. Extending her arm, the tip of the blade touched the guy's Adam's apple, like it was ready to slice him open.

"Think you're tough, don't you, bitch?" he taunted Kate.

"I don't think it. I know it. And you need a bigger vocabulary. How about you—" Kate flashed away.

"Isaac! Go!" Jack ordered.

Just as Isaac flashed away, others flashed in, joining their group.

"You're a fucking joke! Those bubbles won't hold you!" the man who knew Kate taunted. The words had barely left his lips when he puffed out his chest like he was pulling in air. "Now!"

His shout detonated from his throat with the force of a rocket. The walls of the shop vibrated, adding to the already amplified decibels.

As he pushed magic to his hearing for protection, Mirek slapped his hands over his ears. Only a whisper of pain zipped through his skull. The partial dampening of sound from the protective bubble, as well as his magic, and his hands covering them, likely prevented his eardrums from rupturing.

He released his magic's hold on his hearing and realized he'd lost focus with the distraction. Their circle was now surrounded, and even with their total numbering twenty-five, they were outnumbered at least two to one.

"Reece!" Sam called to him, sounding alright. "You got it?"

Reece held out his hands, and the conch he'd retrieved in

South Africa landed in them. The protective bubble around him, shimmered as the object passed through. "Ready!"

"You're outnumbered. Give me the sword and join us or die!" the same guy threatened.

Reece lifted the conch above his head, his protective bubble shimmering once more as the shell passed through the barrier. "Recite!"

Reece, Isabella, Simon, Jo, Jack, and Meredith all spoke together, their voices carrying throughout the room.

"Darkness within as foretold,
Now is time to break your hold."
Take your leave,
No longer to deceive.
Through air and light,
Leave this body and take your flight.
From soul to funnel with utmost grace,
Until you meet your final resting place."

By the time the group recited the fifth line of the spell, the majority of Maverick's minions clutched at their chests. When the group spoke the final word, every minion had fallen to his knees.

"What the hell is going on?" the man Kate knew asked, confusion clear in his tone.

"Reece. Do you have it all?" Jack asked.

"It sure feels like it." Reece lowered his arms, cradling the conch against his chest. He looked up at Sam. "Now what?"

"I didn't think we would test it, so coming up with a way to temporarily contain the evil wasn't part of my plan," Sam said, turning to face Jack. "But... I have an idea. I'm not sure you're going to like it."

Jack frowned. "Isn't anything better than letting it loose again?"

Sam's shoulders lifted in a cringe. "Well... I think we should release it into the people in the infirmary who are in magic comas. I mean..."

Mirek watched Jack to see how he reacted to Sam's wild idea, but he only waited silently.

"If we release the magic among all of them, I don't think it will overload any one person, and we're already monitoring them. We've already proven I was right with quantum entanglement, so if you release the infected people from their magic comas for only a couple of seconds, the additional magic will be absorbed without hurting them, and you safely put them back under a magic coma."

"When the time comes to extract the evil from everyone for real, anyone in a magic coma will need to be released from the coma in order for the extraction spell to work on them at the same time," Jack stated, and nodded, as if assimilating the information.

Simon and the others moved in closer to tighten their circle.

"We'll be able to let you know as soon as we're ready to recite the spell," Simon said. "You'll need to ensure that anyone close to the infected has the original protection spell, so they won't become infected when the magic is pulled from them."

"True. Let's get this over with," Jack said. "Reece, Meredith, Mirek, you're with me. We'll go right to the infirmary. Everyone else can help Ben and Frank round up all these people." Jack smirked as someone in their group groaned, then he and the others were gone.

Mirek strode up to Sam. "I've got to go, but I wanted to check... Are you alright? Your hearing?"

"Yeah, I'm fine. As soon as I felt the vibration, I protected my hearing." She looked around at Maverick's former minions milling about with confusion, then met Mirek's gaze.

She released a long breath. "It was kind of anti-climactic."

He chuckled and wrapped his arm around her waist, directing her over to Ben and Frank. "I don't know… I think I've had enough excitement for a while. Something going smoothly was just fine with me."

Mirek added another wish to his growing list—for the rest of Sam's plan to go just as smoothly as their test run.

SAM GLANCED OVER AT MIREK, leaning against a wall at the back of The Magic Plate. To anyone watching, his hands shoved in the front pockets of his jeans, he would appear relaxed, but she knew better.

Mirek wasn't the carefree type. Being caring and protective were innate to him, and those traits made him worry and watchful. He'd been that way from the moment she first opened her eyes to see him in the middle of the night when she was five years old. Even at ten, he'd worried about her and drained his magic attempting to heal her.

During their years apart, their experiences brought new ways of looking at the world, but deep down, they were still the same people they'd been as kids. Only wiser, and perhaps a bit more cautious.

She gave Mirek a small smile and turned, tilting her head up to look both her dad and Uncle Joel in the eyes. The action tossed her hair back over her shoulder, and she swept it forward around the right side of her face. Her family didn't care about her scars, but she tried not to give her dad any more reminders of the past. Her preference was to stand at an angle, but she couldn't always pull it off, like tonight.

She'd stood after dinner, intending to escape with Mirek, but her dad and uncle walked over to chat. Tuning back into the conversation, she realized they'd been discussing the transfer of the magic to the coma victims and everything else they'd learned that day.

"… can converse, let's hope it will tell Kate if anything else is needed," her dad said.

Uncle Joel frowned. "You're thinking we're missing something?"

"I don't know. It's a case of we don't know what we don't know. This is all new territory for us. I've just learned from experience that we need to prepare…"

Sam continued to listen to their conversation with only half an ear. Her dad was a worrier like Mirek, although he would call himself a planner. She knew he would run through every possible scenario with Jack and her uncle Frank. She didn't know if being an FBI agent had trained him to always look for the worst, or if the FBI attracted that type of person—the chicken and egg thing.

Learning that he'd been duped so completely years ago had probably heightened the trait in the last few months. Since Maverick had been complicit in her faked death, the situation now likely made her dad even more on edge.

At least her plan was working. During lunch at The Magic Plate anyone who had news had reported in. After that, she and Mirek had escaped for a few hours before coming back for a buffet dinner. After they trapped the magic and went back to their normal lives, it would be strange to no longer eat three meals a day in the restaurant, because she'd become so used to it.

Normal. Neither she nor Mirek had ever had that. They would have to figure out what they were going to do with their lives and where they'd live. In the back of her mind, she knew that it still wasn't guaranteed that she would live.

Worrying about it now wouldn't change it, so she pushed the thought from her mind. Thinking about the latest updates they'd received was more positive.

Jack informed them that the transfer of the magic to the coma patients went off without a hitch. Simon let them know that he, Damon, and Jo would be heading back to Maverick's headquarters after dinner tonight, and Sam had already seen them leave.

During Kate's report, she'd explained that the trances holding her, and the other swordsmiths, hadn't been trances at all. Struggling to communicate with them, it had been the sword's way of capturing their attention. Isaac's tattoos had broken down the barrier to communication enabling Kate to have a conversation with the sword.

A conversation with an inanimate object surprised everyone except Isabella. Although she'd never conversed with an object, the way she received information from an object was a close second.

Kate had also said that a spellbook, not the box would need to contain the magic now that the box had been opened. With its seal broken, the box would no longer be able to hold the evil. Once the magic was poured into the spellbook, Kate would plunge the blade into it, sealing it forever.

"Sam," her dad said, laying his hand on her shoulder a few minutes later. "I don't think you've heard a word we've said."

"Uh…" She gave him a guilty smile.

"It's okay. You're probably tired. Why don't you go find Mirek?"

"Okay." She kissed her dad and uncle on their cheeks before finding her mom and doing the same.

"Ready to go?" Mirek asked.

"Yes. I'll meet you there." Sam flashed inside their apartment and kicked off her shoes.

Mirek did the same and took her hand, tugging her to the bedroom. "Are you tired?"

She grinned at his back. "It's kind of late to ask that, isn't it?"

Halting them in front of the bed, he feigned an innocent look. "There are lots of things to do in here. We can…" He gestured to the TV mounted on the wall. "We can watch TV. Or read a book, or…"

"Or?"

Mirek dropped her hand and grabbed the bed's covers and pulled them to the end. He sat on the bed, moving back to rest against the headboard, and held out his hand to her. "We could talk."

She climbed onto the bed to sit beside him, and laughed when he hauled her onto his lap, her legs straddling his. "Talk?"

"Sure. We can talk. After." He held out both his palms, and a small ball of light emitting a soft glow appeared in each one. They floated off his hands and landed on each side of the bed as he conjured two more. He floated those to the nightstands and waved toward the overhead light switch, turning it off.

"Now, we have nice, romantic light to *talk*." His words were romantic, but his smile said pure sin.

Sam loved Mirek's protective, serious vibes, but she loved his playful side too. Getting into the game, she bit the inside of her cheek, trying not to smile. "We should get comfortable to *talk*."

"Right. And how would you like to do that?"

Sam waved her hand between them. Their clothes landed in a heap on the floor. "Like this."

Mirek palmed his hard cock in his fist, stroking up and down slowly. "Yes, like that."

She licked her bottom lip and tried her best for a pouty

expression. "I don't think I'm comfortable yet."

"No?"

"I feel kind of empty."

Mirek's breathing picked up; their game giving Sam a heady feeling.

"Put your hands on my shoulders and lift your ass." Mirek's voice had turned husky.

She watched him watch her as she lifted, and he guided his length to her.

"Oh," she groaned as she slowly lowered herself onto him. Gripping his shoulders tight, she leaned closer to him and dropped all pretense of their game as she rocked back and forth, grinding her pelvis into his.

He took one nipple into his mouth and sucked while he tweaked the other one between a finger and thumb. The sensations were amazing, but not enough. Pulling back, her nipple popped from his mouth.

Sam gripped Mirek's shoulders to gain leverage, and lifted and lowered on his length over and over again. She wasn't worried about his orgasm—she knew he'd come—as she chased her own. Pushing some magic into her thighs to give her more strength, she increased her pace, tilting her hips to change the angle.

His fingers found her clit, and he applied just the right amount of pressure. She slammed down onto him as her body stiffened and she cried out, shattering in euphoria. Mirek thrust up into her, holding her hips against his as his own release took him.

She leaned her forehead against his, waiting for her breathing to return to normal. "Good talk," she said, giving him an exaggerated wink.

He barked out a laugh. Flipping them so she was on her back, he gave her a loud, smacking kiss.

Sam loved that she could be carefree and silly with Mirek.

After they showered together, they laid on their sides in bed, facing each other.

Mirek brushed Sam's hair away from her face, his expression serious. "Jack could call anytime to say that Simon is ready to seal the magic… I don't know what's going to happen, but… please be careful. Okay?" he asked, almost pleading with her.

"I will."

"You promise? We agreed, no unnecessary sacrifices, right?"

"I promise." And she vowed to herself to keep that promise. But they never defined what unnecessary meant.

CHAPTER TWENTY-TWO

December 28

Simon stood in front of the full-length mirror in the bedroom and grimaced at his reflection.

"Still not used to your new look yet, Superman?" Jo asked as she reached up and straightened his collar.

"Are you?"

She shivered and made an expression of disgust. "Hell no, and I never will be."

"Good." He sat on the bench at the end of the bed to put his shoes on.

"What's wrong?"

He swept his gaze down his own body, not being subtle, before meeting hers. "Besides the obvious you mean?"

"Funny... Yeah, besides that."

"I just want this over with. Last night was too close a call..." Pausing, he looked down at his hands—not really his, Maverick's—then looked at Jo again. "I hate that you have to look at me like this."

"Well... your mustache could use a trim, and you are kind

of old." She smirked, and as much as he appreciated the gesture of her trying to lighten the mood, he couldn't joke. Knowing what he was about to do, especially after what had happened the night before, made him too worried to kid around.

"Jo, please be careful today."

She put her hands on her hips and straightened to her full five foot two. "I always am."

"Always?"

"Okay..." Her shoulders deflated, and he bit his lip to stop from smiling. "Maybe not always in the past, but I've been careful ever since the crap with Snake."

"Just be extra careful for me today, okay? You being hurt again is my worst nightmare."

She eliminated the few feet between them and picked up his hand in hers. Closing her fingers over his, the illusion of Maverick's right index finger disappeared. "Oh shit," she said and dropped his hand as if afraid she'd been the one to cut off his finger.

"Maybe don't touch me while I'm looking like Maverick, okay?"

Jo nodded and preceded him to the living room. "I've never looked like anyone else..." She huffed out a laugh. "Duh, obviously. But I can understand that being Maverick is repulsive for you. Even being Lucas couldn't have been as bad... Well... I only knew your version of him, and I liked that version, but..."

"Jo," he said and smiled, hoping it didn't creep her out. "Just tell me."

She let out a breath, and she looked so adorable he would have reached for her if the thought of her kissing him while he looked like Maverick didn't make him want to vomit.

"I know last night we ran into some trouble with Maverick's minions questioning you, but you've been acting as Maverick for weeks now, so that's not what's really bothering you... well... at least not everything. Will you tell me?"

Regardless of the disguise, she saw Simon, and it was only one of the reasons he would love her until his last breath and beyond.

"Every day for over a decade, I relished being the best someone else I could be."

"I know," she said softly.

"Then you saw *me*."

"I'll always see you, Superman."

Simon called on his magic and changed back into in own skin, but stayed in Maverick's clothes. He reached for Jo and lifted her by her waist, knowing she'd wrap her legs around him.

Widening his stance to brace himself, he kissed her with a passion only she'd ever been able to ignite in him.

After a few minutes, he put her down and used his magic to cool his body down; thinking of Maverick with a hard-on was another vomit-inducing thought. Picturing Maverick in his mind, he reverted back to the man's appearance.

If Maverick hadn't been such a despicable human being, he probably would have been considered good looking for an older guy—tall, trim physique, a thick head of hair going silver, and sharp features.

Her hands once more balanced on her hips, her cute purple pixie cut glinting in the glare from the overhead lights. "No more stalling. Although I won't complain about your tactics."

She could never quite pull the stern look off with him because he would always find her adorable. But she was right about the stalling.

"When I lost my trigger finger and knew my career was over, I wasn't upset at first. We were starting our life together, but... I guess... I kept waiting for the regret to set in."

"You thought you'd eventually want to go back to being other people to stop the bad guys, and when that didn't happen you began to wonder if you'd been fooling yourself for years."

Jo hadn't posed it as a question. Again, Simon wasn't surprised that she got him. "Yes. And now that I've been Maverick, and I can help put an end to his madness, I just want to be me again. Last night... I was terrified that someone would catch on—realize that I wasn't Maverick—and hurt you."

Jo took a step toward him, but didn't touch him the way she normally did. She picked up his hand and ran her finger over the rough scar where his own finger used to be.

"You weren't wrong for all those years. I think we just change and grow. The FBI was your calling—at least for a while—and you're meant to do this too. Then we'll continue to change and grow together." She dropped his hand and looked up at him. "Since we've been together, we've never not had a threat hanging over our heads."

He nodded as he processed her words. Jo was right; if it wasn't Snake, then it was Maverick, and now the evil magic that threatened their existence.

"I used to love to teach, and now I'd rather travel the world looking for ancient magic artifacts with you."

"We've got a pretty good gig going, don't we?"

"Yes, and I want to get back to it, so get your butt in gear and let's go."

"Wait." He put his hand on her arm before she could flash. "You'll be extra careful? No Wonder Woman feats?"

"No, none. This Wonder Woman wants to get the job over with and come home to her Superman." She snorted. "God, we're so corny."

"Just the way I like us." He glanced at Maverick's watch—five minutes after ten p.m.— but it reminded him of his old habit. He hoped it was the last day he had to glance at someone else's watch and wrist to remind himself who he was. "Damon is probably waiting. Meet you in the alley?"

"Yes." The word had barely left Jo's lips before she was gone.

Simon flashed and landed in the alley next to her. As they made their way to the front of the building, he looked around. His training was too ingrained for him to casually stroll down an alley, especially looking like the man hated by every uncontaminated magic in the area, and probably by some contaminated ones too.

Maverick's headquarters—the term they adopted the day the man blew up—sat in a row of new high-rise buildings in downtown Blue Mountain. The man's arrogance had been so great that he hadn't even tried to hide his whereabouts. By pure accident, Jack had discovered the headquarters and the day Maverick died, Simon took his place.

"About time, I was beginning to think something was wrong," Damon said as Simon and Jo walked into the building's lobby.

Simon opened his mouth to apologize, then remembered who he was—Maverick wouldn't apologize—and shut it. For months, Simon hadn't had to worry about being anyone but himself, and he'd gotten sloppy.

You got the conch handy? he asked Damon telepathically, not wanting to be overheard.

I can call it in an instant.

When Simon nodded his understanding, Damon spoke out loud to include them both. "Before we go up..." He waved his hand around them. "This protection should blur our images for a minute, unless anyone comes right up to us, and they'll probably think that Maverick did it, anyway."

"What's wrong?" Jo asked.

"I think I solved our little problem from yesterday. I didn't get a chance to tell you because it took me right up until I had to leave to come here. Yesterday, after the test run at Kate's shop, you know Ben and Frank rounded everyone up. Well… Ben said that the guy who had attacked Kate—both last month and in her shop—was almost inconsolable. His name is Brian. He's a family man and Maverick took him from a mall when he was shopping with his wife and two small kids in September."

"Oh shit," Jo whispered. "Does he remember everything he did?"

"Unfortunately, yes. He knows how many people he's trapped and killed. Like I said, he was almost inconsolable. But the real kicker is that he has some powers of persuasion, and that's why he was able to convert so many people. His powers usually only came across as strong suggestions, but they were amplified when he used them in conjunction with the evil."

"Does Brian know how Maverick learned about his specialty?" Simon asked.

Damon shook his head. "He has no idea, but Maverick put some kind of spell on him before pushing the evil magic into him, which made sure he was aware of everything. Brian had no choice but to do whatever Maverick directed."

Simon felt for the guy, but they still had a job to do. "Talk about a case for PTSD if there ever was one, but how is that going to help?"

"Brian can't bring back the people he killed—and Jack and Ben vowed to get him some good counseling because it wasn't his fault—but he wants to help in any way he can. He should be in the penthouse already, putting on his asshole act."

"That's nice of him, but since he's not really under the magic's control, he won't be able to do what we need."

Damon pressed the button for the penthouse elevator. Not knowing what they could land in the middle of, they never flashed onto the floor. "No," Damon said, "but he'll act like he's still under the influence, and he can use his power to persuade someone else to do it."

They stepped into the private elevator a moment later, and Damon entered the code. For the first time since the previous night, Simon felt some of his coiled tension dissipate. If Brian could come through for them, and they could get it done fast, everything would be back to normal soon.

Damon moved in front of Simon, adopting a military at-ease position, like the enforcer he was pretending to be. Jo stood a few inches to the side and behind Simon.

As soon as they entered the building, they adopted their personas because they never knew who could see them. And every time they stepped into the elevator there was a chance cameras could have been placed inside.

Before stepping out of the elevator, Damon scanned for threats and they'd agreed in the beginning that he would be prepared to shut the elevator doors if needed.

When you arrived, something was wrong, Damon said into Simon's mind, keeping his focus on the doors.

Nothing's wrong. I just want this over with. He and Damon hadn't known each other long, but like with everyone in their group, the circumstances over the last year had bonded them all.

Man, I hear ya. "I sense nothing, sir," Damon said, in character.

The doors opened, and Damon checked the foyer of the penthouse that the elevator entered directly into before stepping to the side to allow Simon to pass.

As they'd done every time they played the roles, Jo and Damon used their magic to glamour themselves, but instead of beautifying their looks, they appeared zombie-like, their expressions blank.

Squaring his shoulders and putting on an air of arrogance, Simon stepped around them and strode down the hall. The apartment took up the entire floor of the expansive, luxury building and even included a ballroom, which Maverick had commandeered for a command center.

Out of habit, Simon checked his watch again—quarter past ten. Hopefully their plan not to come back until now had everyone on their toes. The night before, Simon, as Maverick, had a few loyal henchmen announce to anyone they could find that he would be announcing a big plan tonight.

At the door of the ballroom, Simon did a quick assessment of the occupants. Brian sat at the far end of a long table that easily sat fifteen people down either side, and was doing a good job of feigning boredom.

The person who had questioned Simon's authority the night before sat at the head of the table closest to the door, directing two men to threaten some magics that were causing them trouble.

The man went by the name Goose, obviously in deference to Maverick's nickname, as if thinking he'd been referring to the movie *Top Gun*. Goose probably had no idea that Maverick's real name was Forest, and according to Mirek, he'd chosen the nickname because he thought himself to be a true maverick—above others, unorthodox and a true independent—not a fighter pilot.

Simon took a small step to the left, hoping to get caught in Goose's peripheral vision, but not wanting to move too far inside the room. Damon strode around Simon into the room, leaving Jo by Simon's side.

Goose looked Simon's way and leaned back in his chair, stretching one arm over the top of another chair—a cocky move. Goose sneered. "Well... you finally decided to show your fucking face. What're you gonna do now—or is hitting me in the face the best you got?"

From what Simon had seen and heard about Maverick, he wouldn't have tolerated such disrespect, and that was the problem they'd had the previous night. Simon wanted to shut the asshole up, but he couldn't do it the way Maverick would have, nor did Simon want to kill the man. But once the magic no longer controlled Goose, maybe he would be remorseful like Brian. Simon could only hope.

Simon adopted the silent treatment, hoping Goose would interpret the action as Maverick thinking Goose was beneath him.

The night before Simon realized Goose was escalating—he taunted Maverick and threatened to take over. He, Jo, and Damon had to get out fast and regroup. Damon used his power of persuasion to lock Goose in place for a few seconds. Not for long, but a sufficient amount of time for Simon to use magic with enough force to smash Goose's head into the table and knock him out.

Looking at his brash attitude now, Simon feared Goose was a loose cannon.

Jo had come with him every time as her powers of sensing truth had grown substantially since he'd met her, but now all he wanted was for her to be home where she would be safe. He wouldn't tell her that, of course—he wasn't an idiot. Yet for someone who was more beta than alpha—even as an FBI agent—Jo brought out his protective instincts.

Stay behind me, he said into her mind.

Okay.

Simon purposely turned his back on Goose, hoping he

wasn't making the biggest mistake of his life, and moved to the other side of the table, taking the long route.

"What the fuck you doin'?" Goose yelled at him. "Too chickenshit to come near me?"

It took everything in Simon to not turn around as he continued along the length of the table like he had all the time in the world. He was one chair from the end when he heard Jo cry out.

Simon spun around to see Jo suspended in the air about six feet off the ground, then turned to Goose.

He stood, with his elbows at his waist and his hands forward in a taunting gesture, as if to say "come and get me." "You like my little trick, Mav-er-ick?" Goose asked stretching out the syllables, like it would make him seem tough. "I know you're tapping that little thing, so I figured stringing her up might stop your bullshit silent treatment. What the hell is wrong with you?"

Simon looked up at Jo. At first glance, he thought she'd been suspended in the air, but looking more closely, he realized she was sitting in some kind of a bubble suspended in the air. She didn't appear hurt, but he asked her anyway. "You okay?"

"I'm okay. I've had worse."

If Simon wasn't ready to blow his top, he would have laughed at Jo's nonchalance.

Forcing himself to tear his eyes off Jo, Simon met Damon's gaze and lifted his chin toward Goose before nodding. Simon might not be a true alpha, but no one was going to fuck with Jo. Simon needed Damon to put the hurt on Goose while he decided what to do next.

Moving in a flash, Damon stood behind Goose and grabbed his upper arms.

"You might not want to hurt me," Goose said, and Simon

wanted to wipe the cocky grin off the asshole's face. With the wall.

"Oh yeah?" Damon yanked one of Goose's arms behind his back and jerked it upward, forcing the man up onto his toes.

Jo screamed and held her arm.

"I told ya you wouldn't want to hurt me," Goose said, staring straight at Simon. "Ya see… my nice little trick wasn't that I put your cute little piece in the air, it's that I swapped hearts with her. Whatever you do to me, the purple-haired one is going to feel. Tsk, tsk," Goose said, shaking his head slowly. "You shouldn't be surprised since you taught me that trick."

Goose took a step away from Damon and locked gazes with Simon. "Now, you're going to tell me the big news you were boasting about last night, and then I'm going to take over now that you've become a pussy."

"What the fuck do you think you're doing?" Brian asked, stalking toward Goose.

Goose held up his hand toward Brian. "I'm getting back to the plan. I don't know what is wrong with him…" Goose pointed toward Simon. "But since he's not getting the job done, I'm taking over." He paused and looked over at Brian. "You've been acting weird too. You with me or not?"

Brian sneered at Simon before turning to Goose. "Oh, I'm with you, alright."

"Hold them," Goose told Brian and the two minions still in the room, gesturing toward Damon and Simon.

"And don't forget… you try to kill me, you'll kill her," he said, pointing at Jo.

CHAPTER TWENTY-THREE

Brian flashed to Damon's side and yanked his arm, pulling him further away from Goose. Damon made himself stumble, then stood like a zombie as Brian appeared to hold him, but his grip was so light he wouldn't have hurt a baby.

Goose poked Simon in the chest with enough force that Simon had to take a step back to steady himself.

"Now. Tell me what the fuck your big plan is."

Simon—or Maverick—was a few inches taller than Goose, and sneered down his nose at him. "Fuck you. You're a little pissant with an attitude problem. I'm not going to tell you a damn thing."

"We'll see about that. You seem to be forgetting everything you've taught me." Goose waved his hand at Simon, and he dropped to the floor like a bucket of concrete thrown off a roof. Simon clapped his hands to the sides of his head as he writhed around on the floor like a snake that couldn't remember how to make a forward movement.

"Stop!" Jo yelled from her perch in the air.

Damon thought about using his persuasion on Goose, but

he didn't want to tip his hand too soon. He'd used it the night before, but expected that with the blow Simon delivered, Goose hadn't realized Damon's role in the action.

Jo continued to yell between taking large breaths, and Brian's hand stiffened around his arm.

"That's probably enough." Brian snorted in an almost laugh. "If you make his head explode, he won't be able to tell you the plan."

Goose looked over his shoulder at Brian and laughed before looking down at Simon. "Right. Wouldn't want that."

"Pick him up," Goose told the two goons.

When they hauled Simon up by the arms, he was gasping for breath.

Simon slowly lifted his head and sneered at Goose. "You're still a pissant."

"The fuck!" Goose yelled, and waved one hand at Simon and one at Damon.

Damon dropped to the floor and clapped his hands to his head, just like Simon had done.

Time ceased to exist for Damon as his agony—worse than the torture Snake inflicted on him in Mexico—consumed him.

By the time he wished he could pass out, the pain stopped and he sucked in air. Reece had told him about the silent death—at least, that's what he'd called it—and Damon thought he'd understood, but nothing could truly explain the feeling of knowing you're getting air but feeling like you're suffocating while your head was trying to blow apart.

"Get them up," Goose hissed, no longer the cocky bastard he'd been earlier.

Brian hauled Damon up but he wasn't as rough as he made the action look.

"Now, tell me!" Goose yelled, shoving Simon again.

"What do you want to know?" Simon stalled, his voice weaker than it'd been before.

"What is your big plan?" Goose asked.

Simon tilted his head as if trying to remember; Damon knew they were running out of time.

Glancing up at Jo, sitting cross-legged in the air, Damon noticed she looked comfortable. Goose hadn't targeted Jo, only Simon and Damon. Thinking back to what Goose had said—*I swapped hearts with her*—an epiphany hit him. He knew what he needed to do and hoped that his friends would forgive him… if they all lived.

Jack? Damon reached out with his mind.

Here.

We need you and Mirek.

Now?

On my one.

Copy.

With Jack's acknowledgment and part of his hasty plan in place, Damon hoped the rest would work. "Here goes," he muttered to himself and threw a thought at Brian.

On my one, grab Goose.

Not waiting for Brian to reply, Damon called out to Simon. "Hey, Maverick."

When Simon looked in his direction, Goose half-turned toward Damon.

"You trust me?" Damon asked Simon.

"Yes," Simon said without hesitation.

"What the fu—" Goose asked, but Damon cut him off and turned to Jo.

Damon asked Jo the same question. "You trust me?"

"Yes," she said, and when she nodded, he expected Jo had already calculated their odds in her head and was ready for anything.

"Hey, asshole," Goose said as he took a step toward Damon.

Three, he said to Jack's mind and then to Brian's.

Two.

All in one motion, Damon conjured a dagger, raised his hand to his shoulder, and propelled his hand forward.

One, he screamed into Jack's and then Brian's mind, as soon as the dagger left his fist. At the same time, he was already on the move, throwing out his arms to catch Jo. She screamed, and he didn't know if it was from the dagger hitting her in the chest or from the fall.

As Damon lowered Jo to the ground, blood pouring from the wound in her chest, Jack and Mirek kneeled beside him.

"The asshole traded hearts with Jo," Damon told them and moved back to give them room. "If he tried to hurt him, we hurt Jo. I threw a dagger at her, and I'm hoping it hit his heart instead of hers."

"Jo," Simon whispered, sounding more like himself than Maverick. He dropped by Jo's side and clasped her hand.

"Goose is dead," Brian called.

Brian then called out to some of the minions, but Damon kept his eyes on Jo while Jack and Mirek healed her.

"You may have killed the guy," Jack said, giving him a side-eye. "But as soon as he died, Jo's own heart returned to her body."

"The dagger isn't in her heart, but her heart is crowding in next to it," Mirek said with his hands on Jo and his eyes closed. "Jack, pull the dagger on my three…. One, two, three."

Jack pulled out the dagger and Mirek moved his hands to the wound on Jo's chest.

When Mirek opened his eyes and looked up, he gave him a small smile. "Don't do that again… but yes, she's going to be fine."

A fist smashed into Damon's arm, toppling him onto his ass.

He looked up at Simon. "Like Mirek said... don't ever do that again. But... thank you."

Damon nodded and pushed to his feet, not quite steady. As long as he lived he would never forget throwing a dagger into one of his closest friends. The moment the asinine idea had come to him, he had to talk himself into doing it, but he hadn't seen another option.

Jack stood and laid a hand on Damon's shoulder. "You explain everything later. Right now, let's finish what you started."

"He was a traitor," Brian hissed, his act convincing as he sneered at Goose's body laying at a twisted angle on the ground.

Brian jerked his chin toward two of them he'd called into the room "Move his body to the side."

Keeping up with the charade, Brian looked over his shoulder at Simon. "Maverick, if she's okay, we need you here."

Simon walked over and clasped Brian on the shoulder. Damon thought it might have been part for the role and part to find his balance after what Damon had just put him and Jo through.

"Got rid of the traitor?" Simon asked, his tone a perfect imitation of Maverick's harsh bark.

"Yes, sir," Brian said and turned to face the man, standing in the same military at-ease position Damon had been using.

The only difference was that the man sported the zombie expression Damon had seen on too many other faces.

"You said you wanted to give someone the honor of making your announcement," Brian said, gesturing toward the man standing at ease. "James has earned it. He's very powerful."

Damon heard what Brian wasn't saying—that they'd need to be ready to handle the man's power—and expected that Jack and Simon had too.

"Now," Simon said as he nodded at Brian and Damon, and they each moved to James' side and took hold of his arms. The man didn't even glance at either of them.

Damon held out his free hand and called the conch from the safety of his home. Simon took it and said to James, "You have the honor of reciting a spell into the minds of every magic in North America. You will repeat each line I say. Do you understand?"

James nodded but continued to stare straight ahead. "Yes."

Release the comas, Damon said into Jack's mind.

Done.

Simon held the conch's widest end toward James and recited the first line. "Darkness within as foretold, now is time to break your hold."

It wasn't until Simon recited the final line of the spell— *From soul to funnel with utmost grace, until you meet your final resting place*—that James fought against Damon's hold.

"What the hell?" James yelled. "What is this?"

Damon put as much magic persuasion behind his words as he could. "You will repeat what Maverick said. Now."

"Repeat Maverick," Brian told James, and Damon heard the push in his words.

James stopped fighting and recited the final lines of the spell. His body arched toward the conch for only a moment before he righted himself. His gaze was clear and focused as he looked around. "What happened?" he asked, his voice sounding different than before—neither neutral nor angry.

Brian put his arm around James' shoulders. "Come on, let's go find the others and I'll explain."

Simon shoved the conch into Jack's hands and approached Jo.

Damon glanced over at them, relieved to see Jo looking like her usual self as she sat on a chair beside Mirek.

"Never again," Damon muttered to himself and shook his head.

"I still want to hear what happened, but I think this is a ticking time bomb," Jack said, a strange tone in his voice.

Facing Jack, Damon noticed his friend's hands were shaking and the conch was glowing. "Ah, Jack, that doesn't look good."

"Ya think?" Jack asked, sarcasm dripping from his words. "Get to the meadow. I sent an update before Mirek and I flashed here, so everyone else should already be there."

"You really want a large group there when you release that shit? Especially everyone we care about?"

"We need a large group in case we have to erect a protection shield around it and I need people I trust. See you soon," Jack said and disappeared.

Damon told the others where to meet. As he called on his magic to flash, he could only hope that this nightmare would be over soon.

December 29

MIREK LOOKED around for Sam as soon as his feet touched the grass in the field. It was after midnight, but the entire place was lit up like a high school football field during a Friday night game.

Magic balls of light lay in an enormous circle around the edges of the field, just inside where the trees began. There wasn't any snow inside the ring of lights, but patches of white glistened outside the circle in the lights' reflections.

He received hellos and nods. Besides close friends and family, Mirek recognized many of the magic FBI agents who'd been helping them. He also spotted Brian and a few of Maverick's minions there as well.

In the years since Mirek had been separated from Sam and taken from the compound, he'd lived in a small bubble of Snake's and Maverick's making. But now, he had more people in his life than he'd ever had. Only one person was missing—Rocky—and he sent out a wish to the universe that he was safe, wherever that might be.

"Mirek," Sam said softly when he reached her side. He pulled her into a hug and placed a kiss on her forehead just above her burns so she could feel it.

"Damon was just telling us how he tried to kill my cousin," Morgana said, grinning as Damon grimaced.

Mirek could understand where the man was coming from. Years from now, he might be able to joke about what he'd done, but it was equally possible that the decision might always haunt him as well and make him wonder if there had been another way.

Sam got his attention by patting his stomach. "Hey, you okay?"

"Yeah, I'm good. Just tired." It was an honest answer, healing Jo hadn't been as difficult as it could have been. "And I want this to be over with."

"You and me both, man," Damon said. "I've had enough of this—"

"Hello," Jack called out, cutting off Damon's words, as his voice carried across the field.

A hush fell over the meadow, and everyone turned toward Jack.

"For the people who are new to this group... my name is Jack Knight and I, along with my wife, Meredith, are the co-leaders of the new North American magic council. We have the magic contained, and we're now ready to get rid of it for good." Jack held the conch in his hands, and even from where Mirek stood he could see a light green glow emanating from inside it.

"How do you know you've got it all?" Ben asked.

"Your daughter can answer that one. Sam?"

Mirek let go of Sam and she took a few steps forward. She pulled her hair around her face, then held her necklace in one hand, but her voice was strong and steady as she addressed the crowd.

"We can be sure we have it all due to quantum disentanglement—the principle that told us each particle would influence the other, no matter the distance. The spell used to extract the magic was strong—and the quantum entanglement within the magic was even stronger—meaning as soon as the extraction started, no particles would have been able to resist the influence."

"But what if we did miss some?" Fiona asked, her eyebrows drawn together.

Mirek couldn't blame her for being worried. She'd lost her husband due to the greed for the magic box and had almost lost her daughter.

"I don't think that's possible," Sam said with confidence. "But... if it is, the magic would be so insignificant that it wouldn't be able to survive without the rest. It... think of it like a single water molecule from the ocean. Without the rest of the ocean, the one drop will dry up."

"Thank you for explaining, honey. My nerves needed a bit of calming. Okay, Jack. Let's close this sucker up for good," Fiona said, lightening the mood.

"You heard the woman," Jack said. When the laughter died down, he looked serious once more. "We understand what Maverick did to you and we will do whatever we can to make it right. Once we get this—" he paused and smiled at Fiona—"sucker is closed, please come and talk to me or Meredith.

"As you know, Maverick absorbed the magic from the ancient box. But what you may not know is that Maverick died on December first. That magic…" Jack's words trailed off, likely trying to figure out how to describe what happened.

"Left him in an abrupt manner," Stella supplied from where she stood by Ben.

Jack gave her a nod. "Yes. The magic left Maverick abruptly and spread to others. It would have continued to spread if we hadn't extracted it. We were able to locate the original box to enclose the evil, but learned recently that the box would no longer be able to contain it."

The conch began to shake in Jack's hands, and the glowing magnified.

"I think we're out of time folks. Everyone step back to the edge of the circle and place a protective bubble around yourself, just in case," Jack said as he walked over to a spot outside the circle of lights.

"Instead of the box, the magic will be funneled into an ancient spellbook. A sword will then seal the magic inside the book. Kate?"

The spellbook already lay on the ground.

Kate stepped up to the book with the sword clasped in both hands. She stood at an angle to Mirek, giving him a view of both her and the book.

Once more a hush fell over the field as Kate lowered the tip of the sword to the middle of the book and held it there.

Kate lifted the blade off the book and moved to the side to give Jack room to work.

Jack held the funnel to the book, one edge touching, and

tipped it up. Usually magic was invisible, but perhaps because of its malevolence and concentration, a light green shadow was visible as Jack poured.

When Jack finished, the book shook with a small tremor and light emitted from its edges.

Kate touched the tip of the sword to the spellbook again. After less than a minute, she turned away from the book, the sword hanging at her side.

"I can't do it," she said. "The sword… it says the magic is too strong for me."

"It's okay, Kate. I'll do it," Jack said, holding out his hand for the sword.

"It can't be you either." Kate let her gaze travel over the group as if looking for an answer, but Mirek already knew what she was going to say. He knew he'd been in denial, thinking that maybe there would be another way, and the seer had been wrong all those years ago. His entire body felt tense with a pulsing anger at the injustice of what Sam had to do. Hadn't they both suffered enough?

"The sword said only the half-dead one has the power to do it."

Jack frowned. "The half-dead one? Who the fuck is that?"

Sam moved out of Mirek's arms, but he wanted to haul her back.

He and Sam had promised each other that they wouldn't volunteer to sacrifice themselves anymore. But this was different. Sam would no more be able to walk away from this than Mirek would from someone he loved who lay dying. And maybe the two situations were one and the same. He shoved his hands into his pockets so he wouldn't reach for her.

Walking away from her so he could get a grip on his emotions was supposed to be the hardest thing he'd ever have to do.

That was nothing compared to this.

"It's me," Sam said loudly enough for everyone to hear. "I'm the half-dead one."

CHAPTER TWENTY-FOUR

December 28

Sam turned back to Mirek, for the moment ignoring the sudden chatter behind her. Grasping both of Mirek's cheeks, she went up on her toes and kissed him. His lips parted and let her in, her tongue tangling with his as she poured out all her love.

Mirek's hands gripped her hips, hard enough to bruise as he tugged her body against his. She hoped she would live to see the bruises, but the seer's words from when she was sixteen played in her mind. *"I believe I know your destiny. In the vision you were older than you are now... and I saw you die."*

Knowing she was running out of time, she looked into his eyes. "I love you, hero. I will always love you."

Mirek swallowed, and she could see his love for her in his eyes. "I love you too, Athena." He kissed her scarred cheek right near her ear and whispered, "I know you need to do this. But please... please, only do what you need to."

Mirek let go of her hips and walked away. Before she lost her nerve she strode toward Jack and Kate.

Before she could reach the other side of the circle, her parents blocked her path. Their anguish and confusion were as clear as day on their faces.

Her dad held out his hands, and she placed hers in his. "Sam, you need to explain. We don't understand."

"Sam," Jack called. "We're running out of time."

Sam nodded at Jack before looking back at her parents. "I don't know when, but a seer told Daniel Knight, or Snake—I'm not sure who—that I was difficult to kill and I would be useful. Drew staged the fire that killed me. When I appeared to die in the fire it activated my magic specialty, and they took me. The funeral director made it seem like I was in the casket. At least… that's what Mirek and I were able to figure out."

"You're immortal?" Sam could see the anguish on her mom's face morph to hope, and Sam hated that she would have to destroy it.

"No, not immortal, just difficult to kill. Mirek and I spoke to a seer when I was sixteen. She told me that I was the half-dead one and this is my destiny."

Sam could practically see the wheels turning in her dad's mind and anticipated what he was going to ask next. As much as she wanted to lie, she couldn't.

"When Maverick attacked you in Isaac's shop that day… you died, didn't you?"

"Yes. And Jack didn't actually heal me because my body was already healing itself."

Her dad rubbed her hand in both of his. "And when Maverick exploded and Mirek healed you… you died then too?"

"Yes, but it was more than my body could handle that time. If Mirek hadn't healed me, I would be dead."

She pulled her hand from her dad's and gave each of her parents a quick hug, holding on tight for just a moment.

"I've got to go or the magic will release and infect everyone, and next time we might not be able to contain it." She feared if she didn't walk away soon, she wouldn't have the strength to do what she needed to.

"I love you both so much. I've always loved you, even when I was away. Your love sustained me for so long." Her throat burned as she pushed out the last words.

"We love you," her mom and dad said at the same time.

Sam walked around her parents, putting her back to them as she headed toward Jack.

Only a few feet away from Jack, Nate blocked her path. He reached for her, but she moved away. "No, you can't look. I know what I must do, and we're out of time."

"I love you, Sam."

"I love you too, Nate."

Taking the final steps to Jack and Kate, she held out her hand for the sword. Kate hesitated.

"It's okay, Kate. I knew this day would come—a seer told me it's always been my destiny." Sam grasped the hilt, forcing Kate to let go. "Protect your baby."

Kate nodded and walked over to Isaac.

Jack stared at her with intensity, like he could see through to her soul. "That day in Isaac's shop… I didn't heal you."

"I know."

"But you died?"

"I think so, but it wasn't the first time. Depending on what causes it, I can regenerate."

"And this time?" he asked gesturing toward the book, where it vibrated on the ground.

That wasn't a question she could answer. If she said she would die she knew Jack would volunteer to close the book. But he wouldn't survive either. And if she said she knew she would live through it, she would be lying.

"I need to do this, Jack."

He nodded and stepped back.

Sam walked to the book and held the sword's hilt firmly with both hands. Resisting the urge to glance back at Mirek one more time, knowing it could weaken her resolve, she looked down at the book.

Like Kate did, Sam touched the tip of the blade to the middle of the spellbook. Without magical tattoos, she didn't think the book would be able to communicate with her, but her gut said she needed to do it.

I have been waiting for you, the book spoke into her mind.

She was surprised, but she supposed she shouldn't have been. This was her destiny after all.

Are you ready? she asked the book.

A person from beyond must speak first.

The corners of her lips tipped up into an almost smile.

Who? she asked the book.

"Half-dead one." Sam looked up. Floating before her was an almost transparent image of the seer who'd spoken to her and Mirek so long ago.

"So many, both of this world and another, have provided you and the others with support because what you are doing is for all magic people. Past, present, and future."

Sam nodded, unsure what to say.

"When I spoke to you all those years ago, there was something I did not know then."

"What?" Sam whispered, almost afraid to ask.

"The fire that burned you at five awoke your magic specialty, but it could have killed you… What saved you was the love of your parents inside you."

The seer looked over to where she'd been standing with Mirek, but Sam didn't know if anyone but her could see the seer. She'd never seen a ghost before.

"Sam," Mirek said quietly.

Still holding the tip of the sword on the spellbook, Sam turned her head to see Mirek standing beside her.

"The seer called to me."

"What do we need to do?" Sam asked the woman, her image more transparent than before.

"Do not fear what the future holds. Instead… hold on to the love between you. It is strong enough to save you." Then the seer looked directly at Mirek. "You must let her go and trust that your love will be enough."

"Are you telling me that if something happens, I can't heal her?"

"Your love is forever," the seer said as she faded away.

Now! the book shouted into Sam's mind.

Caught up in the seer's words, Sam hadn't noticed the tip of the sword shaking her hands as the spellbook's vibrations increased.

"It's now. Hold me, hero."

Mirek pressed his front to Sam's back, wound his arms around her, and then shifted over to the left, freeing Sam's arms.

She lifted the sword in a two-handed grip.

Pulling on her magic for strength, she thrust the sword downward into the book.

CHAPTER TWENTY-FIVE

*B*eing so terrified he thought he'd jump out of his skin wasn't anything new to Mirek. He'd lived with fear since he was ten years old. Yet, this was the most afraid he'd ever been.

With his arms around Sam's middle, he moved so her side was perpendicular to his front clasped his fingers together and her arms unencumbered.

Her body vibrated against his as she called forth all the might of her magic and swung her arms up.

Her downward stroke hit the book, piercing the leather cover.

Light exploded from the book and he felt the force against Sam's body slam into his.

For a split second he thought of Maverick's body exploding and the impact of the evil magic connecting with Sam and throwing her backward.

Then he was living it.

The energy's clout sent them both hurling into the air.

He sent magic to his fingers in a frantic attempt to tighten his grip around her.

His back hit the ground, knocking the air from his lungs with a force so strong he didn't think he would ever take another breath. Sam laid like a dead weight on his chest, his arms still around her.

Mirek sucked air into his lungs and coughed, causing pain to swell along his spine. Panting shallow breaths, he waited until some of the pain subsided and used his magic to scan himself for injuries. He found three cracked vertebrae in his lower back and healed them before continuing his assessment. Only contusions remained; they could wait.

Holding Sam with one arm, he braced his other on the grass to reposition her. The ground's freezing temperature seeped into him, the cold finally penetrating his senses. He conjured a queen-sized mattress underneath himself and rolled to his side, easing Sam onto it beside him.

Shouts came at him from all directions.

"Is she alive?" Ben asked as the mattress dipped. He and Stella sat on the mattress by Sam's side, opposite where Mirek lay.

Mirek reached his fingers toward Sam's neck.

Then hesitated.

Over the past fifteen years, he'd done the same thing twice.

Both times, her pulse had been absent.

He knew this time it would be no different.

Touching his two middle fingers to where Sam's pulse should be, he waited. He counted to ten, and then fifteen.

Nothing.

The only difference this time was that Mirek wouldn't attempt to heal her. He would give everything he had if he could make her heart beat again, but he couldn't this time.

"Bring her back," Stella demanded, her tone filled with panic.

Mirek conjured two pillows and placed one under Sam's head and tossed the other behind his.

"What the hell are you doing?" Ben barked at him, leaning over Sam and getting in Mirek's face.

With his head feeling as heavy as his heart, Mirek looked up at Sam's dad. "I'm going to wait."

"What the hell?" Ben looked up as if searching for someone. "Jack! Come here! Hurry!"

Mirek laid his head on the other pillow and draped his arm over Sam's stomach, snugging her close to his side. He needed to feel her length against his. She wasn't stiff, only lifeless. Waiting for Sam's body to heal itself might drive him insane, but he would wait as long as it took.

"Jack, you need to heal Sam! Mirek is doing nothing!"

Just like with Fiona, Mirek couldn't imagine what Sam's parents were feeling. He only knew what it felt like to love someone with every part of his soul and be unable to help them.

"Mirek," Jack said softly, as if talking to a wounded animal. He looked more defeated than Mirek had ever seen him. "Did someone visit Sam before she closed the spellbook?"

The only thing Mirek wanted to do was hold Sam until she woke up. But he figured the sooner he answered everyone's questions, the sooner they would leave him and Sam alone.

Mirek pushed up on his elbow but kept his other arm across Sam. "Yes. She was a seer we met in the compound in Mexico when Sam was sixteen. She healed me after... when I needed healing, and she told us about Sam's gift."

"Gift?" Stella screeched. "This isn't a gift! She said she's some kind of half-dead prophecy, but you have the ability to heal her. And you too, Jack. But you're doing nothing!" she leveled at them, like an accusation.

Ben wrapped his arm around Stella's shoulders and paused, maybe speaking into her mind. When Ben met his gaze, there wasn't anything soft in it. "Mirek, Jack. You need to explain. Now."

"You saw the seer's ghost?" Mirek asked, looking at Sam's parents.

Jack should his head. "Only Meredith, Connor, Rowena, and I were able to see her, but we couldn't hear what she said."

"She told us she knew something she hadn't known when she spoke to us years ago." Mirek looked at Stella and Ben and wondered if what he was about to say would help or make things worse, but he knew Sam would want them to know.

"What?" Stella asked, sounding hopeful, even as her eyes were glassy with un-spilled tears.

"She told us that Sam would have died in the fire when she was five if it wasn't for your love. So instead of the fire killing her, it awakened her gift."

Stella's fingers trembled when she pressed them to her mouth as her tears spilled down her cheeks.

"And now?" Ben asked, his voice sounding like his throat was filled with sand.

"The ghost seer said my love for Sam and hers for me would heal her."

Ben's eyes widened. "So, you're not even going to try?"

"The seer told us that our love was forever, and we had to trust in it, and I wasn't to heal Sam." None of it made sense—why Sam was to use her power and yet Mirek couldn't use his own. He had to believe there was a reason and that everything Sam had done had worked. The seer had been right before and he feared going against her could mean he'd lose Sam forever.

Mirek met Jack's gaze. "Did it work? Is the magic closed inside the book?"

Jack scrubbed his face with his hands for a moment, before one side of his mouth tilted up in a partial smile. "Better than that. The book disappeared, taking the evil magic with it."

Letting Jack's words sink in, Mirek laid back down on his side, resting his head on the pillow and pulling Sam tight against him. His adrenaline was wearing off, allowing the cold to seep into him. He conjured a thick blanket and floated it over both of them, tucking it around Sam's other side.

She would be happy that her gift had given her the ability to do something no one else could do, regardless of her sacrifice. For years she'd felt a need to make up for all the evil deeds Maverick and the others had forced her to commit, but she'd been wrong—she had nothing to make up for or prove.

With one selfless act, Sam had righted their wrongs anyway.

"Mirek..." Stella pleaded, forcing him to look at her.

"I need you to do some—" Stella didn't finish as she choked on the words and turned into her husband's arms.

"I know. But I can't. Sam—" A sudden burning in Mirek's throat threatened to strangle him until he could no longer breathe.

He swallowed and tried again. "Sam would want me to follow the seer's instruction. I've heard stories that people who try and circumvent what the seer predicts end up with worse circumstances. I'm not willing to risk that." He only hoped that he hadn't truly sentenced Sam to death by not trying to heal her.

Believing in his and Sam's love was easy. But not using his

magic to save her could kill him. All his organs felt like they were shriveling up and squeezing him from the inside.

If Sam didn't live, he would lie down beside her until he passed onto the next world.

Mirek closed his eyes again and tuned out everything but Sam's body against his.

He opened his eyes when he felt a hand on his shoulder.

Jack crouched on the grass beside the mattress, the sun behind him starting its early morning ascent. "It's almost eight a.m. Meredith got everyone to leave a couple of hours ago, and I finally convinced Ben to take Stella home just now. Do you need anything?"

"No, we'll be fine," Mirek said softly. He and Sam laid in a wide-open meadow, but he felt like they were back in his bunk whispering.

"Okay, I'll check on you every few hours."

"No." Mirek had snaked one arm under Sam's neck, but he gently pulled it out and touched Jack's arm. Mirek needed his friend to really hear him. "Please leave us alone and keep everyone away. When Sam wakes up, I'll bring her home."

Jack looked like he wanted to argue, but waited, as if wrestling with himself. "I'll keep everyone away on one condition."

Mirek raised his eyebrow in question.

"I'll reach out to your mind every four hours, and you answer me."

"Deal."

Jack stood, and Mirek pushed his arm back under Sam and cradled her tighter against him.

A gentle weight settled on him, and Mirek saw another blanket on top of the original one he'd conjured.

Jack stared down at them. "Since the weather's been mild lately, the sun will feel warm, but it won't last. It will set in in just over eight hours."

"We'll be fine."

"You and Sam are not alone, Mirek. Not anymore," Jack said softly, emotion clogging his voice.

"I know. I'll reach out if I need to."

Jack nodded and disappeared.

Mirek conjured a wool cap for Sam and put it on her head, making sure to tuck her hair away from her face and cover her ears.

Without thinking, he had put Sam on his left side, so when she rolled toward him, her left side would be facing up. It was the way they'd always slept. But now, she was on her back, her scarred cheek facing him. He would just make sure he reached around her to cup her left cheek so that when she was able to feel him, she wouldn't miss a moment of his touch. He'd be here for her.

Reaching under the blanket, he lifted her hands and laid them on her chest. They weren't cold like death, but they weren't warm either.

He snuggled against her and let sleep take him.

As promised, Jack reached out to him every four hours and for the first twelve hours Mirek slept in between the messages. Only when nature called did he leave Sam's side.

Using Jack's contacts as a gauge to tell the passage of time, Mirek conjured something to eat every four to eight hours. No matter what he ate, he had no appetite and it tasted like sawdust, but he refused to weaken in case Sam needed him.

When he wasn't sleeping, he spoke to Sam and stroked her arms and face, hoping she could feel him.

"Remember that first night we made love... on your eighteenth birthday?" he whispered. "I was so nervous, but excited too. I've loved you for so long, Sam." He chuckled. "You know what I mean—not in a creepy way—not when we were kids. But when Snake first dumped you on the couch in that body bag... I saw you, your burns, and knew I would do whatever I could to help you. It was during those two weeks while I healed you…"

He huffed out a laugh into the darkness, his breath visible under the moonlight.

"I remember you waking up and trying to figure things out. You didn't cry, and I think you were more worried about me than yourself."

Mirek kissed Sam softly on the lips. "I've been in awe of you since you were five years old."

Over the next two days, Mirek developed a pattern. He would sleep between two of Jack's check-ins and then tell Sam stories between the next two.

On the third day, Mirek conjured himself a watch, one with a GPS that would automatically set to the proper time. The days had begun to meld together, and he didn't want to miss New Year's Eve.

At fifteen minutes before midnight on December thirty-first, Mirek reached out.

Jack?

What's wrong?

Nothing. Just checking in early because it's New Year's Eve.

When Jack didn't respond right away, he figured Jack thought the check-in was over.

Happy New Year, Mirek, Jack said into his mind at five minutes before midnight.

Knowing that his friend was trying to help him celebrate, even in a small way, made him smile. *Happy New Year, Jack.*

Mirek ran his fingers along Sam's forehead at the edge of the knit cap and pictured what she looked like standing under the glow of the streetlamp on Christmas Eve.

It had only been seven days ago. And three days since she'd closed the box—exactly seventy-one hours.

"Remember what I said to you on Christmas Eve? It was right before you found the rift in the dimension. I said, *On*

December thirty-first, let's stand outside and welcome in the New Year in the fresh air under the stars. Well… It's December thirty-first and we're outside in the fresh air under the stars."

He chuckled, watching as he trailed his fingers over her skin. "We're not standing, but lying down is good enough."

At almost midnight, he focused on his watch as the seconds ticked off and counted down out loud for Sam. "Ten, nine, eight, seven, six, five, four, three, two, one." Pressing his lips softly to hers, he said, "Happy New Year, Sam. I love you so—"

Mirek choked on the last word and pressed one more light kiss to Sam's lips. Making sure the blankets were still tucked around her, he laid back on his side and placed his hand over her heart, hoping she could feel his love.

CHAPTER TWENTY-SIX

"$\mathcal{M}$irek, wake up."

I hear you, he told Jack.

A hand landed on Mirek's shoulder. "Wake up, Mirek," Jack said.

Gently pulling his arm out from underneath Sam, Mirek sat up and used his other hand to knead the half-asleep muscles. "What are you doing here?"

"It's almost one a.m."

Mirek frowned. "You came here and woke me up to tell me the time?" Confused, he held up his wrist for Jack to see. "I have a watch."

Jack scrubbed his face with his hands, then sighed. Even in the moonlight, Mirek could see the toll the past few days had taken on Jack.

"Look, you don't have to contact me every four hours, Jack. We'll be okay."

"You're *not* okay." Jack waved his hand at the mattress, his frustration clear on his face. "You're sleeping on a mattress in a field in the middle of nowhere. It's January, and there's snow in the forecast for this week. It's time to come home."

"No." This was where he'd started waiting for Sam to wake up, and he had an irrational fear that if he moved her from this spot, she would never wake. Like if he moved her, he would disturb her healing her something.

"You just going to stay out here forever?"

Mirek stood up and stretched. Since Jack was determined to keep him awake, he might as well use the time wisely.

"No," he said, bending from side to side.

Jack frowned deeper. "No what?"

"No, I'm not going to stay out here forever." Mirek straightened and looked Jack in the eyes. "Look, I know this seems weird, but I started this out here, and I'm going to finish it out here. Sam is going to wake up... Jack, I appreciate what you're doing, but you can stop contacting me all the time."

Mirek gestured toward Jack. His clothes were wrinkled, and he hadn't shaved in days. "You need to look after yourself. Don't worry about us."

Jack looked down at himself as if trying to remember what he was wearing. "I just grabbed this shit from the hamper... It's almost one a.m.," Jack repeated, like he was too tired to figure out what else to say.

"I know, you already told me." Mirek stepped closer to Jack. "Are you feeling alright?"

"There's been a lot going on. The evil's been contained, but it will take a while to get things back to normal. I'm just tired." As if Jack's body wanted to prove its point, he yawned and covered his mouth with both hands.

"Like I said, I'm tired and I'll get some sleep, but right now I'm worried about you... Back to it being almost one a.m...." Jack pulled out his phone. "Now it's after one in the morning, actually. That means it's January fourth."

Jack rested his hands on his hips and raised his eyebrows. "Do you get what that means, Mirek?"

He wasn't dumb; of course he did. A little after one in the morning on December twenty-ninth, Sam sealed the magic—she'd been dead for six days.

Mirek looked over at Sam as he spoke. "I can't give up, Jack."

"You don't have to. Just bring her home." Jack's words were almost unintelligible as he yawned again.

Mirek looked back at him.

"Will you at least think about it?" Jack asked.

"Yes. But… Jack, I won't make any promises, not yet."

"Fuck," Jack sighed after his third yawn. "I don't ever remember being this tired, so I won't reach out tonight, but I will tomorrow… And I might not be able to hold Ben and Stella off forever. They, uh… want to say their goodbyes to Sam."

Jack yawned again and disappeared before Mirek could say anything, but he wasn't bothered by Jack's sudden departure because the man needed sleep.

Mirek looked across the bed at Sam—so peaceful and with no signs of stress marring her features—but no signs of anything else either. He gave his head an internal shake and flashed to the edge of the meadow to answer nature's call before flashing back.

Sitting on the edge of the bed, he pushed some magic into his freezing feet to warm them up and climbed under the blankets.

Adopting his usual position, he put his arm under Sam's neck and snugged her close. As he drifted off to sleep, he heard Rocky say his name.

Lifting his head, Mirek looked out into the darkness and saw his cousin's silhouette backlit by the moon's light. "Jack call you?"

"Yeah. He's worried." Rocky lifted his chin toward Sam. "How is she?"

Mirek kissed her temple and sat up. "Neutral."

Moving over to Sam's side of the mattress, Rocky looked down at her. "Neutral?"

"She's not really dead, nor alive. Not hot or cold." Mirek shrugged. "Neutral."

"Makes sense, I guess."

For several minutes, neither of them said anything as they watched Sam. Mirek put his hand under the blanket and slowly stroked Sam's arm. He'd become almost paranoid with the thought of her thinking he'd left.

Wanting to get comfortable in case Rocky decided to stay, Mirek scooted back a few inches and leaned against the headboard he'd conjured on the fourth day. Rested and not needing to sleep around the clock, he'd wanted something to rest against, but still make it possible to touch Sam—for her to feel him.

He slowly trailed his fingers back and forth along Sam's neck and shoulder, which were still within easy reach. It reminded him of all the times they laid in his bunk and he'd wake up in the middle of the night, as if his subconscious needed reassurance she was still there. The habit stayed with him throughout the years, even when Sam wasn't there. Mirek would wake up to an empty bed.

"Life can't be this cruel," he whispered, sending the words out into the universe.

"Meaning?" Rocky asked quietly.

Mirek noticed Rocky sitting on a chair, a small magic ball of light in his lap. Magic came in handy, but it also put them in the position they were in. He used to wonder how their lives would have been different if they had been born into non-magic families. Then he stopped when he realized it was like being born a tiger and wondering what it would be like being born a turtle—something you couldn't change—so it didn't matter.

"We endured so much over the years…" Images flashed in his mind, like a shuffling of a deck of cards. Them as kids, the compound in Mexico, torture, deaths, but also laughter and love. "Would the universe be so cruel that it would reunite me with Sam only to take her away again so soon?"

Rocky didn't answer immediately. Over the years he'd spoken less and less, weighing his thoughts before he spoke. His experiences did that to him—stole the vibrant, passionate cousin Mirek remembered from when they were young. The same thing happened to Morgana, but recently, he'd seen glimpses of the person she used to be and expected that Damon had a lot to do with that. Maybe someday Rocky would find his person. Someone who would teach him how to forgive himself. Someone who would knock down his walls and find the jokester inside who used to be so much like his brother Reece.

"I honestly don't know," Rocky said quietly, focused on Sam before meeting Mirek's gaze. "But I believe you and Sam were meant to be together. I don't think everyone in this world finds the kind of love you two have."

"And you?"

Rocky glanced at Sam before looking at Mirek again. "You're both special. I hope the universe knows that."

Pushing back his chair, Rocky stood and disappeared it. He placed the ball of light on the mattress beside Sam and picked up a bag from the ground. Mirek hadn't noticed the bag before now, but he had noticed that Rocky didn't answer his question. His cousin thought himself unworthy of love and, like Sam, felt he needed to make up for past sins.

The difference was that Sam had him to love her and show her how much she was worth, whereas Rocky had no one but a family he'd been separated from for decades, and he didn't think he was worthy of them either.

"I brought these for you," Rocky said, passing the bag to Mirek.

Dropping the heavy bag to his lap, Mirek opened it and pulled out books. "*The Lord of the Rings* trilogy and *The Chronicles of Narnia*?" He chuckled and looked up from the books. "This is a lot of reading. You trying to tell me something?"

Rocky shrugged, something he did a lot, as if nothing truly mattered. "I know you'll stay here as long as you need to. Now, you'll be able to escape into fantasy worlds while you wait."

"Thank you… Now that everything's over, are you going to stick around Blue Mountain?"

"Not for now. Ah… if you need me, Jack can reach me." Rocky ran his knuckle along Sam's cheek. "Take care of her," he said quietly and disappeared.

Looking at the bag of books in his lap made him smile. Rocky came across as tough, but he had a heart of gold. His wish for Rocky was that somewhere in his wanderings he would find that somebody who could love him and help him see he was worthy of being loved.

Mirek put the bag on the end of the bed and hunkered back down under the blankets next to Sam. With one hand under her and the other over her heart, he fell asleep.

INSIDE THE BAG OF BOOKS, Rocky had left a bookmark, and Mirek used it when he took a break from reading. He picked up the bookmark and marked his page in the *Chronicles of Narnia*. Rocky had been right—Mirek had enjoyed escaping into the fantasy world.

Checking his watch, he noted the time—almost eleven p.m. on January 4. The days were slipping by, and it was becoming harder and harder to keep up hope.

Earlier in the day, he'd taken a break from reading and laid by Sam's side with his hand on her heart. Arguing with himself, he spent twenty minutes trying to decide whether he should use his magic to look inside her. Would he find her almost healed and have renewed hope? Or see her torn apart like she'd been after she'd absorbed the evil from Maverick's explosion? Would it be too late if he tried to heal her now?

In the end, he respected her wishes and the belief of seers not to tamper with fate, and didn't look. It had been one of the hardest decisions he'd ever made—right up there with not healing her a week earlier.

He would continue to wait.

Disappearing the ball of light he used to read, he crawled under the covers. Leaning over her, he kissed her softly. "I love you, Sam, my Athena. Please come back to me."

After checking to make sure Sam's knit cap was covering her ears and the blankets were tucked to her side, he scooted close, the lengths of their bodies touching. He then got into his usual position—one arm under her neck and his other hand over her heart—and let sleep take him.

Mirek knew he was dreaming as he watched Sam flip through the encyclopedia until she found the page she wanted to show him. He hadn't cared about whatever she'd been looking up, but her excitement was contagious. Listening to her was like watching an animated documentary with a narrator truly passionate about their subject. Sam's eyes lit up as she told him something and bounced in her seat, like she couldn't contain her excitement when she said she remembered another fact.

She lifted her hand and cupped his cheek, and he felt something like puffs of wetness hit his face.

He opened his eyes, disoriented at first as the dream of Sam faded. A puff of dampness, like in the dream, hit his cheek, and then another.

Looking at his watch, the glow from the digital face brought him back to cold-hard reality. It was one ten in the morning on January 5—Sam had been dead a week.

Mirek conjured a ball of light onto his palm and hovered it over Sam. A few soft snowflakes drifted onto her cheeks.

Shifting back a couple of inches, he placed the ball of light between their bodies. The light wasn't strong, but it was just enough for him to see Sam. Snowflakes dropped onto her knit cap and quickly melted away. If the snow increased, he would have to decide if he should conjure something to cover them or finally move Sam inside. Neither option appealed to him.

The longer they stayed in the meadow, the more vindicated he became with his original decision to stay and wait for Sam to wake. He'd often heard magics say they just knew something, whether or not they could explain it—like when Fiona knew her vision of Kate was of the future and that Kate was alive.

Mirek knew he and Sam had to stay right where they were, and when Sam woke, she would see the vast sky—day or night, it didn't matter—and see he waited for her.

He lifted his hand to her unscarred cheek to wipe away the moisture left behind by the snowflakes.

Something was different.

Leaning over her, her cupped her cheek fully, like she'd done to him in the dream. Looking at her closed lids, it took him a full minute before he realized what had changed.

Sam's cheek felt warmer. Not warm like when the sun had shone on them earlier during the day, warm like from body heat.

Both hope and fear welled inside him, one for what the

warmth could mean and one for thinking he was imagining it.

Hesitantly, Mirek moved his hand down Sam's neck and upper chest to where he usually rested it on her heart.

Letting out a slow breath, he closed his eyes and tuned into what he could feel beneath it.

Holding himself motionless—almost afraid to breathe—it took him only a few seconds to feel the most glorious thing in the world—Sam's heartbeat.

Pushing up onto his knees, he extended his two middle fingers, like he'd done exactly a week ago, and placed them over Sam's carotid artery. But unlike the week before, this time, he felt her pulse.

"Sam? Sam? Can you hear me?" He placed a soft kiss on her lips. "I love you, Sam."

Mirek felt giddy, like his heart was going to burst with joy if he didn't share the news with someone.

Jack?

What's wrong? Jack answered after only a few seconds.

Mirek took a calming breath to avoid yelling at Jack in his excitement.

Sam has a heartbeat.

The best news.

Yes, it was.

Mirek cupped Sam's cheek again and placed another light kiss on her lips. They were soft, but not wet. Mirek reached between them and picked up the light ball. Holding his hand out, he looked into the night. The snow had stopped.

"Was that you, universe?" he whispered. As he watched the light cast by the moonlight, he made a promise to himself. No matter how many feet of snow he had to shovel in the years to come, he would never complain. Snowflakes had awakened him, letting him know his Sam was coming back—that his waiting was almost over.

Back under the covers and feeling Sam's heartbeat under his palm, he was dozing off once more when Jack spoke.

Can I spread the news?

Yes. Tell everyone that Sam will be coming home.

It didn't matter when that was—Mirek would be waiting.

CHAPTER TWENTY-SEVEN

It is time for you to return.

Sam didn't recognize the voice in her mind. *Who are you?* she asked them.

I'm your magic.

I've never heard of someone speaking to their magic before, she told the voice.

Because I'm not ordinary magic and this isn't an ordinary situation.

Sam contemplated theorizing advantages for having her magic speak to her. But even the thought of the task made her tired. *Will you speak to me from now on?* she asked the voice instead.

No. This is the only time.

Then why today?

Because you need a push to return.

Sam felt like the voice was speaking in riddles and she was missing something.

Instead of asking another question and getting another riddle, Sam searched her memory. She remembered the test run in Kate's shop, then the lunch. They'd all met again at the restaurant for dinner, and afterward, she and Mirek had made love. And then again the next morning after sleeping in.

Her memory had always been a point of pride with her—her recall was fantastic. Yet now she felt like she was slogging through mud to even pick up the pieces—each one weighted down.

There was something about Simon, Jo, and Damon. Letting go so her mind could relax, the memory finally came. They were going to use the spell to extract the evil from all magics.

Her memories began to flow, the details clearer. Jack reached out to Mirek for help before sending a message to everyone to meet in the field. Like a movie in her mind, Sam watched Kate with the sword and knew it was time to fulfill her destiny.

The spellbook spoke to her—said it had been waiting for her—and the seer she met in Mexico appeared as a ghost. The seer had told them to trust in their love and that it was forever. Mirek wrapped his arms around her waist, and then she lifted the sword.

Like the final piece was falling into place, Sam understood what her magic was trying to tell her.

I must return home. Return to Mirek.

Yes. You have completed your destiny.

Sam realized she'd missed one piece of the puzzle. When the evil magic was created and it could not be undone, the ancestor created a symbol to funnel the magic and the sword and spellbook to close it, but there was one thing he couldn't create.

Oh wow, I was your divine providence.

Yes, Sam. You were created for a future eventuality. As were several others in each generation.

That's what the seer meant by my destiny. Entrapping the evil was all that mattered. I was supposed to die.

Yes... But your sacrifice was so willingly given that I couldn't let you die as a result. With the help from the seer, the sword, and the spellbook, I worked to bring you back.

In shock, she wasn't sure what to say.

Go home to Mirek, Sam.

"... Then he fell on his butt and burst out laughing," Mirek said.

Sam could hear him. And feel him too. The length of his body was pressed up against her side—her right side, like always—and all she needed to do was roll toward him. But her body felt weighted down, like she'd been drained and didn't have the energy to move.

Giving up on moving her entire body, she concentrated on opening her eyes. She needed Mirek to know she could hear him. That she loved him and had come back to him.

Mirek began telling her another story. This time about his cousin Reece. She listened to his voice and tried so hard to open her eyes but failed.

After a few minutes, his voice trailed off, and she feared he would leave. She knew he would always come back, but maybe he was tired of waiting for now. The mattress underneath her—at least it felt like a mattress—dipped as Mirek moved. Only his knees touched her side now.

"I love you, Sam."

Giving up on opening her eyes, she desperately wanted him to kiss her. A memory of Mirek holding up his hands and backing up as he barked out a laugh popped into her mind. She'd just eaten an entire bowl of Habanero salsa with fresh tortilla chips. It was super spicy and so good, but Mirek wouldn't kiss her until she brushed her teeth. She used her magic to clean her teeth and breath, making it minty fresh, but didn't tell Mirek she had. She flashed in front of him, making kissy faces, and goaded him, saying if he loved her, he'd kiss her. He laughed when he finally kissed her, tasting only mint, and then kissed her some more.

Wanting his kiss more than anything now, she pulled on her magic to freshen her mouth. Her magic felt different. It was sluggish and tired, but she knew it was there since she'd talked to it. After three tries, she tasted mint.

She felt Mirek kiss her temple, a brief brush of his lips. "You are and always will be my Athena. I will wait for you." Then his lips brushed across hers.

His kiss was too brief. She wanted more.

"Sam? Sam? Can you hear me? Your breath is minty. Did you do that?"

He kissed her again.

She dug deep for inner strength to make her body move in some small way to show him she heard him—open her eyes, part her lips—it didn't matter what. The more she tried without success, the more tired she became.

"Sam, open your eyes for me. Please."

She could hear the pleading in his voice and wanted so badly to see him. Her eyelids were just too heavy.

"Please, Athena. Open your eyes. I need to see you."

Mirek sounded panicked now. Or maybe it was excitement. Whatever it was, she wanted to see him and to please him.

Magic, can you hear me? Please give me strength. Her magic didn't respond, but Sam pulled on it again and felt it stir more than before. Pushing some to her eyes, she forced her lids to open.

Hovering above her, Mirek—his hair falling onto his forehead and sporting almost a full beard—was the most beautiful sight in the world.

"The sight of your blue eyes is the most beautiful thing

I've ever seen," he said on an exhale. His words were almost identical to her thoughts; they were perfect for each other.

Sam felt her eyes drift close, not having the strength to keep them open any longer. Then Mirek's lips touched hers once more briefly.

"You sleep, Sam. I'll be here when you wake up."

Drifting off to sleep, she knew he would be there when she woke.

And he was. Three more times, she woke—once more in the dark and twice with the warmth of the winter sun on her face—and Mirek was there and kissed her softly.

After that, she was able to speak a few words when she woke, and Mirek helped her drink a protein shake. Only a few sips at first, but each time, she could drink more, had more strength, and was able to say more.

Before long, she could stay awake for several hours at a time.

It was dark again, but the night was clear. The moon and stars looked as if they shone just for them.

"Are you ready to go home now?" Mirek asked softly as she leaned against him.

Every time she'd woken, she asked him what day it was. It had been January eleventh when she'd woken this time, but now it was after midnight—January twelfth—fourteen days since she'd sealed the magic away forever.

When she'd finally been able to stay awake for an hour at a time, Mirek told her everything that had happened. How he'd laid beside her for seven days waiting for her heart to beat. Then another three days for her to open her eyes, and four days since then.

"I suppose we should." She tilted her head to meet his eyes. "Your magic is good, but a bathroom and a shower would be nice."

"Haha, you're hilarious," he said sarcastically, but he couldn't keep the laughter from his voice.

He picked her up and she squealed, making them both laugh. Moving lower on the bed, he repositioned them so they laid on their sides facing each other and tucked the blankets in around them.

"We used to talk in vague terms about a future," he whispered as he cupped her unscarred cheek. "Now I want us to make real plans. I love you, Sam, and I don't want a future without you in it."

She closed the few inches between them and kissed him. "I love you too," she said against his lips. "Make love to me, hero."

"I want to—so much—but not yet. You're not even close to full strength yet."

"You'll just have to do all the work then." Under the covers, Sam fisted his shirt and tugged him toward her. Mirek could have resisted her weak tugging, but instead, he braced his hands on either side of her and covered her body with his.

Mirek looked into her eyes. "Are you sure? I want to make love to you, but just having you here with me..." He paused and smirked. "Alive and responsive is good."

"Ha. You've become a comedian in the last two weeks." She rolled her eyes. "Alive is good and yes, I'm sure." She tugged on his shirt again to bring him down to her, but he resisted. "Please, Mirek. I'm not made of glass."

He lowered his lips to hers and she opened automatically to let him in. She didn't want gentle or sweet; she wanted everything Mirek could give her. He groaned against her and then pulled away. She was about to protest again when he put his finger against her lips.

"We're outside in January," he said as if she'd forgotten. "We're going to be strategic about this."

"Strategic?" She huffed out a laugh and saw her breath in the glow from the ball of magic he'd placed on the side of the bed. "We could just be fast."

He grinned down at her. "We're both comedians tonight… But I was thinking another blanket might work."

Sam felt the weight of a thick blanket as it landed on top of them, already spread out. Mirek lifted one hand and pulled on the edge of the blanket, bringing it up to the back of his neck.

"And… we keep our shirts on," he said as he lowered his body. Sam groaned at the feel of his skin next to hers, loving that he removed their clothes from the waist down. She needed the skin-to-skin connection with him.

When Mirek kissed her again, she closed her eyes, savoring the taste and feel of him. Easing her hands under the back of his shirt she raked her nails along his skin, making him groan.

She would do anything and give anything for this man. He was her other half, and for so long she thought they'd never be together again. Then her magic gift almost took her away from him again. Knowing that it deemed her worthy enough to bring her back for Mirek—so they could have a life together—made her determined to make the best of the future they were given.

"Please, Mirek. I need you." She bit his lip, then soothed it with her tongue and thrust her hips up, feeling his hard length against her.

"Wait. We need a condom," he said as a foil packet landed in his palm.

Sam wanted to tell Mirek to get rid of it. She'd heard there was supposed to be a time and place to discuss important topics, but she'd never seen a list or timetable anywhere. "Do we?" she asked, looking at the condom and then him.

"Do we what? Oh… need it?"

Sam nodded and pulled one hand from beneath his shirt and fisted her pendant. "Do we?" she whispered.

"You don't want to wait?"

She shook her head, not needing to think about her answer. They'd already waited a lifetime. Maybe some people would think bringing children into the mix when they didn't even know where they'd be living or working was crazy, but Sam knew how fast life could be cut short, and she didn't want to waste a moment.

"I want everything with you, hero. Now, later—now and later—it doesn't matter when."

Mirek tossed the condom over the side of the mattress and kissed her as he lowered his hips. The tip of his shaft touched her heat, and they both moved toward each other at the same time, bringing their bodies together. She groaned into his mouth and wrapped her legs around his hips.

For the first time in their lives, they were truly safe and could love each other without repercussions. They made love to each other in the winter night, the moon and stars witnesses to their movements and whispered words of love.

"Come for me, Athena." Mirek tilted his hips in the way that always sent her over the edge and she shattered, finding a bliss only her hero could give her. Mere moments later, he rocked with his own release of bliss, calling her name as he came.

Later, cradled in Mirek's arms, Sam felt truly at peace for the first time in her life. They'd already proven that their love could handle anything the universe threw at them, and Sam looked forward to seeing what else life would bring with Mirek by her side.

EPILOGUE

**Four Years After Sam Destroyed the Evil.
Third Annual Masquerade Ball**

*J*ack flashed to the meadow, landing about a foot in front of one of the stone benches. Using his magic, he melted the thin layer of frost covering the seat and sat facing the vast open meadow.

A few months after Sam destroyed the magic four years ago, Jack bought the meadow and the surrounding land. Not long after that, he commissioned the benches that now circled the meadow. A gazebo followed.

Restrooms were next when picnicking in the meadow became a tradition for their large group of family and friends. Jack could just make out the structure in the distance —built to blend into the trees—in the setting sun's last rays of sunlight. Thinking of the multiple changing tables he had added to the building the next summer, made him smile.

Over five-and-a-half years ago—when the Grand Council had forced a soul jump on him and Meredith, bringing them to this meadow—he never could have imagined what was to come or what part the meadow would play in their lives.

He rubbed his hands together, pushing some magic into them to warm his fingers in the cold December air. Similar temperature to what it had been four years ago. Every New Year's Eve, Jack came to the meadow—not for long—to reflect on how different things could have gone on that night four years ago. His solo visits every year helped him to never forget the sacrifices that were made by so many magics.

The months following hadn't been easy—hundreds of magics had died, leaving behind dozens of orphans—but they'd come together as a council and a community.

Checking the time, he realized he needed to head home to his family. With his hectic family life, he didn't take time daily to reflect on the floor plan and architecture of their living quarters, except on this one night every year.

Several days after the destruction of the evil magic, Meredith told him she was pregnant. It was one of the happiest days of his life. His lips twitched up at the memory of what she told him next—she had already hired contractors to turn three of the empty apartments on the floor into one large one, leaving the three remaining apartments for visitors. Then they'd gotten to work on filling their new enormous apartment—and what fun work it had been.

With one last look at the meadow, Jack flashed inside the foyer of their home and was greeted with shouts of "Daddy," one of the best sounds in the world.

"Hey, Uncle Jack," Madison and Hannah called out in stereo.

Madison, the eighteen-year-old adopted daughter of Rowena and Connor and Hannah, the eighteen-year-old adopted daughter of Reece and Isabella, were like two peas in a pod.

"Hey, back," he said and waited for their eyerolls. They didn't disappoint.

"Meredith asked us to give the kids a snack... well, not the youngest ones, obviously," Hannah said with a laugh. "Dinner is supposed to be served in the ballroom in two hours."

Another thing he wouldn't have imagined—having a ballroom. Meredith and Reece had transformed the fourth floor of the bakery's building from their temporary infirmary into a conference center, complete with a ballroom.

"Sounds good." Jack walked around the large family table and kissed the messy cheeks of each of his six kids while they were strapped into their highchairs and bouncy seats.

After making the expected "yum-yum" sounds when sticky carrots and pieces of cheese were thrust toward his face, he listened to the chatter of his oldest boys. At just over three years old, they could talk up a storm, but their twin brother and sister—exactly two years old—wouldn't be far behind. His youngest girls—only three months old—gave him milk-bubble smiles.

Although with he and Meredith each being a twin increasing their chances of having twins, it didn't account for three sets of twins. Their magic doctor believed their amplified power was the reason for each pregnancy to have been twins. Six kids all under the age of three-and-a-half was more than two handfuls, but Jack was living the dream.

"Where's Meredith?" he asked the teenagers.

"Changing for the party... I think," Hannah said, and grinning, offered Jack a wet rag.

"Thanks." He wiped off his hands and made his way toward the bedrooms. Some days he felt like he'd been sticky for the last three years, but it was a small price to pay for his amazing kids.

"Meredith?" She didn't answer, and he finally found her in one of their four walk-in closets.

She was sitting on the floor crying, clothes and magazines strewn all around her. His take-charge wife wouldn't cry over what to wear; she would find a picture of an outfit she liked and conjure it. And judging by the number of magazines and outfits on the floor, she'd done just that, so there had to be something else wrong.

He sat beside her on the floor and pulled her into his lap. "Bubbles? What's wrong?"

Meredith had been going non-stop for years and wouldn't listen when he asked her to slow down. Maybe he should have pushed, knowing it would eventually catch up with her, like it just may have done.

She conjured a tissue and wiped her nose. "I miss my mom," she whispered as she turned into his chest, fisting his shirt in one hand.

That wasn't exactly what he'd expected to hear, but he wasn't surprised either. Scanning the contents spilled on the floor—looking for details the way he would scan for clues in an investigation—he saw the shoebox filled with old photos.

Listening as his wife sobbed against his chest, Jack's heart broke for the woman he loved. Meredith was the most amazing person he'd ever met. He would do anything for her, but he couldn't fix this.

Five years ago, he learned he wasn't like his father and had finally accepted himself. He had also learned to lean on others.

Picturing Fiona and Stella in his mind, he spoke to them. *We need a mom.*

A few minutes later, Stella and Fiona walked into the closet, both women wearing ballgowns.

"Oh, honey," Fiona said as she kicked off her shoes, hiked up her gown, and kneeled in front of Meredith.

Stella tossed her shoes aside as well and patted Jack on the arm. "We've got this."

"I love you," he whispered to Meredith and eased her off his lap, leaving the moms to work their magic.

A half-hour later, Stella and Fiona, along with the teenagers and Jack's six kids, headed to the ballroom, giving Jack and Meredith a few minutes alone.

"You're beautiful," he said when Meredith emerged from the bathroom draped in a long, royal blue gown.

She stepped up to him and adjusted his jacket collar. "I'm sorry."

"Bubbles, you have nothing to be sorry for. I should have given you more help."

She laughed. "Please, no. Any more help, and I won't know what to do with them. I... I look forward to this day every year, but I was looking for a pair of shoes in the closet and found the box of photos... it got to me today."

"I know," he said softly, because he truly did. He gave her a quick kiss, careful not to ruin her hair and makeup—he'd save that for later—and took her hand.

Jack would always do everything in his power to get her what she needed, even if he needed to bring in others to help him.

Five Years After Sam Destroyed the Evil.
Fourth Annual Masquerade Ball

Jo CHECKED the time on the bedside clock in their swanky London hotel room—half-past eight. Striding over to the desk, she sat and stared at the door as if she could will Simon to walk through it.

He'd told her he'd make his move shortly after the shop closed at eight and flash back to the hotel, so he should be back any minute.

For almost six years, they'd barely been apart. Simon was more than her husband and working partner; he was her best friend. Traveling all over the world, they were making a name for themselves as antique appraisers with both magics and non-magics. It gave them the perfect cover for the work they did for the council, which was why they were in London.

A friend of Catherine and Viktor's had approached the council, two weeks earlier, and requested their help to retrieve an ancient magic book.

A stolen spellbook wasn't usually something the council concerned themselves with if it could be handled by non-magic authorities, but they'd made an exception for this case. The book's owner had graciously opened his library to the council on several occasions when they had needed information, and the council wanted to return the favor.

Luckily, Simon and Jo's contact list had grown substantially over the years, enabling them to easily spread the word about what they were looking for. Within a few days, they had the book's location—a used bookstore in a seedy part of London.

Two magic brothers, known for dealing in stolen magic items, owned the shop. After they contacted their usual buyers, one buyer reached out to Jack, looking for a trade of information.

Sometimes the best plan was the simplest, and that was how Jo found herself waiting in a hotel room while Simon, disguised as the buyer, went to the shop to buy the book. The council provided the money, and as soon as Simon completed the exchange, the magic task force would swoop in to arrest both the shop owners and the buyer, but the buyer would escape.

The transaction would involve multiple lies, with Simon telling the biggest one of all. And although Jo wasn't the naïve woman she'd been six years ago—she understood lies had a place, especially to trap criminals—lies still had the potential to backfire.

By nine p.m., Jo was ready to jump out of her skin when the door opened. The buyer, a distinguished-looking man in his forties, walked in and smiled at Jo. He was wearing the same clothes Simon had on when he'd left as the buyer, but that meant nothing.

"It's me," the man said in Simon's voice and as he walked toward her, his persona fell away. Jo ran to Simon, gripped his shoulders, and jumped—like she'd done so many times before—trusting he would catch her. She wrapped her legs around his waist, captured his lips with hers, and claimed him.

He pushed her back against the sliding glass door to the balcony. With one hand cupping her ass, he wrapped the other around her neck. They feasted on each other as the rest of the world fell away.

When they finally came up for air, he met her gaze. "Loved the welcome. Now, what's wrong?"

Jo felt stupid to admit the truth, but she wouldn't lie to Simon. "I was worried. I..." She dropped her forehead to his shoulder. "I feel so dumb. We're never apart, and you rarely transform anymore, but usually I'm with you..."

"Jo?"

"Hmm?"

"I didn't like being without you either," he said quietly and stepped back so she could drop her legs and stand. "You ready to go home?"

"Yes. And have I told you I love that we can flash five thousand miles at once?"

"Only about a hundred times." Simon laughed and checked his watch. "With the time difference, it's not even three thirty in the afternoon at home, so we'll have a couple of hours before we need to get ready for the dinner and party."

"That won't be long enough to have a nap, but I'm sure I can think of a way to occupy our time, Superman."

"I'll look forward to it. Oh…" He paused.

"What?"

His grin turned salacious. "What dress are you wearing tonight? The red one?"

"*May-be,*" she said, drawing out the word. Jo had donated the red dress she'd worn to the charity event with Lucas—it hadn't seemed right to keep it—and bought an even sexier one the year before. "You're going to have to wait and see."

Jo picked up her bag, but before she could flash, Simon clasped her hand, stalling her, and belted out the chorus to "Lady in Red" in Lucas's voice.

She laughed and pulled her hand away. "Let's go home, Superman."

**Six Years After Sam Destroyed the Evil.
Fifth Annual Masquerade Ball**

DAMON GLANCED at the speedometer and cursed before letting up on the gas pedal. He tried calling Morgana again, but like before, her phone went straight to voicemail.

He contemplated parking his car on the side of the road and flashing home, but ten seconds later, he nixed the idea. If

Morgana needed him to drive her somewhere or pick her up, Damon didn't want to be stuck without his vehicle. It was the same reason he hadn't flashed home from his meeting when he hadn't been able to reach her. But it didn't stop him from wondering if he'd made a mistake.

If his last meeting of the day hadn't been at a downtown restaurant with non-magics, he would have flashed home, instead of being stuck on the road panicking about his wife while trying not to break any traffic laws.

"You're an idiot," he muttered to himself when he had to stop for a red light. He should have canceled the meeting, but Morgana hadn't wanted him to. He'd been meeting with a promising start-up, and the investment looked like it could be profitable for both sides, but the client was only in town for the day. Now that he'd cinched the deal—which looked even more lucrative than he'd first thought—he still thought he was an idiot. Nothing and no one were more important than his wife.

He lived to make Morgana happy, but no amount of magic, money, or persuasion could give her what she wanted most. One of her biggest wishes was to be a mother and, on their honeymoon, they started trying to get pregnant.

Four years and three miscarriages later, they stopped trying and Morgana went back on birth control. That had been two years ago—right after Meredith had given birth to her third set of twins.

Damon had suggested adoption, and Morgana was more than willing to do that, but she also wanted to have the experience of being pregnant. Wanted to feel their baby growing inside her. He couldn't argue with that, and when she'd told him four months ago that she wanted to try one more time before they looked at adoption, all he could do was agree.

This morning, just before he left the house, Morgana

admitted that her last three periods had been so light she wasn't sure about them. And for the last three days, she'd been nauseous.

His heart had skipped a beat. Before each of Morgana's miscarriages, she'd been nauseous for several days.

Damon had wanted to call Jack or Mirek to check on her, but she didn't want them. She said she'd call her magic doctor and had practically booted Damon out of the house. Morgana managed to get an appointment for two p.m., the same time as his meeting.

He pulled the car into the garage and flashed directly into the house.

Morgana sat curled in the corner of their large sectional, and even from several feet away, he could tell she'd been crying.

"Aww… Angel," he said under his breath.

Bracing himself for bad news, he sat in the middle of the couch and pulled her onto his lap.

All he'd ever wanted was to love and protect her, but he couldn't protect her from heartache. He didn't offer platitudes—didn't say everything would be okay, because he knew none of that would help.

She lifted his hand from her lap and put a crumpled piece of paper in it. With everyone popping out kids over the last six years, he'd seen his fair share of ultrasound pictures and recognized the thermal paper right away. Oh fuck... was someone else pregnant and gave the picture to her?

Unless... He lifted her chin to look into her eyes. "Morgana? Whose baby is in the picture?"

She shoved her hand down beside them and picked up a black T-shirt he hadn't noticed. He'd seen the shirt many times—Meredith had worn it during all her pregnancies. Printed on the front where the wearer's ribs would be were a set of ribs with a red heart behind them. In the space below, were two baby skeletons high-fiving each other.

"Meredith lent me this," she said and looked up at him, her eyes red as tears spilled down her cheeks. "I'm going to wear it to the party tonight, instead of my dress, with my mask."

"Tonight? You mean…" He stared down at the paper in his hand.

"These are happy tears." She pointed to the paper. "Twelve weeks and healthy."

He was the luckiest man alive—he already had his angel, and now he was going to have two more.

Seven Years After Sam Destroyed the Evil.
Sixth Annual Masquerade Ball

Meredith reached across the table, clasping Madison's cheeks in both hands, and kissed her forehead.

From her spot tucked out of the way against a stack of books, Rowena couldn't hear the conversation, but Madison beamed up at her aunt. Connor must have said something because the people in the front of the long line of waiting readers broke out laughing.

"Did you catch that?" Meredith asked as she walked toward Rowena, holding her signed hardcover book.

Rowena chuckled. "The public smooch you gave my daughter? Yes, but not what was said."

Meredith grinned as she opened the cover of the book. "I got to be a crazed fan… told her how much I loved her and that she was my favorite author."

Rowena leaned over to see. *"To Meredith, my biggest fan,"*

Rowena read the inscription out loud and then burst out laughing at the inscription Connor added. "That's my husband for you."

"I know." Meredith closed the book and looked at the line. "I can't believe the line. Well... I can... but it's still crazy."

Rowena followed her cousin's gaze. The line snaked through the large bookstore and out the door, along the sidewalk. "Madison was so nervous... it's not just her first book signing, but it's in a huge store in Manhattan."

"And for her first book too." Meredith gave Rowena a quick one-armed hug. "When you told me seven years ago that you wanted to adopt one of the orphaned teenagers, could you have imagined yourself standing here?"

Thinking back to that time, Rowena hadn't even been thinking about the future. All she could think about was the present and the heartbroken fourteen-year-old she'd met who had just lost her mom—her only parent and family— due to the evil magic. Madison had been shy, introverted, and so lost.

Looking at her now, laughing with her fans, and sitting beside Connor—the only dad she'd ever known—she shone.

"No," she said, finally answering Meredith's question. "I don't think I was able to look even a week into the future. Whenever I'd dealt with grieving teens before I was always able to send them back home to their parents... She's amazing." The love she felt for her husband and daughter still grew every year.

"Has Madison figured out what she's going to do when she graduates in a few months?"

"She's got some ideas, and her criminology degree gives her options—she's even had some job offers—but no, she hasn't decided yet."

"Well... there's no rush." Meredith looked at the time. "It's almost midnight... "Why is the signing on New Year's Eve?"

She chuckled. "I didn't even ask and just marked the calendar, or I would have forgotten because of a million other things."

Rowena smiled at her cousin. "Mrs. Biggest Fan… Madison and Connor didn't give you an advanced copy?"

"They tried, but I wanted to buy my copy here and show Madison my support. Connor…" She waved her hand in his direction. "This is old hat for him. Although, writing a book with his daughter is a first."

"It is, but they've already planned three more books… Anyway… the murder in the book happens in Manhattan on New Year's Eve at midnight, thus the reason we're here and missed the annual dinner. But there'll be more dinners."

"Exactly. Are you—"

Meredith's words were cut off when someone yelled a two-minute warning until midnight.

"That's my cue to leave," Meredith said. "I'll go to the bathrooms and flash from there. But I was going to ask… are you three going to make it for the ball and midnight?"

"Yes. Everything will shut down here at one a.m. and we'll flash home. With the time difference, it will only be eleven there. We'll have lots of time."

"Great, I'll see you at the ball," Meredith said and headed to the back of the store.

When someone yelled the thirty-second warning, Rowena walked over to her family. Madison and Connor stood. He wrapped an arm around her and his daughter and they counted down to the new year together. The crowd cheered when he dramatically leaned Rowena back in his arms and kissed her. He kept it short, and when they straightened, he took a mock bow.

Connor laughed and Madison rolled her eyes at both her parents before they went back to signing books. Rowena and Connor had both come so far in the past seven years. No longer feeling they weren't worthy of love, their lives were now brimming with it.

Eight Years After Sam Destroyed the Evil.
Seventh Annual Masquerade Ball

Loud laughter from five of his seven kids greeted Reece when he arrived home.

"Have Grace and Nora already gone over to help Jack and Meredith with their brood?" he asked while walking into the kitchen.

His middle girls, both fifteen, had taken over from Mackenzie when she went to college the past fall. And Mackenzie had taken over from Hannah and Madison, Rowena's daughter, three years before that, when they'd gone to college.

"Yes, they went over early to give Meredith and Jack a break," Mackenzie said while dishing out snacks for Brooklyn, Aiden, and Logan.

Hannah grinned and pointed at her siblings. "Mom said to feed the monsters because dinner will be late."

Aiden stood and pounded his chest, like he was Godzilla. "I can be a monster."

"Me too," Logan said, copying his brother. Two years younger than his older brother, Logan had been only two when Reece and Isabella adopted children from two families whose parents had been killed by Maverick. At first, Logan had hidden behind Aiden, but now at ten, he was as loud as the others, and Aiden's mini-me.

Brooklyn rolled her eyes. "You are monsters." At thirteen,

his youngest daughter was a great kid, even despite coming into her teenage attitude.

"Oh, you're monsters alright," Reece said playfully as he pretended to take Aiden, and then Logan, in a headlock.

He chatted with his kids for several minutes as they caught him up on their days.

Reece loved listening to all his kids and was thankful the girls had decided to go to college locally, because he wasn't ready for any of his kids to leave the nest.

"Where's your mom?" he asked his eldest daughters.

"She's still at work."

"I'll go see if she needs help closing up. We'll be back soon."

He flashed from their apartment to the third floor. Then he released the spell between the second floor and third floors, allowing him to access the second floor and the gym. He'd implemented the extra precautions, not allowing anyone without permission to go above the second floor, because his children lived in a building frequented by strangers.

Most of his family still lived in the apartments two buildings over, but when he and Isabella adopted seven kids, his family and friends had come together quickly to renovate an entire floor in the bakery's building. Meredith put her own renovations on hold to ensure that Reece and Isabella's kids—the four girls from one family and a young girl and her two little brothers from another family—all had their own spaces. Daily living was hectic, but the past seven years had been the best of Reece's life.

While their apartment had been under renovations, Meredith—always looking ahead—approached Isabella to run the gym she was setting up, and be the head trainer. Now, with four full-time and six part-time trainers working for her, Isabella's gym was the preeminent one in the city.

Even with her busy schedule, Isabella didn't usually work late on New Year's Eve, a night they both looked forward to every year. More than eight years ago, when he'd bought Isabella a mask in New Orleans, he'd promised her a masquerade party. It took him a little over a year, but he'd made good on that promise.

The New Year's Eve after Sam sealed away the magic, Reece created the inaugural Masquerade Ball, preceded by an enormous buffet dinner. Tonight marked its seventh anniversary, and he was as excited for this one as he'd been for the first.

As expected, when he walked into the main area of the gym, the lights were dim and the music off. Isabella didn't approach him as she usually did. She sat on a workout bench with a piece of paper in her hand, looking dejected.

The day before, when a letter arrived from her parents' attorney, they both knew it couldn't be good news. He'd wanted to be with her when she opened it, but she'd said she would open it later and made an excuse about needing to do something for the kids. And he didn't think her avoidance had anything to do with needing time to process the letter's content on her own.

He kneeled in front of her, resting a hand on her thigh. "Cupcake?"

Her eyes were dry, but filled with sorrow, when she looked up. "I didn't know he died."

"Your dad?"

"Yeah. He died over eight years ago... He was at a restaurant with some co-workers when the place was attacked. Just like what happened to me and Kate. He refused to join Maverick and they killed him."

"Why did they send the letter now?"

"My mom died six months ago from cancer. The lawyer said she didn't seek treatment. She... when I told her about

Mateo and where I was, she didn't tell me about my dad or want to see me. But…" Isabella held up the letter. "She left me everything—not that we need it—but… she didn't even write a message."

She waved the letter in the air. "It's only from her attorney. Nothing from her… I don't need money from her, but a note, or a phone call, or…"

Reece sat on the bench and pulled Isabella into his arms. She collapsed against him, and he wished he could absorb all her hurt. After Mateo died, she said it took her years to finally realize that no one could make someone be a better person. A person had to choose it for themselves—but that didn't mean she would stop wishing for someone to be better. Like for her mom to realize what she'd done and to love Isabella.

Nor would Reece stop wanting to be strong for her, even while knowing that vulnerability wasn't a weakness.

Isabella put some space between them to wave her hand in front of her face, giving herself a light glamour. "Don't want the kids to ask questions," she said, pointing at her face.

He leaned over and kissed her slowly. A kiss definitely not safe for work. When he pulled back, he sent his magic out to lock all the doors.

"Are you up for going tonight?" he asked. New Year's Eve was one of his favorite nights of the year, but he would stay home and cuddle with his wife if that's what she needed.

She gave him a sly smile. "Of course I'm up for the party. I told you my dress this year is emerald green. I'm expecting a mask to match."

"You are, are you? Well, I guess we'll just have to go home and see what's there."

Every year he bought her a new mask and he'd outdone himself this time. But no mask, or anything else he could give her, could even begin to match the joy she'd brought to his life.

Nine Years After Sam Destroyed the Evil.
Eight Annual Masquerade Ball

KATE DIDN'T MAKE a sound when she flashed inside the apartment they were borrowing for the night. Silently, she reached over and hung her garment bag on one of the hooks by the door. It wasn't often that she had the chance to observe all three of her guys without them knowing.

Curtis lay on the couch, his head propped on the armrest, his legs extended along the cushions, all his attention focused on his dad. They'd named Curtis after her father, but he was so much like his own father—serious and quiet, also easygoing and patient. His talent for drawing had been evident from an early age, but now at ten, his drawings were incredible.

Austin, her eight-year-old son, sat curled in a chair, a sketchbook in his hand, his brow furrowed. He was named after his father's brother, but he was just like his mother—passionate, quick to anger, and could hold a grudge. She and Isaac used to joke they'd mixed up their kids' names.

Isaac sat on the floor and leaned over Curtis's leg, drawing on him with a fine-tipped marker. It was a semi-regular occurrence, and with both parents sporting tattoos, she had known her boys would want their own. Isaac had told the boys early on that having tattoos drawn on with marker was better than real tattoos because they could enjoy them, and when they eventually washed off, they could get more. So far, the concept was working.

As Isaac leaned over the couch, creating his design, it reminded Kate of being trapped in another dimension nine years ago when Isaac created her own tattoo. It wasn't only his position that reminded her—she'd seen him tattoo many times over the years—it was the time of year, and even more so, the day. The holiday season always brought out her memories of being trapped in the room with Isaac. Especially Christmas Day and New Year's Day.

Those two days reminded her they were given second chances, both with each other, and as a community of magic people. She'd be forever grateful for Isaac's perseverance, her mom's vision, Sam's genius, and everyone who helped save them.

At forty-two, there were days when being trapped seemed like a lifetime ago, and other times a comment or a look from Isaac could easily transport her back to that time and how they'd fallen in love. She didn't feel quite as sexy as she had back then, when Isaac tattooed her, but he told her often that she'd always be his Turquoise. At thirty-nine, he was still her lumberjack.

His beard was full and neatly trimmed, but now he only kept it during the winter months, claiming it was too hot during the summer. It didn't matter; she'd take him any way she could get him.

And tonight, they'd take each other—oh boy, would they. She smiled at her own little joke. The New Year's Eve ball always wore the boys out. They were similar in age to Meredith and Jack's kids and would burn lots of energy running around the ballroom with their friends and then sleep like the dead for ten hours. Perfect.

Isaac looked up just then and smiled. As soon as her boys followed their father's glance, her quiet observation was over.

"Mom. Look what Dad's tattooing on me. It's my design," Curtis called from the couch, holding up a drawing.

"Mom. Mom. Come see," Austin said, almost bouncing out of his chair.

She walked over and gave each of her guys a kiss and admired their talent. Perching on the edge of Austin's chair, she watched Isaac work.

"How'd the day go?" Isaac asked, not looking up.

"Good, the materials arrived."

"And the new apprentice?"

Kate smiled. "So far, she seems great, and she fits in with the others." In the years since being trapped, she and Isaac had both expanded their businesses—adding apprentices—and Kate had chosen to work only with magic females. Was it sexist on her part? Maybe… but she loved teaching women as eager to break from the stereotypes as she was, and her business was thriving.

"Okay, Curtis," Isaac said to his son. "You're done for now. Go check it out in the mirror in the bedroom."

"Thanks, Dad." Curtis scrambled off the couch, heading for the mirror, with his brother right behind him.

Isaac groaned and twisted to lean against the couch. "I'm too old to sit on the floor."

"Oh yeah?" Kate straddled his lap, placing her knees on either side of him. "What hurts?" she asked quietly. "How about I kiss it and make it feel better?" She gave him a grin that was anything but motherly.

"That sounds like a great idea, but…" He laughed as the boys came stomping back. "Later. I'll hold you to it, Turquoise."

"My pleasure, my lumberjack." She kissed him softly and then laughed when her boys made kissing noises in the air.

"That's so gross," Austin said, flopping down on top of them.

She'd happily let him think that for many more years, but eventually he'd realize what it took her years to learn. Kissing and sex were fantastic, but nothing could beat forging a bond with someone you loved.

Ten Years After Sam Destroyed the Evil.
Ninth Annual Masquerade Ball

MIREK PULLED on his coat and stepped out onto the balcony, closing the sliding glass door behind him. Leaning back against the wall, he shoved his hands into the front pockets of his jeans and looked out over the city.

The night was cooler than it had been ten years ago while he laid on a mattress in the meadow waiting for Sam's heart to beat again. Most days, he was too busy living and enjoying life to think about that time. Except every year around New Year's Eve he made a point of remembering. Not because of how he'd almost lost Sam, but because it was when their lives truly began. To him, it was a rebirth.

He conjured himself a glass of twelve-year-old single malt whiskey, something Jack and Damon introduced him to years ago. Lifting the glass toward the skyline, he made a toast to the universe. "Happy birthday, life," he whispered into the night and took a sip. That first smooth swallow was always his favorite.

At the sound of the sliding door's soft *swoosh*, he turned his head and smiled at his wife. She shut the door behind her and came to him, getting right up in his space. Another one of his favorite things.

Her lips were cool and soft, and he tasted mint as the subtle scents of honeysuckle and orange flooded his senses.

"Mmmm, hello," Sam said softly when she pulled back.

"Hello." He conjured her a glass of wine and passed it to her.

She moved to his left side and leaned against the wall too. "Did you make a toast already?"

Mirek rotated to his side and Sam did the same. "Yes, but I knew we'd do another one together." He held up his glass and she did the same. "Happy birthday, life," they said at the same time, and then both took a drink.

As if by unspoken agreement, they rotated again, their backs against the wall, and stared out into the night. He'd started the toast on the first New Year's Eve after she destroyed the evil. They'd stepped onto one of the ballroom's balconies to get some fresh air and enjoy a bit of quiet as a break from the masquerade party. Since then, they'd always come outside for their toast. A couple of times, before life became too busy, they flashed to the meadow for it.

He reached down and clasped her free hand. "Freezing," he said, and pushed some warmth into his fingers to wrap around her ice-cold ones. "How was your day?"

"Oh."

He heard the excitement in her voice and met her gaze.

"A patient I met at the beginning of my psychiatry residency… I think I told you about that night—a young guy who'd been so high he walked in front of a bus—I saw him today. We bumped into each other in the hallway of the clinic, and he thanked me. He's been in recovery for four and half years."

Mirek disappeared both their glasses and took her face in his hands. "I'm so proud of you, Athena."

She looked down for a moment, before meeting his eyes. "I didn't do much… just talked to him."

"You did enough to make an impression on him, and because of that, he has a new life."

He kissed her softly, then wrapped his arm around her, pulling her into his side as they turned back to look over the city.

"I ask you this every year," she whispered. "And I always will…"

"I know." He waited for her next words, knowing what they'd be, and contemplated how he would answer this time.

"Did you ever imagine we'd be where we are today? I… I don't mean in this luxury apartment… but… together. With three beautiful children, me a psychiatrist working in addictions, and you working for the council?" She laughed and shook her head. "Some days the last ten years feel like they flew by, but other days… all that studying and getting through my residency…"

"And don't forget… while giving birth to Taren in med school and then Caleb and Charlotte at the end of your first year of residency." Mirek smiled. Their conversations had changed over the years, from Sam deciding to go to medical school, to the pressures of attending, to having children, to her residency. Regardless of what they'd gone through each year, she always asked him the same question.

He asked her about it once. She'd told him that she wanted them to always remember what they'd endured, and never take what they had for granted. Two things were easy to do—forget how you got where you are and get so caught up in daily activities that you're constantly on the go—and then you never stop to look back and see that you have an amazing life, even if you didn't imagine it exactly what it could be.

"I'll never forget what it felt like to be totally exhausted in my residency, pumping milk for Taren, and realizing I was pregnant… The best mistake we ever made."

"It was." And he'd never forget holding her as she cried

and wondered how she'd keep going. Luckily for them, they weren't alone anymore; they had a lot of help. But even if they hadn't, he knew Sam would have made it work. His wife was the strongest, smartest, most capable person he'd ever met.

"Speaking of our children…" She grinned. "Where did you ship them off to?"

"Damon and Morgana's. Morgana said that sometimes five kids are easier than two because they occupy each other." Mirek wasn't so sure about that, but he didn't argue because it meant he got some alone time with Sam.

Sam bumped his shoulder. "So… You going to answer my question? I like hearing your variations of 'no.'"

Mirek huffed a laugh. He always said "no", because no one could see their own future, not even a seer.

"My answer has two parts this year… Every year I tell you that if you'd asked me that eleven years ago—while Rocky and I were still under Maverick's lock and key—I would have said no, I couldn't imagine the life we have. I couldn't see a way out, without Maverick coming after you. But… ten years ago, while I waited under the stars for your heart to start beating again, I would have said yes."

"Really? You've never said that before."

Sam lifted her eyebrows in the same way she questioned the kids when she knew they were hiding something. The skin on the right side of her face didn't rise quite like the left side, but her expression still meant business.

He smirked. "Yes, really. While I held you in that meadow, I knew I just had to wait. I'd been waiting for years to be with you… For us to be able to live our lives like we wanted— without being controlled—to be free to love each other…"

Mirek paused as an image of the seer's ghost came to his mind, as clear as she'd been floating in front of them ten years ago. "The seer said our love is forever. And maybe I say "no" every year because I couldn't imagine the exact details and I'm happy to let life continue to surprise me, instead of trying to guess what it has in store for us."

Disappearing their glasses again, he ran his knuckles along her cheek. "But details can change. What I did know was that our life together would be full of joy, we would support each other, tackle anything that came our way, and love each other like no one else could. I also knew that I just had to wait for you to wake up so we could have our forever. I'll always wait for you, my Athena."

Without saying a word, Sam grabbed his hand and ushered him inside their apartment. He chuckled as she led him toward their bedroom.

Even though he'd been looking forward to the ninth annual Masquerade Ball, he would enjoy it just as much when they arrived a little late.

Eleven Years After Sam Destroyed the Evil.
Tenth Annual Masquerade Ball

STELLA LEANED on the railing and could just make out the silhouettes of the mountains in the distance. Some years she went to a balcony on the other side of the ballroom and looked out at the city. But tonight, the mountains called to her.

"Needed some quiet time?" Ben asked as he placed a blanket around her shoulders, and pulled her to his side.

"Thanks," she said and kissed his cheek.

She chuckled, thinking about his question. "Yes. Is it me or does it get louder each year?"

A laugh rumbled in his chest. "It's not you. It definitely gets louder every year. And I thought at our age it wouldn't be quite so loud because our hearing was supposed to go."

"Hey, don't talk like that. I want lots more years with my grandchildren. I'm a young sixty-three. And you're..." She paused and laughed at Ben's mock indignation.

"I think the words you're looking for are a spry seventy-three."

"Ah, right... that's what I meant to say."

They lapsed into silence for a few moments as they stared out at the night. New Year's Eve always seemed to be a time for reflection. Over the years, she'd spoken with her kids—her three biological and the fourteen her heart had adopted as adults—and they all agreed. They partied and they reminisced, so thankful for all they had in their lives.

"Any specific memory on your mind tonight?" Ben asked quietly.

"So many...We've been through some hard times, and I'd never want to relive Sam's death, but I wouldn't want to wish away the twenty-two years we had without her either." Her daughter had become two people in her mind—Julia, her little girl, and Sam, a woman who'd come into her own. There was no in between.

"Agreed. Those years gave us Travis and Nate and a lot of good memories."

"The eleven years since Sam and Mirek came back to us and destroyed the magic have been pretty spectacular, though."

"They have." He tugged her around so they were chest to chest. "But it all started with you."

She huffed a laugh, her breath forming a cloud in the soft lights from the ballroom. "How do you figure?"

"Thirty-five years ago, if you hadn't had the courage to

trust me in that alley and then take my hand so many times over the years, we wouldn't be here today."

Tilting her head, she captured his lips with hers. Their kisses didn't always have the same urgency as they used to, but there was no less passion.

They pulled apart when Reece's voice boomed through the speakers and welcomed everyone to countdown to midnight for the tenth annual masquerade ball.

While still wrapped in each other's arms, they turned around to see their family and friends through the glass doors, but stayed where they were.

They counted down with the others and kissed again to welcome in the new year. She and Ben had welcomed in so many years together, and she wanted many more.

Ben's mention of the alley brought an image of the memory to her mind. Back then, she'd taken a risk by trusting him. Then she'd come to love him, but it wasn't until years later that she realized she did more than love and trust him.

They'd become two halves of a whole. When he'd walked up to the railing earlier, she hadn't needed to look to know it was him because she'd known instantly. It hadn't been his cologne or his footsteps. Deep inside her—maybe her magic or maybe something in her soul—recognized him as her other half, and always would.

She'd trusted him a long time ago to be there for her—to love her—and he'd never stopped. And nor would she. She'd always trust their love to handle whatever the universe brought their way.

Thank you so much for reading *Forever in Love* and the rest
of the In Magic series!
This is the end of the series, but who knows… you might see
the gang and their children again in the future.
But right now, you can read about a family of brothers who
have been cursed.
Turn the page to get a glimpse of
Cursed to Love

CURSED TO LOVE

**Falling in love is the only way to break the curse... If it
doesn't destroy them first...**

Blake Akerman's first love crushed his heart. Reeling from
the pain, he swore off love forever.
His heart doesn't care that he just discovered his family is
cursed, and to break it, he must fall in love. Or that the curse
haunts him with ghosts tortured by heartbreak, as if that
would make him want to fall in love. Not likely.

Then the universe lands his first love, Paige Goshko, right in
the middle of his path.

She's everything he remembers and loved. Except now she's
a single mom out of an abusive marriage, homeless, and
determined never to be reliant on a man again.

Just because he's sworn off love doesn't mean he won't help a
friend. And if helping her leads to a second chance at being
friends—with some benefits on the side—why not?

As long as he guards his heart.

Too bad the curse didn't get the memo, because as it grows stronger, they're forced to risk not only their hearts, but their lives, to break it. If they're not too late…

Find *Cursed to Love* at all your favorite online vendors:
https://books2read.com/cursed-to-love/

IN MAGIC SERIES

Lost in Magic

Truth in Magic

Found in Magic

Courage in Magic

Love in Magic

Forged in Magic

Forever in Magic

CURSED TO LOVE SERIES

Cursed to Love

Cursed to Dream

Cursed to Wither

ABOUT KJ WARAWA

Paranormal romance author KJ Warawa had worked every job under the sun, including swimwear seller, switchboard operator, legal secretary, sign language interpreter, soldier, massage therapist, and process improvement advisor, before settling into the career she'd always dreamed about: Author.

She still loves processes and spreadsheets, doesn't love massaging feet, and is currently living out her own love story in Alberta, Canada.

STAY IN TOUCH WITH KJ:
Join KJ's Newsletter at
https://kjwarawa.com/free-book/
to receive a FREE book, exclusive deals, special offers, behind-the-scenes info, and learn about new releases, plus more!
www.kjwarawa.com